The sun's rays stream into the small room, and I pause on the edge of them. I've never been afraid of the sun. So why am I now? It used to illuminate my world, make it seem worth fighting for. But now . . .

Oh, God. Did it happen? Did Victor turn me?

I hold out my hand and tentatively ease it forward, exploring the empty space in front of me, unsure of where the sunbeams truly begin.

I watch the light kiss the tips of my fingernails. No burning.

I expose more. Up to my knuckles. No stinging.

Finally I plunge my whole hand into the bright rays, letting the golden glow wash over my skin. It feels wonderful. When I offered Victor my blood, I was certain that I would never again watch a sunrise, would never again experience its perfect illumination.

Yet here I am in a hospital with morning sunlight filtering gently through the window and dancing over me. I have to admit I'm slightly disappointed.

THE DARKNESS BEFORE DAWN NOVELS

Darkness Before Dawn
Blood-Kissed Sky

Blood-Kissed Sky

A Darkness Before Dawn Novel

J. A. LONDON

HARPER TEEN

An Imprint of HarperCollins*Publishers*

HarperTeen is an imprint of HarperCollins Publishers.

Library of Congress Cataloging-in-Publication Data is available.
ISBN 978-0-06-202066-6

Typography by Michelle Gengaro-Kokmen
12 13 14 15 16 CG/RRDH 10 9 8 7 6 5 4 3 2 1
❖
First Edition

For Robin Rue and Beth Miller,
who believed and worked to make it happen

Prologue

"She is awakening," the vampire, as ancient as the rocks that surrounded him, announced.

"Good. Then the time draws near," Sin said.

"Will she come?"

"When I'm done, she'll have no choice." Sin paced the small cavern. Everything was bathed in darkness except for the area where a tiny crack in the ceiling spilled just enough moonlight to reveal the throne and the old vampire hunched over by the weight of centuries.

When the sun rose, he would flee, forever cursed with the fear of its bright light and the pain of fire scorching his skin. Yes, this vampire, the oldest that remained, was still afraid. . . .

So unlike Sin. Born a Day Walker, he was the first of his kind. He never slept, had no quarrel with the sun and its warming brilliance. He was the next evolutionary step for vampires. And his plan, started so long ago, was finally reaching its pinnacle. A grand scheme that seemed written into the very stars—as unchangeable, as predictable, as inevitable as they were.

Soon. So very, very soon.

Chapter 1

*Death isn't what I thought it would be. It's an acute aware-
ness, a consciousness. A chill that seeps deep into my bones.
Most surprising of all, though, is that it's not ethereal. It's solid,
substantial—hard stone, narrow ledges, steep drops.*

*The black sky is laced with stars. A high moon visible over the
snow-capped peaks cloaks everything in cascading blues and grays.*

*I've been wandering aimlessly through this mountainous
maze for what seems like forever.*

Ever since Victor killed me.

*Victor Valentine. Vampire. How could I have fallen for him—
knowing what he was?*

*How could I have willingly given him my blood—knowing it
would mean my death as a human?*

*How could I have accepted becoming a monster—knowing it
was a life I would detest?*

He warned me: Once he tasted my blood, he wouldn't be able to stop. He would drain me. I would die. So here I am, waiting for him to bring me back as a creature of the night like him.

Did he change his mind? Did he decide that I would hate him too much if he turned me? Or is the metamorphosis from human to vampire a slow process that seems to take an eternity?

I begin to hear a soft lyrical sound. Almost as if this place is singing to me. A voice suddenly echoes from within the stone.

"Find me."

"Victor?" I rasp, desperate to be with him again—but it's not his voice summoning me.

"Find me."

I don't want to answer. I don't want to search. I'm suddenly afraid. More afraid than I've ever been.

"Find me!"

Air fills my lungs and I feel as though a cord is attached to my spine, yanking me backward . . .

My eyes spring open to stark, white surroundings. Where am I?

"Someone get Dr. Icarus! She's awake!"

Through a dense fog of confusion, I watch as a petite woman in light blue scrubs rushes to the bed and begins adjusting dials, checking a bag that is dripping fluid into my arm. Then she leans over and smiles at me. "Hello, sweetie. Welcome back."

Does she know I was in the land of the dead?

"Where's Victor?" I croak. I can hear the beeps on the heart monitor going faster. "Why isn't he here?"

"Easy, sweetie. The only Victor I know is the new Lord Valentine, and you sure wouldn't want him to be in this room."

He's alive! Thank God. I was afraid my blood hadn't been enough. But if it was, then why am I here? Why didn't he kill me? Turn me? I had accepted that I would become a vampire when I offered him my blood. I had felt a sense of relief that the battle was behind me, that the differences between us would no longer separate us.

If I wasn't in the land of the dead before I opened my eyes, then where was I? I have to find Victor, discover exactly what happened. Why am I now in this cold room and not in his warm arms? I try to sit up and the nurse gently pushes me back down.

"Relax, you're not going anywhere in your condition."

I force my breathing to even out, my muscles to go limp. She's not the one with the answers. But who is?

A door creaks open. She steps away, and another face hovers over me. It's not as kind. It looks to be all business. Maybe that's the reason his hair deserted him: He wasn't any fun.

"Miss Montgomery? Miss Montgomery, can you hear me? I'm Dr. Icarus. You're at Mercy Hospital. Do you know why you're here?"

Should I know? What happened after the darkness engulfed me? I give my head a slight shake and pain ricochets through it.

Everything is so fuzzy, so distant. Their voices echo along with my own. I feel like I'm in a dream. Before—that strange world in the mountains—seems more real. Now it's like all my memories are running away, heading toward the dark corners of my mind, and I can't snag the one I need. I don't know how I got here.

"I was . . ." I start, but instinct keeps me from finishing. I was with Victor in a crumbling apartment building. He was dying. He fought my brother—Brady. Oh, God, Brady. A sharp pain pierces my chest as though a stake were thrust into my heart. All these years I thought he was dead. I thought vampires had killed him—but they chose a worse fate for him. They turned him. No, not *they*. Sin. Sin, who attended our school. Sin, who dated my best friend, Tegan Romano. Sin, who earned our trust, and then betrayed us all. He stood alone as a new breed of vampire—a Day Walker. How could we have known he thirsted for our blood? By the time he showed his fangs, it was far, far too late.

He sent Brady to kill Victor. He almost succeeded, but my love for Victor is stronger than Sin could ever comprehend. I rub my neck, remembering the pain of Victor's fangs sinking into my flesh, but I can't feel any healing wounds or scars.

"It's strange," the doctor says, observing my movements. "You arrived a few heartbeats away from death with two deep punctures in your neck, but they healed completely within a couple of hours. I've never seen anything like that. Most vampire bites take days to mend and scar tissue develops. Even your tattoo is completely intact."

I have a crucifix inked on either side of my neck. Even

though they don't ward off vampires. My brother had them as well, which was the reason I had the ink work done. In honor of him—when I thought vampires killed him.

"How did I get here?" I ask.

"A week ago some guy brought you to the ER. He took off once he saw us tending to you."

Victor couldn't risk exposing himself as a vampire, or what he had done to me. If anyone thought he'd attacked the city's delegate, he'd have a difficult time convincing people he wasn't like his father, Murdoch Valentine. Murdoch was Denver's overlord until Victor overthrew him.

"We gave you blood transfusions, but you went into a mild coma," the doctor continues, interrupting my thoughts. "No doubt it was your body's defense mechanism kicking in so you could recover from the ordeal. It's a miracle you're alive. Can you tell me what happened?"

"Strangest dream," I say.

"You want to tell me about it?" the doctor asks, turning to his charts.

"I don't really remember anything. Just that it seemed . . . real. I mean, right now, this all seems like the dream."

"But you don't remember anything from it?"

It was so vivid while I was in it, but trying to recall the images now . . . it's like my mind is fighting me. "My head hurts."

"I'll get you something for that, but I can't medicate you too much; we need to make sure your body is stabilized."

The door opens. My guardian, Rachel Goodwin, enters. She is always put-together in dark blue suits, with her brown hair clipped up neatly. But right now she's wearing jeans and one of my fading T-shirts. She looks as though she hasn't touched a brush or makeup in a week. As soon as our eyes meet, she drops whatever she's carrying, hurries across the room, and hugs me hard.

"Oh my God," she says. "I go out for a few seconds to grab a bag of chips from the vending machine, and you wake up."

I squeeze back, so very glad to see her. Like me, she works for the Agency—which is responsible for protecting the city—serving as my mentor, guiding me in my role as the city's delegate to our vampire overlord.

"Tegan," I whisper hoarsely, tears stinging my eyes. "Do you know what happened to Tegan?" She's been my best friend forever and the last time I saw her she was in a crumpled heap on the floor after Sin plunged his fangs into her neck. Did he kill her? Did he turn her?

"She's fine," Rachel assures me. Releasing her hold on me, she tucks my hair behind my ears.

"What about Sin? Did we get him? Tell me he's dead."

Sadly she shakes her head. "Not yet."

"Do we have any leads? What are we doing to find him?"

"Shh. You don't need to be worrying about that yet."

How can I not worry about it? Sin may be Victor's half brother, but they're nothing alike. Victor sees a future with humans and vampires together, while Sin sees . . . I haven't a clue. His plans are still unfolding, which makes him all the more dangerous, especially to those who know him.

Like Tegan. Poor Tegan. She loved him. "I need to see Tegan, Rachel. I need to see her."

"I know, I know. I'll call her." She pulls out her cell phone.

"She's not ready for visitors yet," the doctor explains, but Rachel just holds up a warning finger to cut him off and then dials anyway.

Half an hour later, the doctor and nurse have left and I'm surrounded by some of the most important people in my life. Even with all these blankets over me, I feel exposed. I've never much enjoyed being the center of attention. Right now I feel like Dorothy awakening after her trip to Oz. Only I didn't follow the yellow brick road. Victor took me down a rabbit hole into the darkness of the vampire world.

Rachel gives me another hug that almost strangles me. Jeff gently pulls her away.

"I'm glad you're awake, kiddo." He pats my shoulder. He's a bodyguard, watching over Rachel and me when we move about the city on official Agency business. Although lately he has been hanging around even when we have no business, and I'm pretty sure his relationship with Rachel has moved beyond simply professional.

"We all are," Clive Anderson says, his voice weary but still commanding authority.

He's the director of the Agency. My boss. I already know

that my report to Clive will leave out a lot of details—mainly those that involve Victor and how much I've come to care for him.

"The Night Watchmen that Sin turned—at least tell me that you got them."

The Night Watchmen are the most respected group in the city, dealing with any vampires who breach our wall. Somehow Sin infiltrated them and did the unthinkable: He turned some of them into vampires. He corrupted the incorruptible.

"We called a special meeting of the Night Watchmen," Clive says. He explains that they locked the doors, and brought out buckets of blood. The Day Walkers couldn't stop their fangs from dropping and those who hadn't been turned staked them. "We're confident we got them all. We haven't had a Day Walker attack since."

"But that's just the Night Watchmen. What if there are others Sin turned?"

"Then we'll be facing an absolute nightmare come to life. We'll be at war all over again. Only this time, the enemy can walk in the sun."

"But you shouldn't concern yourself with that right now," Rachel says, knowing that I could discuss this issue with Clive for hours. "We weren't able to contain the news that a Day Walker exists. Too many kids at the party saw Sin at school. But at this point, we have no proof that the turned Night Watchmen were in fact Day Walkers. Still, we've increased the guards on patrol, and the Night Watchmen are working day shifts. We're doing what we can. You just need to get well."

I look past her to Tegan. She's petite with short blond hair that frames her pixie face and makes her startling green eyes stand out. They used to be so vibrant and bright. Now they're dull, and it's all Sin's fault. She's studying the floor as though she's searching for a crack she can slip through.

"Can I have a moment alone with Tegan?" I ask.

"Sure," Rachel says, squeezing my hand before ushering out Jeff and Clive. When the door snaps closed in their wake, Tegan gives a startled jump.

"Tegan?"

Finally, she looks at me. Tears are welling in her eyes.

"I could really use a hug," I say, knowing she needs one a lot more than I do.

She rushes across the room and wraps her arms around me.

"I didn't know Sin was a vampire," she whispers brokenly near my ear. "Oh, God, I'm so sorry."

I hold her close, rocking her slightly, like she's the patient instead of me. She has a set of small, neat stitches on her neck. Why don't I? What if Victor *did* turn me? What if I am a vampire? They heal quickly; they don't scar.

"No one knew what he was," I reassure her. I hate what he did to her. I need to get out of here, find him, and make him pay.

"I should have known," she insists.

"There was no way to know."

"I loved him, Dawn, I loved him, and now I hate him."

I rub her back. "I know. I know it hurts."

She breaks out of my embrace and paces the room. "I just feel so stupid. How could I have not known?"

"No one knew. Not even Victor. Vampires can sense other vampires, but not Sin. No one knew what Sin was."

She stops with her shoulders slumped in defeat. I hate seeing her like this. She's always been ready for any adventure, grabbing all the fun she can from life. I'm afraid Sin has stolen that spontaneity and joy from her.

"I thought he was the one, you know?" she says in a low, self-effacing voice. "I've never been in love before and I thought . . . I thought he was everything. He bit me, Dawn." She jerks her head up and I see the first sign of fire and life in her eyes. "He sank his fangs into me—without even asking! I mean, how rude is that!"

"Very rude," I reassure her.

She dries her eyes, gives a few little sniffs. "Yeah, well, I plan to sink my stake into his heart without asking."

"I'll help you do it."

She gives me a quick smile before she furrows her brow. "I wasn't the only one with a vampire in my life. Victor is the new Lord Valentine. Why didn't you tell me what he was?"

I hear the edge of betrayal in her voice. Michael and Tegan had met Victor, but they'd thought he was a Night Watchman. And I hadn't corrected them. "I was afraid it would put you in danger."

"You told me you liked him, but how could you if he's a vamp?"

"It's complicated."

"Do you love him?"

I groan. "I don't know. I care for him deeply, but we're not a couple, if that's what you're asking. Humans and vampires never work out."

"You got that right," she mutters.

I know Tegan is struggling with everything she went through. In some ways, what she endured was worse than what I did. Vampires have been screwing with me for as long as I can remember. Even when I began to care for Victor, I was wary. I didn't commit my heart completely.

Tegan thought she was falling for a human.

"I hope he's dead," she says quietly.

I know she's talking about Sin. "I hope so, too."

The door opens and the nurse strides in. "Sorry, visiting time is over."

"One more minute," I plead.

"Nope. You've got a lot of recovering to do."

I give Tegan another hard hug. "It's going to be okay."

"I'll try to sneak back in when she's not looking," she whispers.

My heart lifts at a shadow of the old Tegan.

The nurse flaps her hands at Tegan like she's a bird that needs to be shooed away. "Now go on."

When I'm finally alone, I feel exhausted, but my mind is racing with so many questions that I can't sleep. I can't stand being in the bed. I throw back the blankets, sit up, and swing my legs over the side. I ease my feet to the floor and when I stand my knees buckle. I catch myself by bracing one arm on the bed and grabbing the IV stand with the other hand.

I can't believe how weak I am, but I'm also determined. Using the stand for support, I shuffle toward the window. The sun's rays stream into the small room and I pause on the edge of them. I've never been afraid of the sun. So why am I now? It used to illuminate my world, make it seem worth fighting for. But now . . .

Oh, God. Did it happen? Did Victor turn me? Is the vampire instinct to fear the light already in my blood?

I hold out my hand and tentatively ease it forward, exploring the empty space in front of me, unsure of where the sunbeams truly begin. It feels like I'm pushing toward an invisible Venus flytrap: one that may snap close, or one that may let me pass.

I watch the light kiss the tips of my fingernails. No burning.

I expose more. Up to my knuckles. No stinging.

Finally I plunge my whole hand into the bright rays, letting the golden glow wash over my skin. It feels wonderful.

I step fully into the sun and press my cheek and body against the glass of the window. Closing my eyes, I absorb the warmth. When I offered Victor my blood, I was certain that I would never again watch a sunrise, would never again experience its perfect illumination.

Yet here I am in a hospital with morning sunlight filtering gently through the window and dancing over me. I have to admit I'm slightly disappointed.

The door opening interrupts my thoughts, and I know it's the nurse, coming to poke and prod me some more. "Just give me a few more minutes," I say.

"I'll give you all the minutes you want," a deep voice replies.

I spin around, nearly losing my balance. Grabbing the sill, I lean back against the window to steady myself. "Michael."

Michael Colt. He's always worn his wheat-colored hair cropped short, but it's grown out some as though he couldn't be bothered with it. Just like Rachel looks as though she misplaced her hairbrush, Michael looks like he lost his razor. But the stubble on his jaw makes him appear tougher, older.

His cheek sports a healing gash and a yellowing bruise. His lower lip is slightly swollen. His arm is encased in a cast and I remember the crack that echoed down the alley when Brady broke it. But Michael didn't stop fighting.

"Rachel called me," he says. "I got here as soon as I could."

Of course she called him. Michael and I have been friends forever. Then a few months ago, we became more. Rachel thinks we're still a couple. But then so does *Michael*. I never got a chance to tell him that we couldn't be together anymore, that I had strong feelings for someone else. For a vampire.

Michael approaches me cautiously, as though I'll shatter if he moves too quickly. "I was afraid I'd never see those pretty eyes of yours again," he says.

It's cheesy, but my throat tightens as I fight back tears. "Oh, Michael."

Suddenly his arms are around me, and I'm clinging to him.

"I keep having nightmares about that monster that hauled you away," Michael says, his voice low, guilt-ridden. "I'm sorry, Dawn. I'm sorry I couldn't stop that . . . thing."

That thing? Brady. How much do people know? Rumors and half truths can spread very fast in a week.

"That *thing* was Brady," I say quietly, struggling to get out his name, as though I don't deserve to even speak it anymore.

He pulls back to look at me. "Your brother?"

I nod, but dizziness assaults me. I sway. He grabs my arm.

"You need to sit," he says, guiding me into a chair in the corner. He crouches in front of me. "You probably shouldn't be out of bed."

I give a little laugh. "When have I ever done anything I'm supposed to?"

He grins, and I gaze into his familiar brown eyes knowing that I'm going to have to hurt him. I don't want to, especially after everything we've gone through lately, but it's not fair to him for me to pretend my feelings haven't changed.

"So Brady, how did he become that thing?" Michael asks.

I tell him how my brother was turned by Sin all those years ago, but honorable Brady wouldn't feed on humans. He fed on vampires instead, not knowing the horrible consequences that awaited him. He became infected with the Thirst, a madness that turns vampires into the worst kind of monsters. They become rabid, craving vampire blood and destroying any human that stumbles across their path.

"How did you get away?" Michael asks. "If Brady was that powerful, how did you escape?"

"Victor. I don't know how he found me, but it's a good thing he did, because if he hadn't—"

"Victor?" he interrupts, obviously unwilling to let me paint Victor as a hero. "The *Night Watchman* you introduced me to who is now our new overlord? Old Family right in our midst and you never said anything. Why didn't you tell me the truth about him?"

"I couldn't risk placing him in danger. With Victor on the throne, we won't need the Night Watchmen. We won't need to be afraid. Victor will keep the vampires out of the city."

His features turn to stone. "What fantasy world do you live in? Nothing's changed, Dawn. If anything, it's all worse."

That can't be true. Not after all the challenges we faced, the dangers we escaped.

"Is he the one who took your blood? Who almost drained you?"

Oh, God, I know he's not going to like it, but I can't lie to him anymore. Michael deserves so much more than I've given him. If I can't love him like he deserves, I can at least be honest with him.

"He was badly wounded, dying—"

He shoots to his feet, walks to the window, and gazes out. I want to go to him, but I'm suddenly so tired. My body feels like it's weighted down with guilt and betrayal.

"You *willingly* gave him your blood?"

"He could have taken it all. He could have turned me, Michael, but he didn't. He brought me here. I don't know where he found the strength." My blood would have revived him, but it would have taken time for his gashes and torn flesh to heal. I imagine him staggering through the city, trying to get me to a hospital in time. "Please, don't tell anyone that he was the one who pierced my neck. People will think he's a monster like his father. They won't understand."

"I'm not sure I do, either." He's staring out the window, his jaw tight, his fists clenched. I don't know what to say that will make this any easier for him.

Finally he turns back to me, and I see in his somber eyes that he's come to the painful conclusion—

"You were seeing him, weren't you?"

"Not like you mean. Our paths crossed from time to time—"

"And you fell for him. How could you be so stupid?"

Knowing he has a right to be angry, I struggle to stand. "Michael, I'm so sorry. I was going to tell—"

"Save it for someone else, Dawn. I'm done listening to you."

The door opens and the nurse strides in, pushing a wheelchair. She comes up short as she notices Michael. "Young man—"

"I'm already on my way out." Michael takes two steps, then stops and turns back to me. "I'm glad you woke up. And no matter what I just said, no matter what I might say, that'll never change."

Before I can even respond, he's brushing past the nurse and slamming the door behind him. Watching him go, I know that everything has changed.

Chapter 2

I want to leave the hospital so badly. I know I'm still weak, but it feels like there is so much I need to do: make sure Tegan is really okay, straighten things out with Michael if that's even possible, and see how the Agency has held up without me. And, most importantly, talk to Victor.

Unfortunately, the nurse who came into my room isn't carrying my discharge papers. Instead, she gently guides me into the wheelchair and leads me down a hallway, saying that the doctor wants to "run some tests." I expect those tests to involve having some blood drawn, maybe getting an X-ray or two. Instead I find myself wheeled to a psychiatrist's office.

The lighting is dim, just enough to reveal the wooden walls, potted plant, and old furniture. A man, who I can only assume is the psychiatrist, spins around from his place at the window, like we've surprised him. Small but incredibly thick glasses make his gray eyes bulge, giving them an all-seeing, all-knowing glare that betrays a cold, calculating intelligence. He's unnaturally thin, as though he spends all his time lost in books and journals, nourishing his mind but forgetting the needs of his body. His black hair and mustache are perfectly trimmed.

"I'm Dr. Schwartz," he says after the nurse leaves. "Don't worry, Miss Montgomery. Your being brought to me is nothing to be concerned about. We just need to verify that you're firing on all cylinders."

"You need to make sure I'm not crazy," I say.

"We don't like to use those kinds of terms. But you have been through a very stressful experience, which can create certain anxieties. Compound that with a week in a light comatose state, and, well . . . we just want to make sure you're as healthy as possible before leaving our care."

And before I return to work. I can feel Clive's influence in this room. He cares about me, maybe too much. I've been through more than most seventeen-year-olds and he has to be questioning how much more I can take before I break. Or if I'm already broken.

Can't have a schizo delegate negotiating to protect Denver's citizens. But I know I'm fine, and I need to get out of here. So I sit down on a couch across from the doctor and he runs through the basic questions with me. I know exactly what he wants to hear, so at times, I fudge the truth just enough.

No, I've had no thoughts of self-harm.

No, I haven't felt "the blues."

Yes, I'm eating fine—or as fine as one can when dining on hospital food.

Yes, my grades were good before the incident.

Yes, my relationships are steady. Steadily falling apart, but I keep the last to myself. I've lost Michael and I'm not sure where things stand with Victor.

"Before all of this," I say, "everything was great. And my friends came to see me as soon as I woke up, and it was like nothing changed. I'm looking forward to getting back out there."

"Good. Good," Dr. Schwartz says. "I know you're lying to me, but good."

Uh-oh. I swallow hard and want to backpedal through my answers, but he just raises his hand.

"I have no plans to put you in a straitjacket," he says. "You're a teenager; you've been through a lot; you have a very stressful job. A certain amount of leniency must be given in light of all that. In fact, if anything, you're too sane. Most people in your position would've cracked by now under that much responsibility. But not you. I'm worried that you might be repressing things. Does that sound reasonable to you?"

"Yes. I've always thought that if I bury my feelings now, I can dig them up later when I have time to deal with them." Good answer, but the truth is that I don't ever want to dig them up. They're too painful, make me feel weak. I have to be strong, make my parents proud of me. Finish the work they started.

"That can create a very shaky foundation," he says.

A silence falls and I try to psychoanalyze *him*. What's he thinking? Have I sealed my own fate? So what if I keep certain emotions from getting out of control? It's worked, hasn't it? What's the alternative? Cry my heart out in a darkened corner every night? No thanks.

"I'd like to try something with you, Dawn," he says. "Dr. Icarus told me you had a dream that seemed very real."

"It was nothing. It was just . . ."

"Most dreams are nothing, just little neurons in your brain still firing while you're trying to sleep. But what interests me is what was going on inside your mind while you were in that coma. Your psyche may have taken the time to . . . rearrange things. To catch up. To unbury all those repressed feelings."

"Fine. I'm up for anything that will get me out of here. What do you want me to do?"

"Draw."

He brings out a pad of paper and pencil, then hands them to me.

"I'm not a very good artist," I say.

"All the better."

Dr. Schwartz goes around the room and dims several of the lights further until my eyes have to adjust. I struggle just to see the sketch pad on my lap.

"Okay, now lean back and relax." His voice has shifted to something soothing, mesmerizing.

Tilting my head back, I close my eyes.

"Think about that dream," he says softly. "Where were you?"

"A mountain," I say.

"Draw it."

This is really stupid and I open my eyes in protest.

"No," he says. "Keep your eyes closed. Just let your hand do the work. And think. What else was there?"

Fine. Let's get this over with.

"The moon," I say, eyes shut, pencil on paper.

And the stars, of course. A lot of them. It was a clear night. I was in the middle of nowhere, far away from a city.

I groped along the walls. My fingers touched something—a deep groove, deliberately created, not something formed by erosion. I outlined it. Too many lines, too many curves. Why is it here? What does it mean?

"I turn to look at it," I say.

It's just a symbol. But it's familiar. I've seen it before, but where? In another dream? No . . .

The symbol is complex, like several characters combined into one.

"I can't really explain it."

My heart was beating fast. My heart *is* beating fast. I can feel my pulse, the blood pumping through my veins, ending at my fingertips, controlling the pencil.

Enough of this.

I open my eyes. I'm no longer in the room, but on that mountain. Rocky cliffs surround me. And a voice calls from within the stone.

"Find me."

I put my hand against the symbol, feeling its contours, knowing every little detail. No bigger than the palm of my hand, but I can sense that it's significant. It's pulsing, drawing me in.

*I never woke up from the coma. The hospital, the visitors—
none of it was real. I'm still trapped in my own mind.*

"Find me."

*The voice is growing louder, raspier. I don't dare answer. I
don't know who it is. I don't know what he wants. But I'm scared,
scared that I've become lost. I'm compelled to move toward the
voice.*

"Find me!"

Someone grabs me—

Help! Oh my God, help me!

"Dawn!"

I'm back in the dark room. Dr. Schwartz is across from
me.

"I was there," I say.

"You were dreaming."

"No. No! I was there!"

"It felt very real, that's all," he says. "Made more powerful, perhaps, by your time spent in a comatose state. You
may be having some difficulties differentiating one reality
from another. Don't worry. That'll fade in a matter of days
as your sleep cycle returns to normal."

He turns on the lights. The world seems so hazy, a
gigantic fog settling over my mind. Nothing seems real and
I have to convince myself that it is.

"I heard something. A voice. It said, 'Find me.'"

"Hmmm . . . interesting."

He writes it down on my chart and I'm frightened of
what else is on there. Then I look down at the drawing I
made: It's scribbled nonsense, completely blacked out. The

pencil in my hand is worn down, the sharp point eroding as I dragged it across the blank paper.

But then I see it. The symbol. The one in my dreams.

Knowing that he'll collect this drawing, possibly to record my psychosis, I flip the page and quickly copy the symbol, then quietly rip it out and place it in the folds of my hospital gown.

I hand the sketch pad back to Dr. Schwartz and give him a reassuring smile.

He smiles back.

I just hope that my smile doesn't look as fake as his.

After the session I'm wheeled back to my room. I hate feeling like an invalid, but I take some comfort in the fact that they didn't deliver me to a padded cell.

I wake up to find the sun has set. The blinds at the window are raised and I can see the night. The session with Dr. Schwartz must have been more tiring that I thought. He told me that getting my sleep cycle regular again was important, but that doesn't look to be happening anytime soon. My schedule is still really off. Of course, as a delegate, I wasn't on much of one anyway. School during the day, but dealing with Valentine and vampire problems at night. I wonder if Victor is awake.

I wonder a lot of things: mostly how soon before I go out of my mind. I have nothing to distract me from my thoughts—no newspapers, no TV.

I buzz for the nurse. She's a different one from this morning: large and bulky. Her uncompromising expression tells me that I'd better be dying to have bothered her. Unfortunately for her, I've dealt firsthand with vampires. It's going to take a lot more than a stern look to cause me to retreat.

"Can I get a TV in here?" I ask.

"No TV. Doctor's orders."

"Why?"

"He doesn't think it would be good for your health."

Since the war that pitted humans against vampires, programming is limited to what we can produce in the city. For the most part, it's awful low-budget soap operas, but as far as I know they never killed anyone. Even though sometimes they make me gag. We have local news, but we get very little communication from the other cities.

"How about a newspaper, then?"

"We don't have any here."

"None? It doesn't have to be current. I want to catch up on what's been happening since I've been out of it."

"You really don't."

With that cryptic statement, she turns toward the door. "Be sure to eat your supper. The more quickly you regain your strength, the sooner you can leave."

The door slams in her wake. I glance to the side and notice the tray on wheels standing nearby. Reaching over, I pull it toward me. I lift a domed lid to unveil a gelatin that wiggles, potatoes, and grilled fabricated chicken. Yuck! I'm in the mood for a hamburger. Or steak. A real steak with warm juices oozing out of it. My parents splurged and bought the real stuff to celebrate when Dad became delegate to Lord Valentine. Only it wasn't really a celebration. We were all just trying to pretend it was good news. We knew how dangerous it would be for him to travel outside the city walls at night. We were trying to show we weren't scared.

I place the cover back over the food. Not interested.

I notice a small white box. I open it. Inside are two pieces of chocolate. There are places for four. A note is scribbled on the inside of the top of the box.

Sorry! You should have woken up while I was here. A girl can only resist so much temptation. Figure best friends share anyway, right?

Tegan was here? Maybe I'm not as recovered as I think. Now I'm fully awake. Maybe I should call her—but I have no cell phone. I'm doomed to boredom.

But just as I think that, the door opens, and I know my next visitors will not be boring. Vampires never are.

"Where's Victor? Is he okay?" I ask.

"Relax, my brother is fine. Almost recovered and back to full strength." Faith is quite possibly the most beautiful creature I've ever seen. She has perfect skin, vibrant red hair, and an hourglass figure. Her eyes are the same sharp blue as Victor's, but they look more seductive, if that were possible. Her red leather pants hug her legs all the way down to her six-inch matching heels. How does she stay upright in those things? Her scarlet blouse doesn't leave much to the imagination and I'm tempted to point out that she has a couple of buttons that are feeling neglected. She *looks* to be nearly my age, although she's been around for two hundred years.

"Then why isn't he here? Why are you?"

Richard Carrollton takes my hand and presses a kiss to it. "Victor's new responsibilities as overlord keep him pretty busy. I'm glad to see you've regained your color."

Old Family vampires are elegant, suave, sophisticated. Comfortable with what they are. Humans who are turned—Lessers—never quite achieve that beauty. Richard Carrollton is Old Family and it shows with each movement he makes. Like Victor, he's well dressed and well manicured. His jeans and buttoned shirt are crisp. A small clump of his long brown hair is braided and decorated with leather wraps that line one side of his face. Like all Old Family vampires, he's gorgeous. He's different from Victor. More party boy than poet. But they're two sides of a similar coin. I can understand why they're good friends.

"You've been here before?" I ask.

He gives a casual shrug. "Victor had us keeping watch."

"Were you in the city that night?" I ask, knowing I don't have to clarify.

Richard nods. "We did what we could to contain it."

"What about Sin? What happened to him?" If they destroyed him, they might not have told the Agency. Vampires have a tendency to keep vampire business to themselves.

Faith moves nearer to the bed. "My creepy half brother got away. We don't know where he went. Victor has hunters out looking for him."

"He . . . he turned my brother. Brady."

"He's apparently obsessed with your family," Faith says. "He may even be the one who killed your parents—possibly at Father's bidding. We don't know."

"But your father said it was rogue vampires—"

She purses her lips as though I'm the silliest thing. "Well, he certainly wasn't going to confess that he was behind their deaths, now was he?"

"But why would he kill them? What would he gain?"

She gives me a pointed look. "Think about it, Dawn. What did he gain?"

The answer slams into me, making me dizzy. "Me as delegate," I whisper, forcing out the answer, trying to make sense of it.

He had requested me, and what the mighty Lord Valentine wanted, he got. No one questioned why he would want a seventeen-year-old girl, still in high school, to serve in such an important role, yet I had always wondered.

"But why?"

"Who knows? But you were there the night he confronted Victor. He kept saying you were special."

"Special how?"

"That's the mystery," Richard says. "Victor has been going through Murdoch's journals searching for some clue, but as you can imagine, almost a thousand years' worth of handwritten text is slow going."

I sigh with the futility of it all. "Waste of time. I think Valentine was just referring to me being a pawn because he knew that Victor and I . . . I mean, that Victor . . . that I—"

"That my brother would die for you?" Faith asks.

"He wouldn't—"

"He almost did." She rolls her eyes toward the ceiling. "And that is strange because vampires are not normally emotional creatures. Not when it comes to matters of the heart."

"I disagree," Richard says. "I believe vampires can love. Deeply."

He's not looking at me anymore. He's focused on Faith, not bothering to mask his feelings for her. She refuses to meet his gaze. How can she ignore him? I know they have some sort of history, but I've only recently met them, and we're not yet to a phase in our friendship where we pour out our souls to one another. I can't imagine that we ever will be. She starts to fidget with her pearl necklace, running her slender manicured fingers over it, creating little clacking noises. Seeing the usually calm and cool Faith flustered makes her seem almost approachable.

"Hospitals give me the creeps," she finally says. "Let's find the blood-storage room, grab a midnight snack, and get out of here."

"Your wish is my command," Richard says.

She rolls her eyes again. "You can be so—"

"Romantic?" he asks.

"Banal." She turns her attention back to me and lays a small package on my lap. "Hospital gowns have never been very fashionable."

She walks from the room.

"She's not as uncaring as she acts," Richard says. "Valentine didn't tolerate weakness in his children, including showing emotions."

"You love her, don't you?"

"Let's just say I understand her." He turns to leave, stops, looks back at me. "Just so you know: What you did for Victor means a lot to us. You could have left him to die."

"No, Richard, I couldn't."

I see in his eyes that he understands. I didn't save Victor because I knew that his being alive was best for Denver. I gave him my blood because I didn't want to live in a world without him in it.

When he's gone, I open the package that Faith brought me. A crimson nightgown shimmers in spite of the dim lighting in the room. I run my fingers over it. It has to be real silk. Only the fabulously wealthy can afford something like this—and Old Family vampires have wealth beyond measure.

I imagine wearing this for Victor. I slam the box closed, then my eyes.

In spite of Victor being willing to die to save me—and me being willing to die to save him—the reality remains: He's a vampire. I'm not.

I lay back, stare up at the ceiling, and listen to the nighttime streets far below. The hum of the city, so subtle now, slowly fades until I hear nothing but the wind. Then that, too, disappears, and I hear the night. The quiet, the silence of the moon.

I turn off my lamp, welcoming the plunge of shadows.

Whereas so many of us now fear the darkness, I'm beginning to draw comfort from it. This world without light, this world of midnight sounds calms my breath, calms my heart. I feel its grasp slowly enveloping me, and all I can do is thank it for being there.

For always being there.

Chapter 3

I don't know how long I stare into the night before I hear
footsteps. Several of them. My heart speeds up along
with them. They're moving with purpose.

A strange fear takes hold and I'm tempted to try to escape
through the window, but then Rachel comes through the
doorway. Attila the Nurse is right behind her.

Rachel smiles. "Hey, kiddo. You ready to go home?"

I jerk my gaze back to the window to make sure—

"I'm not complaining, but it's night. Seems an odd time
to break me out of here."

She suddenly looks uncomfortable as she sets a small
duffle bag on the foot of my bed. "We just thought it would
draw less attention."

As a delegate, I do usually have to deal with the media
following me around. I'm actually surprised that no one

has barged into my room with a camera and microphone. I can only assume that the Agency provided guards to make sure that didn't happen.

"Well, whatever the reason, I'm ready," I say.

The nurse comes over and removes the IV from the back of my hand. I'm fascinated by a drop of blood that beads up and rolls in slow motion along my skin. The nurse slaps a bandage over the wound and the spell holding me mesmerized is broken, the tiny droplet absorbing into the cotton, taking shape like some red butterfly with broken wings. She proceeds to remove other monitoring devices that were clamped on me or stuck to my skin.

"Thanks," I say when she's finished.

She just glares at me before pivoting on her squeaky shoes and leaving the room.

"What *is* her problem?" I ask.

Rachel ignores my question and just pats the bag. "Get dressed. I'll be outside."

She doesn't have to tell me twice. I pull my long black hair back into a ponytail. It feels great to shed my drafty hospital gown and pull on the clothes she brought me: well-worn jeans, a black tank top, and a black hoodie. I place the box of chocolates and the gift from Faith into the bag. I give the room a final glance and hope I never have to come back here.

When I join Rachel in the corridor, I'm surprised by how quiet it is. But not surprised by the two guards standing by the elevator. I have no doubt that Faith and Richard charmed them in order to visit with me. Or maybe they found another way in. Vampires are very resourceful.

"Aren't there any other patients?" I ask.

"Not on this floor," Rachel says. "VIP only." She tries to smile like it's a little joke.

"You mean only people who are in danger and need twenty-four-hour guards posted at the entrances."

"Let's just say it's easier to watch you when there's no one else around."

Normally I'd call them out for being overprotective, but maybe they aren't this time. Sin may have gone underground, but he's still a threat. Plus not everyone in the city appreciates my role as delegate.

We quickly make our way to the elevator and step in. The two bodyguards join us, standing like ever-present statues ready to spring to life.

"Now that you're well, Clive wants to debrief you soon," Rachel says, the elevator rumbling downward. "There've been a number of developments since . . . since the party."

Yeah, I can just imagine.

We step out of the elevator and into the lobby. Two more guards are standing nearby. They acknowledge us with a jerk of their heads. The lobby, like my own floor, is empty, the lights dimmed or turned off completely. It's so eerie here with no one around—like it's a ghost hospital.

Jeff is outside, waiting for us beside the Agency town car. "You're looking good," he says with a bright smile.

"And how about me?" I ask teasingly, pretending that I think his comment is for Rachel.

"You're looking good, too," he says with a wink, indulging me.

"Will you two knock it off?" Rachel says, then gives me a pointed look. "Yes, Jeff and I are dating." She ducks into the backseat.

"Awesome," I say as I join her. "About time you admitted it."

On the drive home, I welcome the sight of familiar places. I spot the Works, a sprawling mass of steel pipes reaching out to the sky. Out of the top plumes the constant blue smoke, created from the processing and burning of coal, which fuels the massive generator that provides electricity to the city. It also coats the city in soot, giving it a blackness that mirrors the oppression we faced under Valentine's rule. It'll be different with Victor. The darkness won't seem so dark.

"Can we take a detour by Day Street?" I ask.

"I don't think that's a good idea," Rachel says.

"Please? I just . . . I need to see it."

I notice Jeff studying Rachel in the rearview mirror, waiting for her decision.

"Okay," she finally says.

Day Street is what all of Denver is working toward becoming. When the sun sets and the shadows lengthen and creep between the buildings, huge streetlamps come on and chase back the darkness, making people feel safe.

But at this time of night, in spite of the bright lights, the street is completely empty. It wasn't abandoned before Sin wreaked havoc. A few people could always be seen taking in the evening, feeling the warm glow of the halogen bulbs, pretending for a moment that they weren't afraid, that they were the masters of the night.

Then I spot the Daylight Grill. It's a popular teen hangout. Or at least it was. Now it's boarded up. This is where we held the Teen Initiative party.

I started a campaign to get teens to donate blood in an attempt to increase our supply and keep Lord Valentine satisfied. The reward for donating was a free ticket to an entire night of dancing, food, and live music. As the sun set, we locked everyone into the Daylight Grill so no vamps could get in and ruin the fun. Unfortunately, the vampires were already there. Sin had decided to use the venue to reveal that he was the first Day Walker to ever exist. He did it by unleashing hell.

Jeff slows the car to a crawl. Flowers, plush teddy bears, and burning candles create a memorial in front of the building. Pictures of people my age—some I recognize from school—are mounted to the boards covering the space where the windows once were. And words have been scrawled in dripping red paint that gives a sinister feel to the messages left.

We won't forget.

We love you.

Vampires will pay.

Death to Dawn.

My chest tightens painfully with the last one, because I'm pretty sure they aren't referring to the sunrise. I swallow past the lump in my throat. "How many died?"

"Twelve confirmed," Rachel says in a raw whisper, and I know she didn't want me to have to face this yet. "Three are still missing."

As we roll past, I can't seem to tear my gaze from "Death to Dawn."

"Is this why we left the hospital at night?"

"During the day, people gather there, chanting, protesting. We weren't sure we'd be able to control the crowd if word got out that you were being discharged."

Jeff turns the corner and speeds up, maybe fearing that our little detour did more harm than good.

"People blame me," I say, almost trancelike.

"It's not your fault, Dawn. People don't know where to direct their grief and anger. You're a symbol, that's all. The Daylight Grill is going to be renovated and it'll reopen. It may take a while but things will return to normal."

Normal wasn't so great.

"Blood donations?" I ask, trying to make this conversation professional when it is painfully personal.

"No one's donating. People are advocating that we break the VampHu Treaty, that we fight the vampires."

"But this was all Sin's doing. People have to give Victor a chance to show that humans and vampires can work in harmony."

"People aren't in the mood to listen right now, Dawn. Even the Agency isn't trusted. We have to repair our reputation."

I try not to sink into despair. I had such hope for the future. Now it's just like Michael warned me: Things are worse.

When we get to our apartment building, Jeff sees us safely inside before leaving. Rachel and I take the elevator to our floor. I breathe a sigh of relief when we walk into our apartment. At least here, everything is the same. No, not quite. Rachel and I aren't slobs, but things are just a little too pristine. "The hospital didn't have any newspapers. So where are ours?"

"I tossed them already."

"Rachel." I give her a pointed look.

"You don't need all that mess in your head yet."

"It's already in my head." I pull my hair free of the ponytail. "What day is it anyway? Do I have school tomorrow?"

"Friday. And about school, the Agency has decided to hire a tutor. You'll take lessons here."

"Why?" And then it hits me. "Because of what people are writing on the wall at the Daylight Grill?"

"Clive just thinks it'll make things easier on you."

"No."

"Dawn—"

"No, Rachel. I'm not going to become a prisoner in this apartment or hide out. The Teen Initiative was a good idea. It worked. We were finally able to meet our blood quota. No one could have anticipated the arrival of a vampire who could walk in the sun and would throw Denver into chaos."

"We'll talk about it later."

She can talk all she wants, but I'm going to school Monday morning. I'm not weak and I don't scare easily. If I retreat into hiding, Sin will have won a little bit of his war. I'm not going to be one of his victims.

"Try and get some sleep," she says as she hugs me.

I squeeze her back, grateful she's in my life. I know she and Clive mean well, but I have to do what's best for me.

I walk into my room and close the door. It's so good to be here. Home.

I glance at the clock on the bedside table. It's a little after midnight. I should be tired, but I'm not. Maybe a warm shower will help. I unpack my duffle bag, putting the few items in it away. The last thing I take out is the picture I drew for the shrink. I trace my finger over the symbol. My palm tingles and it's almost as though my blood sings, "Find me."

What the hell is that? I place it gently on my desk, unsure if it holds secrets, or is just an image of my psychosis. I should destroy it, crumple it up, throw it away, but something holds me back. This stupid piece of paper feels alive. . . .

God, what is wrong with me? I scurry into the bathroom and study my reflection in the mirror above the sink. I'm not even sure what I'm looking for: proof that I've somehow changed or reassurance that I'm the same. I'm thinner than I was and my blue eyes look too big for my narrow face. Leaning in, I pull my black hair to the side and scour my neck for any signs of a vampire bite. It's like my crucifix tattoo was never even touched, let alone punctured. Strange.

I comb my fingers roughly through my hair. Too much doesn't make sense. I have to visit Valentine Manor. I have to talk to Victor. I need to see for myself that he's all right.

He told me that we couldn't be together, that I was his weakness and his enemies would use me against him. And Sin did exactly that.

But Victor came anyway. He risked his life for mine, just as I risked mine for his.

The last thing I remember isn't his eyes, but his breath on my neck, the smell of his hair combined with the coppery scent of my own blood, the feel of it running down my skin. And his tongue lapping at the precious, life-giving fluid. I felt his strength growing with every beat of my heart, every ounce of blood that flowed through my veins and into his; but I need to see for myself that he's fully recovered. I must go out to Valentine Manor. Tomorrow night.

"It's a date," I whisper with conviction to my reflection.

Turning away, I start the shower, strip out of my clothes, and climb into the tub. The warm water feels wonderful cascading over me. After being bound to a hospital bed, everything seems more sensitive. It's almost as though I can feel each individual drop. The lilac shampoo and soap I use is sweeter than it was before. Maybe because it hasn't been opened in so long. I could stay here forever, enjoying the sensations, but the water is beginning to lose its warmth.

I turn it off, step out, and blot all the water from my skin with a towel. I slip on my cotton pants and tank top. It's hard to believe such simple things can be an absolute luxury.

Turning off the light, I go into my bedroom, disappointed

not to find a vampire sitting on my bed. The first time Victor came to my room he threatened me, threatened to kill Rachel if I screamed. But even then, as much as I hated him for being a vampire, I instinctively trusted him, sensing that his threats were bluffs. I never told anyone about his visits. I miss him terribly now.

I turn off my light and crawl into bed. I stare at the door to the balcony, wishing, hoping Victor will come through it. But he doesn't.

Chapter 4

*T*he mountain. The rock walls surrounding me. The pathway
ahead, which I inevitably follow.

*A shadow darts past, not too far from where I stand. It disap-
pears into the inky blackness where the moonlight can't reach it.*

*"Hello?" I whisper, but just my voice echoes back to me from
the emptiness.*

"Hellooo?"

Nothing.

*My bare feet feel the rough, cold rock, and I kick up a pebble. I
hear it skittering over the hard ground, then silence. Seconds pass.*

Ping!

Thump.

*I realize I'm at the edge of a crevice. I could slip over at any
moment. Would I fall into eternity?*

I pick up my pace. The mountain juts out and I hug the wall, my toes gripping the edge of the cliff. I make it past the corner. The mountain curves inward and I have more room, but still I can feel the walls squeezing in on me, their emptiness somehow taking form, pushing on me.

The darkness goes on forever, its dimension infinite, able to hide anyone . . . anything.

I want to rush forward, but I'm held here by something I can't define.

"Find me."

How? How can I?

"Find me."

Who are you?

"Find me!"

My world collapses, and then comes together again. I'm in bed, sweating, my breaths short. It's still dark.

"They're getting worse, aren't they?"

The voice is not the one from my dreams. It's familiar and comforting; it grounds me in this world rather than one of illusion.

"Victor!" I can see his silhouette so clearly with the moonlight streaming in through the window. He's sitting on the edge of my bed. Reaching out, he tucks my hair behind my ear, his palm skimming along my cheek. I welcome the warmth of his skin. Old Family vampires are born vampires. They're warm-blooded, have heartbeats just like us. But they need to drink human blood for sustenance. "You're okay. You're really okay."

Lunging up, I wrap my arms around him. He puts his

around me, holding me tightly. I can smell the earthy rich-
ness of his unique scent and hear the rapid thudding of
his heart. Mine is beating out the same rhythm. He has
an inexplicable hold on me, and I wonder if things will
change between us since he took my blood. I think of that
moment when his fangs pierced my skin. While I was con-
scious I experienced a mixture of pain and ecstasy. Since
then, whenever I've thought about it, I've been unable to
determine which sensation was stronger.

"I can't stay long," he says. "I just had to see you, to
know you were truly awake. Now I can finally sleep."

"I'm so grateful you're alive. They say someone brought
me to the hospital. That was you, wasn't it?"

He eases away. "Yes."

Leaning over, I turn on the lamp so I can see him more
clearly. He's as gorgeous as ever. His black hair brushes over
his shoulders. He's wearing a black T-shirt and jeans. He
would blend in with the night, but here in my blue bedroom he stands out. And I'm glad, so glad he's here.

"You *did* have the strength to stop taking my blood," I
say. "I know you were afraid you wouldn't."

"I barely drew away in time," he says, his voice a rasp.
"Your blood . . . is unlike anything I've ever tasted before.
So sweet. It was like . . . it held power over me. I can't
explain it."

He turns his back on me and plows his hands through
his hair in frustration. "Even now, it calls to me."

"It's just because it was fresh—"

"No, it's more than that. I nearly killed you, Dawn. I

pride myself on my control. For me, human blood is nourishment, a necessary evil, and nothing more. It's always been like that, until you came along. You bring out the monster in me, Dawn."

My neck starts to throb, right where Victor drew blood. Maybe it's the pounding of my heart setting it off. It's kicked into high gear ever since I realized Victor was near. As though it's calling for him, he turns back to me and skims his fingers along my tattoo. He appears mesmerized.

"I have no scars," I say to bring his attention back to my eyes.

"I gave you a blood kiss."

Just when I think I know everything about vampires, I learn that I don't. "What's that?"

"I sealed the wound with a kiss. Vampire saliva carries a weakened version of our rejuvenating properties, but it's enough to heal a bite mark. In the days before blood could be safely drawn and stored, when we had no choice except to take blood directly from the source, it was a way to ensure our donor didn't bleed to death and that he could remain anonymous, if he wanted. Most did."

"Tegan had stitches from Sin's bite."

"I doubt he took the time to properly tend her wound."

"But you did."

"You say that like I'm a hero. I should have never taken from you to begin with."

"I offered, Victor. A gift. It would have been rude not to accept. And I know how Old Family vampires adore etiquette."

He releases a soft laugh, relaxing a little. Old Family vampires have rigid codes of behavior. I had to learn all these silly rules—how to walk, how to curtsy, how to sit like a lady—before I met with Lord Valentine. I hated all of it. But there was kind of a grace to it. And I don't want Victor to regret taking what I offered.

"Victor, I've been thinking about Brady."

"You can't feel guilty, Dawn. What you did, you did out of love for him. You set him free. In his final moment, he was thankful for what you did."

My head knows that, but my heart is having a difficult time accepting it. Brady thought the blood of an Old Family vampire could cure him of his affliction—reverse what Sin had done and turn him back to a human. He abducted me to lure Victor into his trap. Victor had four hundred years to develop his fighting skills, but with Brady's Thirst-increased strength they were well matched. I decided which way the tide would turn. I chose Victor. We killed Brady together, both our hands on the stake. No, not killed. As Victor said, we set him free.

Brady never wanted to be a monster. He'd gone insane. All he wanted was to be cured.

But there is no cure for the Thirst or vampirism—except death.

"I want to give him a proper funeral—"

"I knew you would want that. I was going to arrange a burial for him, but when I returned for him the next night, I discovered the sun had turned him to ash."

"But he was a Day Walker, immune to the sun."

"I was as surprised as you. Day Walkers are a new

phenomenon. There's so much we don't know about them, but apparently after one dies, he's simply a vampire and the sun is once again his enemy."

The image of Brady's body turning to ash saddens me, the sunlight scorching him until nothing remains. But I close my eyes tighter, and see him drifting through the wind, up and up, to rejoin the beautiful sky that he loved. Maybe . . . maybe it's better that he be up there than buried in the ground.

I open my eyes. We could go on for hours about the dangers of the Day Walkers, even more so about the Thirst. But right now I want to talk about us. I know it's unwise to tempt us both, but still I sink back onto the bed, bringing him with me until we're lying on our sides, face-to-face.

"What did you mean when you said, 'They're getting worse'?" I ask.

He cradles my face, skims his thumb over my cheek as though he can't stand to not touch me. "When you were in your coma, I knew you were dreaming. Your eyes fluttering, your body sweating, jerking slightly. Every time I thought you'd wake up, but you didn't. I was worried you'd be trapped forever in some kind of nightmare world. I was afraid that even though you were right in front me, I'd never be able to reach you."

"You were there? When I was in the coma?"

"Every night. Just long enough to make sure you were still breathing."

"Faith and Richard said you weren't coming into the city."

He grins. "I don't tell them everything."

The most Victor and I have ever shared is an amazing kiss, but I'm closer to him than I've ever been to anyone in my life. It's more than the fact that we faced death together. We saved each other, in more ways than one.

"How did you know I was here?" I ask.

He brushes his fingertips over my neck, over the place where he drew blood. "I saw you leave the hospital. I was hoping the nightmares would stop. Are you dreaming about me taking your blood?"

I see the worry in his eyes; the thought that he's responsible for my nightmares is unbearable to him. "No, no. It's weird. It makes no sense. I'm wandering through a mountain, and someone is calling to me to find him. It seems so real that I'm always disoriented when I wake up. The doctor had me talk to a shrink. He says it's nothing. Just my subconscious trying to figure things out."

"Humans are so complicated."

"And vampires aren't?"

"Maybe it's just you who's complicated." He releases another soft laugh.

I enjoy that rich sound for a moment. It seems like since we met it's been nothing but drama and near-death. I have to cherish these precious moments, because they're so rare.

He's still stroking my throat and I'm growing warm. He's looking into my eyes but every now and then his gaze flicks down. Then finally it doesn't come back to my eyes. His nostrils flare and I imagine he can smell my blood, because I can hear it thundering between my ears.

"Is it hard being overlord?" I try to distract him.

His eyes shift back to mine. "Harder than I expected. I'm going to have to demand more blood."

"Rachel says people have stopped donating. They're frightened."

The muscle in his jaw clenches. "They'll have reason to be if they don't give blood."

Shoving him back, I sit up. "That sounds like a threat, Victor."

"If vampires don't get human blood, they'll turn on themselves, become infected with the Thirst. Then no one will be safe. You've seen what it does. Do you really want that to come to Denver?"

A chill runs through me and I rub my arms. "Of course not. But . . ."

"But what?"

"You can't just demand blood. You know that doesn't work."

Victor seems to lose patience. "I need blood. End of story."

I swallow hard. "Then you'll have to talk to the delegate, and right now, I don't want to shift into delegate mode. I just want to be Dawn with you. I don't want you to be the overlord. I just want you to be Victor." *My Victor.*

"It's not something I can turn off, like a light switch." He rolls to a sitting position, his feet hitting the floor, his back to me. I want to press myself against him, curl around him. "I thought you were different, Dawn. I thought you understood."

"And I thought you were different from your father."

He comes up off the bed in a blur of fury. Old Family vampires can move that quickly, that smoothly. I know I should be frightened, but I've never been scared of Victor. Even in the beginning when I first realized what he was. I hated him. But I was never afraid to stand up to him.

"Never compare me to the Bloody Valentine," he grounds out.

I jerk up my chin. "Then don't act like him. You once told me that bullying humans into giving blood wasn't the way to handle the tenuous relationship that exists between our kinds."

He plows his fingers through his hair. "I didn't realize how bad it was out there. Father never talked about it. He kept control over the Lessers with an iron fist; if one of them stepped out of line, he killed him. I don't want to do that, so I need blood to stave them off. I don't have time to be diplomatic. Once they've been fed, they'll listen to reason."

"The citizens of Denver will listen to reason," I say. "Have you held a press conference? Have you tried talking to the people? Your father never did that; this is how you can show that you're different from him."

"After Hell Night, they don't care what I have to say."

"Hell Night?"

He groans. "That's what they're calling the night of the Teen Initiative party. You know how the media is; they need a catchy sound bite."

"And an appropriate description."

"Unfortunately, Sin damaged the human-vampire

relationship. It may be beyond repair at this point."

I clamber off the bed to face him evenly in order to give more weight to my words. "I believe in us, Victor. With you as overlord and me as delegate, we can make things better for humans *and* vampires."

Pain crosses his features. "Don't, Dawn. I've told you before that you're my weakness. There can be nothing between us. Nothing. So, I wanted to tell you in person . . . I'll be requesting a new delegate."

Is he serious? He has to be; he wouldn't joke about that. And it hurts so badly, like his hand is wrapped around my gut, squeezing tighter. I always complained about the difficulties of the job, how I never wanted it. But now that it could be taken away, I realize it means much more to me; it has started to define me. I'm not sure how *not* to be a delegate.

I want to be professional, but this is personal.

"When did I become such a liability to you? I helped you overthrow your father. I saved your life. I've proven that I'm not afraid of what you are!"

"You should be!"

Victor looks at me with those sharp eyes, a haunting anger in them. Not at me, but at himself. I remember that look from long ago. Before I loved him . . . before we meant so much to each other, I saw that look.

"What are you so afraid of, Victor?"

"I'm afraid of what I'll do to you. We can't be together, Dawn. Not professionally. Not . . . romantically."

"Then why are you here?"

"Because it's difficult to let go."

I barely see him move, but suddenly I'm in his arms again, his mouth hot and demanding on mine. I scrape my fingers up into his hair and hold him close as he deepens the kiss. I want this forever, but it's never felt so far away.

Victor draws back. He presses his thumb to the erratic pulse at my throat. What song does it sing to him? I see his teeth clench, and his fangs begin to grow. He releases me and steps away. "I don't understand. It's like your blood is a drug that overpowers everything else. I want *you*, Dawn. And yet . . ."

"You can control it."

"I don't know if I can. I have to go."

He heads toward the balcony with purpose. I could keep him here with a single word. But he has to leave. If he doesn't, things between us will change dramatically, and I'm not sure I'm ready for that. He'll take us places I'm not prepared to go. Not yet, anyway . . .

Suddenly he stops, his gaze falling on my desk. He lifts the paper that I snuck out of the shrink's office. "What's this?"

"Nothing, really. Just something I see in my dream."

He faces me then, his brow furrowed. "This dream that seems so real?"

"Yeah."

"How does this symbol come into play?"

"It's carved into the side of the mountain."

"Strange," he says, studying the drawing carefully. "It's

Ancient Vampiric. It hasn't been used in a thousand years, at least."

"Why would it be in my dream? I've never even seen it before."

"I don't know, Dawn."

"Well, what does it say?"

"I don't know that either. Like I said, it's ancient. Vampires don't even use their own language anymore, let alone the ancient version of it. All I know is that it's a character or symbol from a long time ago."

I look at it with him, hoping this new information will help me pick out something different. But it still just looks like a mess of lines to me.

"Well," I say, "who does know Ancient Vampiric?"

"You'd have to find an Old Family vampire, one old enough to remember this. I'm not sure if there's any alive. As you know, Old Family stick together, but they also have an unfortunate tendency to kill one another."

"No humans know this stuff, huh?"

Victor looks up, his expression troubled. "Actually, there was one."

"Who?"

"Your father."

Chapter 5

The next morning, after Rachel leaves for work, I find myself studying the symbol and thinking about Victor's revelation regarding my father's knowledge of Ancient Vampiric. I shouldn't have been surprised. During the war, my father was an intelligence officer. He was known as the foremost expert in vampirology. He helped draft the VampHu Treaty that brought a final end to the war. And before he became a delegate, he was a professor of vampire studies at the local university.

Much of his work from the war is archived at the Agency, and I can't help but wonder if I might find some clue there regarding the meaning of this symbol.

I head to the Agency, sunglasses in place, my hoodie pulled up over my head so I'm not easily recognizable and am less likely to run into any "Death to Dawn" advocates.

Strapped to my thigh is a leather holster and stake that Victor gave me shortly after we met. I have another stake tucked into my boot. Beneath the high collar of my shirt is a chain-link choker to protect my neck. Just because there have been no incidents since Hell Night and the Agency thinks they destroyed all the Day Walkers doesn't mean none are around. Besides, Sin is somewhere and I want to be totally prepared if he steps into my path. I'm going to take him down.

I hop on a trolley. It carries the usual Saturday crowd. Looking out the window, I can see the city move by lazily. Few cars are on the street, and those that pass us are usually Agency-owned. Gasoline is rationed—by the Agency. For the most part, people walk or "ride the rails" of the trolley.

As we near the center of the city, the government district, everything becomes cleaner, brighter. Once the war ended, the rebuilding efforts began in the center and expanded outward. But progress has been slow. Supplies are scarce. VampHu outlawed any sort of mass distribution vehicles. No airplanes, no eighteen-wheelers. One train is allowed to travel across the country delivering goods from one city to the other. The only thing in abundance anymore is fear, and hatred for the vampires that made us into this. I think about what Victor said last night, how the citizens wouldn't want to listen to him now. Sadly, in the light of day, I think he's right.

I spot the Agency building long before we reach it. In the heart of the city, it looks like a giant crystal cigarette.

It's a tower of windows reflecting the sun outward. Its brightness is the perverse opposite of the despair that surrounds it.

I step off the trolley and walk the last couple of blocks. The guard in the lobby waves me through. He's always taken his job seriously. Doesn't even offer a smile or ask how I'm doing. That's fine with me. I'm on a mission and I want to get in and out before Rachel is alerted that I'm here. She and Clive have become too protective.

I take the elevator to the basement floor, the archives. Stepping into the short, dimly lit hallway, I greet the man sitting at the receptionist table.

"Hello, Calvin."

"Miss Montgomery," he says. "It's been a while."

Calvin is in his midtwenties and has shaggy hair. His thick glasses are always sliding down his nose in an attempt to escape. A harmless guy who I think might live down here. Someone Tegan could make look good with just an hour of his time. But I don't think he'd keep it up. Besides, he may not have an hour to spare: A road twenty miles long could be made out of all the documents and books in this massive archive, all waiting to be categorized by this one-man army.

"I'm still waiting on that date you promised me," he says. "Remember? For finding out the original birthplace for Murdoch Valentine. It wasn't easy."

"Or very useful," I say. He was born somewhere in eastern Europe. A country that disappeared centuries ago. I remember hoping it would give me some edge in my first encounter with Valentine. I don't know what I was thinking. I guess you can never have too much knowledge about your enemy, though.

"Well, maybe I'll let it slide, then," he says. "What can I help you with today?"

I show him the symbol from my dreams. He studies it in much the same way Victor did.

"It looks like Ancient Vampiric. I haven't seen this in a long time."

"Any idea what it says?"

"Not a clue. The only thing I can tell you is that it's probably a name. It's so complex, you know? Not a common word, but a collection of sounds, if that makes any sense."

"Kind of. Like the name of a person?"

"Or a place. No way of knowing."

"I heard that my dad knew some stuff about Ancient Vampiric."

"Some. Not a whole lot. I mean, don't get me wrong, your dad was a genius with this kind of thing. The leader in vampire historical studies. But this language is so rare, only a handful of surviving documents use it at all, not nearly enough for accurate translations."

"Do you have any of his notes down here?"

"Yeah, follow me."

Calvin takes me down the halls of bookshelves, each one holding its own history of events long past and long forgotten. I'm staring at the life's work of men and women gathering dust, just as they themselves do now.

Calvin eventually stops in front of a shelf and pulls down a large box.

"Here you are. This is the carton you'll be interested in. It contains the notes he made during an expedition to Romania. He went during the war when it was incredibly dangerous. But the government hoped he might be able to find information about the way vampires worked, some hidden weakness or something. He was in charge of finding their origin. I don't think he had much luck, but his notes on Ancient Vampiric are in here. You can take this to that desk. Just check out with me when you're finished."

At the simple desk with its single lamp that probably hasn't been used in years, I empty the box. I trail my fingers over a leather-bound journal. It's held closed with leather strips, tied in a loose knot by my father. I remember walking into his office and seeing him secure it. What secrets does it hold? I think about the hand that wrote it being the same hand that tucked me in at night. It's almost like he's here with me now.

I spread out various documents and begin studying them. Most are notes that don't seem very helpful, more like observations of vampire ruins. Dad looked through ancient castles, the older the better. Especially the cellars, where Old Family vamps might've hidden during the day.

After half an hour I find something interesting. In a plastic protective sleeve is a very, very old piece of paper, yellowed and brittle with time. It's filled with symbols and characters from a language I couldn't even begin to decipher. But beneath it is a stack of papers labeled "Ancient

Vampiric Text." I begin reading it, placing my father's voice over my own:

> Carbon dating puts this document back at least two thousand years. The ink itself is strangely advanced and well preserved, leading me to believe that the vampires who created this knew it would need to last. I found it kept in a cool, dry room, high above the ground in case of floodwaters. The placement was purposefully careful. . . .
>
> This Ancient Vampiric text is the most complete I have ever found. Unfortunately, without more characters, or a direct translation into ancient Latin, it will be impossible to make any meaningful deciphering of it. However, I do believe that this may be a document of great importance, by noting what appears to be fourteen signatures at the bottom. . . .
>
> This could be the Genesis of the Fourteen Families. I gather that from the unique, single characters, spaced in such a way to make it appear as a contract. These symbols are repeated throughout the document, and I believe it may be some kind of agreement. Perhaps, and this is just speculation, an agreement regarding where each of the families' domain of influence will be. . . .
>
> Also of note is a symbol that appears to be very similar in complexity to the unique fourteen signatures. However, it is not in line with the signatures. This leads me to believe that the symbol in question is not an Old Family, but rather a single notation for the Fourteen Families as a whole. Perhaps they used this complex symbol whenever referring to themselves as a single collective. . . .

He drew the symbol, and my hands begin to shake. It looks exactly like the one I have in my pocket.

Dad thinks it was the collective signature of the Fourteen Families. I've never seen it on any other vampire documents. Then again, I've never seen this language. Vampires adopted whatever language the humans who surrounded them used.

Maybe, then, this symbol is just something deeply buried in my subconscious. Dad worked on this before I was born, but if he kept his notes in the house, it's quite possible I looked at them as a child. Could this symbol, which he painstakingly drew, have burned itself deep within my memory banks? It's possible. While I was in a coma, my brain was "sorting things out," as Dr. Schwartz said. Maybe it found this symbol lurking somewhere and brought it forward. It doesn't mean there's any reason to its being, just some misfiring neurons scattered throughout my mind.

I'm not sure whether I'm more at ease or not. But at least I have something to go on.

I look through the box again, and at the very bottom, find something that calms my hands instantly: a picture of my mom and dad. They're young. I don't see wedding bands on their fingers. This must've been while they were dating! They're sitting at a table outside a restaurant; maybe a friend took the photo. They seem so happy.

I used to gather the photos of my family, take them to where we once lived, and burn them one by one. It was my method of letting emotions out. I never told anyone because it sounds so insane, but it was the only way I could keep from snapping. That place was where I housed my emotions, not my heart, because it can't handle the burden.

It ended up being the last place where Brady and I were together. I can never go back there again.

I hold up the photo and know that this will never feel the burn of flames. Like the document next to it, the Genesis of the Fourteen Families, this is the beginning of Mom and Dad. There's something pure and perfect about it. So I take it with me when I leave. I figure Calvin would forgive me if he knew.

The other things that I've taken, though, my father's journal and notes—he probably wouldn't forgive me for that.

Chapter 6

My stolen items tucked securely in my backpack, I take the elevator up to the lobby floor and head for the door. Avoiding eye contact, I keep my head down. The last thing I want is for someone to stop me for a conversation, delay my exit, and possibly discover what I've "borrowed."

"Dawn Montgomery."

A chill skitters up my spine and I slam to a halt. The very, very last thing I wanted was to run into Roland Hursch. Since day one he had a problem with me being the delegate and he wasn't shy when it came to being vocal about it in front of cameras: I was far too inexperienced, far too immature, and definitely far too young.

I turn on my heel and angle my chin defiantly. The wealthiest man in town is decked out in a sharp gray suit. His salt-and-pepper hair is perfectly styled. "Mr. Hursch."

"I'm glad to see you've recovered from your ordeal." He's wearing a smug expression. I might try to read something into it if he didn't always have his face set the same way. It's like he wears a mask. "Lila's been concerned about you."

Lila. His daughter, my nemesis. If she was worried it was that I'd pull through.

"Thanks, but she doesn't need to worry about me."

"You must be relieved to have the burden of being delegate removed from your shoulders."

Alarm bells ring in my head. How does he know? Victor told me only last night. It's not official. Neither Clive nor Rachel has said anything. "What are you doing here?" I ask, knowing his distaste for the Agency usually keeps him far away from here.

"I'm meeting with Clive, to get my marching orders."

I study him, trying to figure out what he's talking about. "I don't understand."

He grins widely, his eyes filled with the righteous indignation that accompanied his TV rants against vampires. "Why, Miss Montgomery, I'm the new delegate to Lord Valentine."

"Roland Hursch? Really? Roland Hursch?"

Rachel jumps to her feet like a bomb has gone off beneath her desk when I burst into her office, slamming the door behind me, but going to Clive wasn't an option since Roland Hursch was on his way there. I can only breathe the same air he does for so long before I start to feel poisoned.

"Who told you?" she asks.

"He did. In the lobby just now."

"I'm sorry you had to find out that way," she says. "I was told only this morning. It's the reason I was called in—to put the reports together for him. I was going to break the news to you tonight." She comes around her desk to face me. "I know this isn't what you expected after all the sacrifices you've made for the Agency, for the citizens—"

"Has Clive totally lost his mind?" I can see the distress in her eyes because she thinks I've just learned I'll have to step down. But Victor already told me that my delegate days were over. I just didn't think he meant, like, right that second. I start pacing as Rachel leans her hips against her desk and folds her arms over her chest.

"Roland Hursch?" I repeat because my brain just doesn't want to absorb that possibility. "He's always spouting anti-vampire propaganda. For years, he's been advocating that we stop giving blood to vampires."

"It wasn't Clive's choice. Lord Valentine requested him and, as you know, the overlord chooses the delegate. None of these changes are a reflection on your work—"

I wave my hand to cut her off, because I'm not looking for sympathy. "I'm not worried about that." I'm just trying to figure out what Victor is thinking. He needs someone on his side, someone who believes in him. If it's not going to be me, it should be Rachel, someone who I can convince to give Victor a chance, someone who values my opinion. But Roland Hursch? If he were on fire and I pointed it out to him, he'd tell me that I was too young to understand what

I was seeing. So yeah, he's not going to listen to anything I might tell him about vampire relations.

"But why—never mind." Victor is no fool. He's adopting the old adage of keeping your friends close, but your enemies closer. He must see Hursch as the main obstacle to him getting his precious blood. If he can control Hursch, he'll control the supply. But I don't think Victor knows what he's getting into.

"Your job now is just to finish school," Rachel says kindly.

I stop my pacing. "I could help you train Hursch."

"Believe it or not, the new Lord Valentine believes all the Victorian etiquette rules you had to follow are pointless."

I can't help but smile. Victor would think that. He told me I wouldn't have to wear the corset and long Victorian dress when I came to see him. Of course, that was when he was still planning on me serving as delegate. But now that he knows his father wasn't the only one willing to use me to get to him . . . I'm a liability.

"Roland Hursch will actually be taking a limo out to Valentine Manor," Rachel continues.

"Lucky guy," I say, remembering how uncomfortable traveling in the horse-drawn coach was.

"We'll continue to offer you protection until this Sin guy is apprehended," Rachel assures me. "And we'll call on your vampire expertise from time to time. Like your father, you have keen instincts and insights where they're concerned. But for the most part, Dawn, embrace this opportunity to regain your youth."

I expected to feel glad. Instead I feel untethered. "It might be too late for that, Rachel."

She gives me a nod and a look that indicates she thinks I might be right. "What are you doing here anyway?"

I shrug. "I wanted to check some stuff in the archives."

"Now, see," she says as she shoves away from her desk, places her hand on my shoulder, and begins ushering me toward the door, "that's precisely what you need to stop doing. Go home, read a romance, take a bubble bath, sit on the balcony, and do absolutely nothing."

Do absolutely nothing? Is she kidding me? Sin is out there, Day Walkers may still be among us, the Thirst is a threat, and the citizens have stopped donating blood. Doing *nothing* is not in my near future.

On my way home, the trolley rattles beneath me, the seats feeling more uncomfortable than usual. My day took a turn I wasn't expecting, but I don't have to be a delegate to search for Sin. I'm lost in my thoughts when my phone vibrates. It's a text from Tegan:

Can I come over? Wanna catch up.

I text her back to meet me at my place.

An hour later I open the front door and let her in. We hug. She seems frail somehow and that worries me. "Are you okay?" I ask.

She pulls away from me. "Yeah, sure. Isn't everyone when they're attacked by a vampire?"

She starts walking through the living room, picking things up, putting them back down. I feel so inadequate.

I'm not sure how to comfort her. "Want some coffee?"

"No thanks."

"How about some hot chocolate?"

She stops her aimless wandering and smiles at me. "I never say no to chocolate."

I grin at her before heading to the kitchen. "Thanks, by the way, for bringing me some candy in the hospital."

"I'm so glad you're out of there."

"Me too." I start making coffee for me, hot chocolate for her. "I've just been so tired today. I keep waking up at night and sleeping during the day. The doctor said I'd get back on a normal sleep schedule soon."

I hand her a mug of hot chocolate, then pour myself some coffee, drink half, and refill the cup again. I peer over at her. "How are you doing?"

"Not sleeping. Day or night. When I close my eyes, I keep seeing that gaping mouth and those fangs. Those awful fangs. They hurt going in." She rubs her neck. "Then it didn't. It started to feel good. How could it do that?"

"I think they must release some sort of numbing—"

"It wasn't numb. It was almost . . . pleasurable. That thought makes me sick. That I could want it." She glances around in shame, as though afraid someone might hear her. "Where's Rachel?"

"At the Agency. Come on. Let's go to my room."

In my bedroom, Tegan immediately notices my dad's notes on my desk. I was studying them again before she arrived. I'm not sure why I'm drawn to them, why I think they hold some secret.

"Already back on the job, huh?" she asks.

"It's a side project," I say, not ready to reveal that I'm no longer a delegate.

Tegan picks up the piece of paper where I drew that weird symbol, the one from my dreams and the one I found in my dad's studies.

"What's this?" Tegan asks. "It'd make a cool tattoo."

"I don't know, I keep seeing it in my dreams. It's Ancient Vampiric."

"How do you know that?"

"Victor told me."

Her green eyes widen. "Victor was here? When?"

I sip at my coffee nervously, acting like it's no big deal that an Old Family vampire pays me visits from time to time. "Last night. Just for a little while. He wanted to make sure I was okay."

"Maybe that's why you're so tired today."

"Maybe." I shrug. "Probably."

I cross the room, open the balcony doors, and wander out. It's so bright, and I realize how rarely I spend time here during the day, but how often I have a visitor waiting for me here at night. Victor . . .

I become aware of Tegan's presence beside me, taken a little off guard that she could move so quietly. I can feel her studying me.

"So you and Michael," she finally says. "I guess things are over between you."

I think about his parting words. He's such a decent guy. Why couldn't I have loved him enough? It would certainly have made my life simpler, but apparently my heart isn't looking for simple. "Yeah. We're completely over. I told him when he came to see me at the hospital."

Those words leave an emptiness in me.

"Nothing is the same anymore," Tegan says.

I point to a banner suspended over the street with rope.

"The Sunshine Carnival is the same," I say, looking at the cartoony images of tents, fair games, and the sun that hasn't shined that bright since before the war.

I used to go every year. I remember when I was fourteen my parents started letting me go by myself. The whole thing is designed for teenagers, by teenagers—students operate all the rides, make all the food, and sell various items they've made through the year to raise funds. It only runs during the day, so I guess my parents thought it was the best place for me to try out some newly gained independence. Of course, one time I saw them at the edge of the carnival trying to hide. I think I was sixteen before they ever fully let me go by myself.

Six months later, they'd be gone from my life completely.

"I'm not going," Tegan says.

I'm not particularly in the mood to go either, but I'm bothered by Tegan's announcement. She was the ultimate party girl. It's something else Sin stole from her, and it makes me angry.

"I think we should go," I tell her.

"Why? It's stupid. Just a bunch of silly stuff."

She's the one who has taken a lot of vamp psych classes, the one obsessed with analyzing why vamps do things.

She's always applying what she's learned to me, but right now I'm the one who's reading her. "If we stop doing what we normally do, Sin wins."

"I hate that creep. It's like I can't get him off my skin now. And every time I close my eyes I feel his fangs and . . . I hate it!"

I understand how she feels. Whenever I close my eyes I feel Victor's fangs plunging into my neck. But I don't hate it. I wish I did—somehow that would bring normalcy into my life, the familiarity of my hatred toward vampires. Everything changed, even before that night. Victor showed me they weren't all the same. And when I felt his fangs, I felt his closeness, I felt his heart beating. Now, as though I'm peering through a kaleidoscope, I catch glimpses of all the moments we shared, and hear the little whispers we spoke, even when we weren't speaking at all.

"It's okay," I say, putting my arm around her, drawing her in close. "He'll never hurt you again."

I won't let him.

I feel her relax against me, but I don't want her going to that dark place in her mind that Sin inhabits. "So," I say with false cheer. "The Sunshine Carnival. Will you be my date? Because Victor can't be it."

Her lips twitch. "Yeah, I guess. I've got nothing better to do."

I grin. "Then why aren't we there already?"

Chapter 7

Tegan and I ride the trolley to the Sunshine Carnival. Every year it's held in an immense, empty parking lot that has no real purpose now that we have so few vehicles. The yellow lines have faded with time; the asphalt is pitted and crumbling as weeds work to reclaim what remains. The carnival, however, has brought out a crowd.

Most people are wearing bite protection and sporting visible stakes. A lot of Agency bodyguards and police are wandering about. Even the Night Watchmen, wearing their balaclavas and identifying medals, are present.

I sense Tegan tensing beside me. "Think any of them are Day Walkers?" she asks.

"Highly unlikely."

"Since the party, there hasn't been a single attack

during the day," she says. "So maybe we're all paranoid for nothing."

"We're not paranoid. We're alert. There's a difference."

"Feels the same."

I stop walking and face her. "Tegan, look, a lot of people are here. And the Agency has people on guard to handle any trouble. We're going to be fine."

"I know, I just"—she rubs her neck—"I'll feel better when they catch Sin."

"He's a coward. I think he ran off with his tail between his legs." At least that's what I'm hoping he did.

"You're right. Let's have some fun."

We stop at a booth and pay our entrance fee. When we step through the gate, we're greeted with laughter, shouts, and squeals. The aromas of melted sugar and cinnamon waft around us. A guy with a white painted face is juggling balls. A girl is prancing around playing a violin. I see a man walking along holding a large hoop. A little dog keeps jumping through it.

It's like we've stepped into a carefree world.

"Okay, I'm already glad we decided to do this," Tegan says. "Let's get some cotton candy." She grabs my hand and pulls me toward the food tents.

Behind them, I see the top of a small Ferris wheel. I recognize the familiar echoing ding as someone swings a huge mallet down hard enough to make a puck travel up the rail and hit the bell. That particular challenge has been at every carnival for as long as I can remember.

I buy a big bag of pink cotton candy to share with Tegan,

recognizing the girl selling it, but I'm not sure from where. Did we have a class together?

"It's nice to see you here, Dawn," she says with a genuine smile, and I wish I could remember her name.

"Thanks. It's good to be here."

As we walk away, I whisper to Tegan, "Who was that?"

She shakes her head. "Looks familiar, though." Then she's stuffing a wad of spun sugar into her mouth. I join her, loving the way the sugar melts on my tongue.

While we wander, for the first time in a long time I actually feel like a seventeen-year-old high-school girl. It's always been delegates and Valentine and Old Family and vampires. But now . . . now I can just breathe in the air.

Kids from school pass us, weave in and around us. Some acknowledge us with a quick word or smile; some look away like they're embarrassed they saw us.

"People are weird," Tegan says, taking the last of the cotton candy.

"Yeah." But I can't help but wonder if any of them spray-painted "Death to Dawn" on the side of the Daylight Grill.

Out of the corner of my eye, I notice Lila Hursch. She's easy to spot with her red hair gathered into a ponytail on the right side of her head. She spies me and starts sashaying over with her two favorite clones flanking her. When she reaches us, she doesn't even pretend to be civil.

"You really screwed up," she says. "With the Teen Initiative, the party, everything. You should be left outside the wall, for the vampires. You didn't protect us, Dawn. That's why Daddy is now the delegate."

"Your dad the delegate? Dream on!" Tegan says with a bark of laughter. Then she looks at me, no doubt expecting me to confirm that it's a joke.

But Lila's words are like sharp little daggers. I didn't do my job. At least not that night. But I can't let any vulnerability show because it'll just feed her meanness. As for "Daddy," he's the delegate because Victor wants to control him.

"You're really special now, aren't you?" I ask.

"Daddy will make sure the vamps understand their place."

"Oh, they understand their place. We'll see soon enough if your daddy understands his. And I'm already really bored with this conversation." Edging around her, I can sense her hatred burning holes in my back. One of the reasons she and I have never gotten along is that she's always wanted Michael for a boyfriend. Then when I became the delegate and all the attention was focused on me, her ego took a bruising. She needs the limelight.

Tegan catches up to me. "Why didn't you tell me about Hursch?"

I shrug. "I just found out this morning. No official announcement has been made."

She grabs my arm, stopping my forward momentum. "You still could have told me that you weren't the delegate anymore. Lila doesn't know what she's talking about. You didn't do anything wrong."

"I made mistakes, Tegan, but I'm no longer the delegate because it complicates my relationship with Victor."

"I bet. Do you ever feel like we're caught in a whirl-wind? Sometimes I just can't catch my breath."

"I know exactly what you mean. That's why we need to be here. New rule. Let's forget about everything that happened during the past month and just have some fun."

"I'm with you. Let's do it." She nudges my shoulder and winks. "And let's avoid Lila."

"Absolutely."

We walk over to the games section. Guys are throwing balls at glass bottles, tossing small rings onto pegs, trying to win the overstuffed bears for their girlfriends. None of them are doing very well.

Ding!

"There you go, man!" a carny yells.

Ding!

"Ha. How many stuffed animals you got? This kid's on a roll, folks. Come and watch."

Ding!

I see Michael raise a large mallet and bring it down on the tiny seesaw, sending the puck flying upward and slamming into the bell. He's wearing a black sleeveless T-shirt, and his arms are bulging and tight from swinging that heavy mallet around.

"He's so hot," Tegan says with appreciation.

"You mean because he's sweating?"

She punches me in the arm, then grows serious. "Do you miss him?"

"Yeah, but when I look at him, I just see a friend. I don't get that crazy excitement that used to make my heart do little flip-flops."

"Think he'll give me that big stuffed cat he just won? I love cats."

Last year, all his prizes went to me. I still have the stuffed bear and dog sitting on a shelf in my bedroom.

"All right, all right," the carny says. "You've won enough; let someone else give it a shot."

Handing back the mallet, Michael collects an armful of furry toys. I don't see any pride or satisfaction on his face, and I wonder if he simply was taking out some of his frustration regarding Sin. Or even me.

As he starts giving his prizes to the little kids surrounding him, Tegan skips over to claim the one she wants. He grins at her. His bruises have faded a little more, and now he's sporting a soft cast on his wrist. His gaze shifts past her to me. Growing serious, he finishes handing out his bounty.

"That's all I've got," he says, and the kids scamper away.

"You're a hero," I tell him as I approach.

"Don't worry, I'll be the villain tomorrow." He shoves his hands into his jeans' pockets.

A heavy silence falls. It never used to be this way. We grew up together, spent so much time together. So many of my good memories contain Michael. I hate this distance that separates us now.

"So . . ." Tegan says, breaking into the awkwardness that exists between us. "Why don't we ride the carousel?"

"I've got some stuff to do," Michael says. "Have fun."

"Like what?" Tegan demands.

"Stuff."

"Yeah, right. Come with us," she urges, and I know she's trying to rebuild a crumbling bridge. "I mean, you're not here with anyone, are you?"

"No. Just me."

"Then hang around with us. At least for the carousel."

He looks at her, then me.

"It'll be fun," I say. Like old times. Although I know that's not true. I'm not sure we'll ever be completely comfortable with each other again.

"Okay, sure, why not?" he asks. "Let's go."

As though knowing that Michael and I need a few minutes, Tegan charges ahead of us, and I can feel the tension surrounding us growing thicker. I know I have to say something. I have to use this moment to explain.

"Michael, listen, about Victor. I was going to tell you about him. That night. Hell Night. After the party."

"And what were you going to say? That you were serving as his blood diva?"

"No," I snap, then reel in my anger. I hurt him. I can't expect him to be happy about all this. "He never saw me as a source of blood." Until death was coming for him, but I'm not going to tell Michael that. "We . . . I care about him. But I care about you, too. I want us to be—"

"Don't you dare say friends." He stops walking and faces me. "He's a vampire, Dawn."

I realize Michael is struggling with that fact. Maybe it would have been easier for him if I'd fallen for another guy from school.

"Yeah, I know. Who would have ever thought—me and a vampire, right?"

"It's not funny."

"I'm not laughing. And I understand that you're angry and need time. Just don't shut me out. And don't tell Tegan, but you've always been my best friend."

He tightens his jaw, shakes his head. "I hate the F-word."

"Hey, come on, guys!" Tegan yells, interrupting us. "It's getting ready to start."

We hurry over and follow the next group of riders as they're being loaded on. When I step onto the wobbly platform, I quickly claim a horse. Tegan takes the one beside it. Grabbing a pole, Michael stands between us.

The ride starts and we begin slowly revolving, the entire fairground moving past us in a soft blur, like so much of my life lately. I can't remember the last time that everything seemed sharp and uncomplicated.

I glance over at Tegan. Clutching her stuffed cat, she's wearing a small smile and her eyes are closed. Michael grins at her, then his gaze clashes with mine. It's hard being with him like this. The music spilling from the speakers is loud, trapped beneath the canopy. It doesn't provide the best backdrop for conversation, but watching Michael saddens me. He meant so much to me for so long.

"Other than dealing with how messed up things are between us, how are you doing? Really?" I ask.

"Everything changed Hell Night, Dawn. I'm more focused on my training. A lot of my weaknesses were exposed."

Michael's always hard on himself, especially when it comes to this. He'd been taking extra after-school body-guard and vampire-hunter classes. His goal was to one day become a Night Watchman. Not that he'd be able to tell me if he ever achieved it. Night Watchmen are notoriously secretive so they or their families don't become vampire targets. Lord Valentine didn't trust the Night Watchmen. I suddenly realize that I don't know how Victor feels about them, but surely he understands they are needed as long as vampires infiltrate the city.

"How is that going?" I ask.

"Good. It's just taking up more of my time."

"Michael, I want you to know—"

That I'd never meant to hurt you gets cut off by a shrill scream.

Tegan's eyes pop open wide and she's glancing back. "What was that?"

It wasn't someone winning a prize or someone too high up on the Ferris wheel. No, it was chilling.

Michael's gone into warrior mode, his body tensed and alert.

We see the ride operator running away. As the carousel continues on, we're treated to a view of the crowd fleeing in all directions.

"Something's wrong," Michael says, helping Tegan get off her horse.

I don't wait for assistance. I just slide off, hitting the platform, feeling it shake beneath me. Another scream echoes around us. It's much closer, on the carousel itself.

People are scrambling off their wooden animals, grabbing kids, jumping off the spinning platform onto the ground. It isn't high up, and it isn't moving fast, but the fear causes most people to stumble before getting up and running.

Then I see what they're running from.

A Day Walker.

He appears around the curve, blood running down his chin. He's laughing, his hands covered with the same dark crimson, wiping it against the painted horses and dragons, smearing it against the brass poles.

Tegan, Michael, and I draw our stakes. The vampire advances toward us, taking his sweet time, dancing between the poles, even doing a twirl, laughing the whole way like some psychotic ballerina. He's older, not a teenager at all. Then I think about the Night Watchmen who were turned by Sin. Am I looking at one?

"Be careful," I say.

"Be careful!" the vampire mocks.

Another scream has us jerking our heads around. A patrol guard is struggling with another Day Walker. This one is a girl, my age, the one I bought cotton candy from just a moment ago. Now I realize where I've seen her before. I didn't recognize her from school; I recognized her from the Missing Persons posters after Hell Night.

Sin got to her, and now she's gotten to us.

"Let's go!" Michael yells.

Jumping off the carousel, we land awkwardly, but quickly regain our footing. Michael dashes over to help the guard fighting off the girl.

"Run!" I order Tegan, taking up a defensive position, facing the carousel.

"No way," she says.

I feel her back against mine; she's watching for another surprise while I want to get this vamp on solid ground. We could run, but that would leave this guy searching for a new victim.

"Do you know who I am?" I shout.

Grinning broadly, he leaps off the carousel. "Dawn Montgomery. Sin sends his regards."

"Walk away now or you won't be returning with a message."

A high-pitched shriek cuts across my words. I dare a quick glance over. The guard is prone, a stake is protruding from the girl, and another vampire is squaring off against Michael.

Turning my attention back to the waiting vampire, I wonder why he hasn't attacked yet. Maybe killing me isn't on his agenda. I don't want to consider what is. "Look at your friend!" I shout. "Do you want to end up like that? A stake can kill a Day Walker just as easily as any other vamp."

"You can't take me down," he taunts, opening his mouth wide, his fangs glistening in the sunlight.

He charges—

I dart around him and leap back onto the carousel. Tegan runs to where two more Day Walkers are engaging Michael. They disappear from view as the ride rotates, and I see the Day Walker who charged me jump onto the moving platform.

"You can't escape, Dawn."

"I don't want to." I have a stake. All he has are fangs. When humans are turned, they gain a vampire's arrogance, and it becomes their greatest weakness.

He catches up to me, facing me, with the horse moving up and down between us.

"I need you to come with me," he says. "Don't make me kill you."

He reaches across to grab me. The horse goes up. I duck beneath it and force the stake through the soft flesh below his ribs, angling it up and pushing twelve inches of finely honed metal into his heart. He stumbles back, falls into the sun, and is now at its mercy. He is dead before he hits the ground.

I rush over to help Michael and Tegan, but ash begins swirling around them as the slain vampires become glowing embers in the sun. Michael reaches out and grabs my wrist with one hand and Tegan's with the other.

"Let's get the hell out of here."

Chapter 8

It would be better for half the city to be on fire than to have gone through what happened earlier this afternoon. Rumors are running rampant that hundreds of Day Walkers are out there, wandering the streets at will.

Michael escorted me straight to the Agency, then took Tegan home. I can't stop thinking about the people we saw along the way who were in shock. One woman stood in the street screaming as though she thought a vampire would sink his fangs into her at any moment. Others were angry, throwing things against store windows, looting, pillaging. Most people, though, were rushing home, striving to find security behind locked doors and barricaded windows.

All the police and Night Watchmen had to be called out to restore order. Clive made a brief appearance on television to state that only a handful of Day Walkers exist, and that they will be hunted down by the Night Watchmen. The same Night Watchmen that no one trusts anymore.

"What's this bastard trying to accomplish?" Clive asks.

Rachel and I are in his office, at the top of the Agency building in the heart of the city. We can look out and see the walls. I'm surprised I don't see a mass exodus, a line of people stretching from here to the horizon, everyone leaving at once, taking their chances in the wild, desolate countryside. Maybe that'll come tomorrow once calm is restored and they've finished packing.

Clive looks at me. "Guess Sin is still around."

"Probably." I scowl. "One of the Day Walkers told me he sends his regards."

Clive summoned Roland Hursch, since he's the new delegate, but he has yet to show. I wonder if he's cowering somewhere.

"This is my fault," I continue. "I had to go to that stupid fair."

"Don't be ridiculous!" Clive shouts, standing up quickly. "This isn't anyone's fault. We have to figure out how to identify these Day Walkers and destroy them. And this Sin fellow. We need to find him, too. I'm putting a bounty on his head. If he's still in the city, we will track him down and—"

Before he can finish, his phone rings. He lets out an angry sigh and picks it up. "What? Wait. Who? Impossible. No, let them in. Let them in immediately. I don't care! Just do it!"

He slams down the phone. "We've had an interesting

development. Seems Sin wants to speak to us as well. He's sent us a messenger."

We go to the window and watch a white carriage, pulled by six powerful white horses, come down the main street. Even from this distance I can tell the citizens are turning their heads, concerned by what they see, even if they don't understand it. Vampires embrace past eras; the Victorian period was their golden age and most are more comfortable with the trappings from that time. The carriage stops outside the building, and when the door opens, it seems like the sun itself steps out. From my place on the top floor all I see is flowing white. Then it's gone, heading through the entrance.

"Okay," Clive says, taking us back to his desk. "I'll do the talking, but you ladies give me a signal if you're catching something I'm missing."

When the door opens, a woman—with tan skin, hair so blond it nearly outshines the sun, and a low-cut dress in a shade of white that seems impossible in this dirt-filled world—enters. She's beautiful, complete perfection. Her soft smile reveals her pointed fangs.

"Director Anderson, a pleasure to meet you," she says, her voice angelic.

"The pleasure is mine, I'm sure," he says. "And who graces us this fine afternoon?"

"My name is Eris. I've been sent as an emissary from Sin to discuss certain matters."

"We welcome you. Please be seated."

"That won't be necessary. I won't be staying very long."

"I see that you're a Day Walker," Clive says.

"Indeed. Sin has blessed me. He chooses so few, and those he does are eternally grateful for the gift."

"And what of those he doesn't choose? Is he kind to them as well? Do they gain his pity?"

"No. Those unworthy quickly find themselves . . . unnecessary."

"Even Day Walkers need human blood," Clive retorts.

"For now . . ."

Clive's brow furrows and I can tell that he isn't sure how to respond. He's not catching what she might be alluding to. I'm not sure I am, either, but something about what she said tickles the back of my mind.

"What about you, Eris?" I ask. "Can you give the same blessing? Can you create a Day Walker?"

She looks right at me. Her eyes are a piercing green, nearly transparent.

"Dawn Montgomery," she says. "How wonderful to finally meet you. I've heard so many fascinating things."

"Odd. Sin never mentioned you."

"And you didn't answer her question, Eris," Clive points out.

She gives me a patient smile, as though the prodding came from me. "Only Sin can create a Day Walker."

I wonder if Sin meant for her to reveal a weakness in the system.

"But obviously he's not strong enough to control them," Rachel says. "Several just attacked the citizens."

"He is more powerful than you can comprehend," Eris

answers, a biting edge slipping into her calm.

"If he's so powerful, why isn't he facing us now?" I ask.

"You do not disappoint, Dawn," Eris says, her eyes glittering with leashed anger. "Sin warned me about you. He said that I had to tread lightly, that you were too smart for your age, too clever. Too willing to sacrifice."

"I'm not flattered by anything he says."

"Not yet, you aren't. But you will be. When you serve him, you will accept his generous compliments."

"Yeah, like that's ever going to happen. I'd stake myself first."

Eris's stare turns cold. She seems to be speaking from another world entirely, and I realize that she isn't young. She has to be one of the first Sin ever turned. Behind her voice is infinite knowledge and experience. I imagine many have defied her, but few have ever won.

"You are so unenlightened. You will bow to Sin one day, Dawn. Whether you stand up afterward will be your choice."

I grind my teeth, knowing that even if I wanted to stake her I wouldn't be fast enough. No, I'll have to let her slide. For now . . .

"What does Sin want from us?" Rachel asks, maybe trying to keep my temper in check by changing the subject.

"It's a simple request, really: Dawn Montgomery."

I expect her to continue, but she doesn't. That's what Sin wants? That's why he sent her?

"Me?" I ask.

"Yes," Eris responds. "You are to come with me."

"And if we refuse?" Clive asks.

"Then Sin will take the entire city of Denver, and you will lose Dawn anyway."

Clive laughs. "Impossible. Sin already tried that little stunt, remember?"

"Yes, the, oh, what did you call it? Teen Initiative party? Very cute."

I hate her even more. There was nothing cute about kids I roped into volunteering their blood being slaughtered.

"Yeah," I say defiantly, "that is what we called it. And Sin failed. Miserably."

"That depends on his objective," Eris answered curtly. "To spread fear? To incite panic throughout the city? I'd say it was a rousing success."

"The point remains," Clive says, his voice louder than someone negotiating with a vampire should ever use, "Sin tried and still we stand strong."

"I wouldn't be so sure of that," Eris says. "The true potential of our Day Walkers has only begun to unfold. Look what they've done already to your poor city. Half a dozen of them cause a tiny amount of mayhem at a carnival, and the city nearly buckles. Imagine what a hundred of them would do."

"There aren't a hundred Day Walkers," Clive boasts without any way of knowing.

Eris simply smiles and lets out a petite, closemouthed laugh. Then turns back to me. "Come with me, Dawn, and all the Day Walkers in the city will leave right now. You can save this city, and everyone within its walls. Isn't that what you've always wanted?"

"I'm supposed to take your word as guarantee?" I ask.

"All I can offer is my word."

I want to say it isn't enough, but I can't think of anything that would be enough—except for Sin's surrender.

"What does he want with me?"

"Why, your conversion, of course."

To turn me into what he is. The thought of him sinking his fangs into me makes me ill.

"You have seventy-two hours, Dawn," Eris says.

"And after seventy-two hours?" Clive asks.

"I can assure you that you won't want to find out. The walls of Denver aren't nearly as thick as you may believe."

"You're forgetting something, Eris," I say. "We're not fighting Sin alone. We have a new vampire overlord, and he won't appreciate another vampire taking over his city. He'll stand by us. He and his army of followers."

"Ah, yes, Victor Valentine. We're well aware that the citizens aren't being as generous as they once were with their blood donations. That will create problems for your *overlord*."

I'm left to wonder if Sin's plan all along had been to frighten the citizens and turn them against Victor. Is he that cunning?

"Without blood," Eris continues, "Victor's minions will have no choice except to turn on one another, and he'll be too busy fighting the Thirst to care about what is happening within Denver's walls."

"You're wrong. Victor can take care of the vampires and the humans."

"Hmmm . . . perhaps Sin overestimated your intelligence." Eris turns back to Clive, all her haughty arrogance shimmering off her. "Sin only asked that Dawn be delivered, but not how. If you have to bind and gag her, I'm sure he'll understand. You've always measured your actions by the greater good, Director. What is one life for thousands?"

As she strides majestically from the room, I walk to the window and look out over the city. I hate to admit it, but her final point was a good one. One life. Mine.

Can I live with myself if I'm too selfish to give it up?

Chapter 9

"You should have seen her, Victor. She was an ice queen. Beautiful and cold. It's hard to believe the sun touches her."

Clive sent Rachel off to start working on a PR campaign to lessen the tension in the city after the Day Walker attack. Somehow Victor heard about it. Like his father before him, he no doubt has spies in the city. I couldn't get angry about that because this time it worked to our benefit. He arrived at the Agency two hours after sunset. Clive called me back in to serve as an advisor. Roland Hursch isn't here, but I'm not surprised. It seems he's not trusted yet with delicate matters.

Hursch did finally make an appearance earlier, though. He said we should give in to Eris's demands quickly, that I should surrender myself before anyone else is hurt. Clive packed him off to help Rachel with the PR campaign.

Now Clive, Victor, and I are sitting in Clive's office. Victor requested that the lighting be low so we don't make ourselves into a target. Only the lights from the street and the distant Works are filtering in through the windows, giving a secretive air to our meeting.

"Have you ever heard of her?" Clive asks, looking over at Victor.

"No. But I didn't know Day Walkers even existed until Sin showed up. My father always referred to his other son as a freak of nature, but he never clarified in what way. He kept him hidden, was appalled by the very thought of him. I didn't know what he looked like. Or his name, for that matter."

Clive fills three glasses with scotch from a decanter, setting one before Victor, who is sitting perched on the edge of the desk, and one before me, where I'm sitting in my usual chair in front of his desk. I'm not sure if he's forgotten that I'm not old enough or just thinks the solemnity of the occasion warrants it. Victor reaches for his, and I watch him take a long, slow swallow. He's drinking for the sensual experience of the taste. His body doesn't absorb alcohol. He'll never get drunk. I can't claim the same, so I let mine sit. Besides, I'm giddy enough because of his nearness. As much as I hate everything that happened today, I can't deny that I'm glad to see Victor again.

He dressed up for the meeting. He's wearing a navy blue suit. The point of a red handkerchief with two interlocking Vs stitched perfectly into it peers out of the breast pocket. I'm not sure I've ever seen him looking quite so Old Family, quite so . . . lordish. I miss the Victor I knew before he took his father's place. The Victor who made his home in an abandoned movie theater in a run-down part of the city. The Victor who enjoyed watching musicals.

He was more approachable then. Now he's all business. He's barely looked at me.

Clive walks to the window and stares out. Before us, the midnight sky is calm, as is the city. The police and Night Watchmen restored order. They're still patrolling, but very few people are out. Normally, well-lit parts of the city would still have some kind of life in them, but not tonight.

"Eris admitted that only Sin can create Day Walkers," Clive explains.

"I'm surprised she would give that information freely," Victor says.

"I don't think he wanted us to know, but she was angry . . . not thinking things through," I say.

"So if we kill Sin," Clive muses, "the problem of the increasing Day Walker population is solved. Then all we have to do is destroy those he created."

"Realistically, how many Day Walkers can there be?" I ask. "If only Sin can create them, could there be very many?"

"Probably not," Victor admits. "It's actually more fatiguing for an Old Family to turn a human into a vampire than it is for a Lesser to create a vampire. I think it comes back to nature trying to restrict how much impact we could have on growing the vampire population."

"He's right," Clive says. "As much as we like to demonize the Old Family, during the war, it was mainly Lessers turning people, not Old Family. That, and the V-Process."

"The what?" I ask.

Victor appears uncomfortable and when it's clear that he's not going to explain it, Clive continues.

"It was the code word the vampires used for their rebirth centers. Once vampires took over a city, the humans had two choices: be turned or killed. Most chose to be turned. But it was too cumbersome for a vampire to feed from all the humans, then kill them, then give them their blood in order to resurrect them. So, they mechanized the whole process. Imagine a factory where humans were turned. They were strapped to chairs, their blood drained, then a massive shock stopped the heart—"

"The shock was designed to be merciful," Victor interrupts to clarify. "Saving them the agony of a prolonged death."

His words are brittle. He obviously doesn't like talking about this. I can't blame him. It's barbaric.

Clive continues, "Vampire blood was then introduced into their system through a vein. They were reborn. Day in and day out, it never stopped."

"The Vampire Process," I say.

Clive nods.

"Would Sin have access to one of these factories?"

"They were destroyed after the war," Victor assures me.

"But if even one remained—"

"No. The task of destroying them was given to me. I

made sure they were all burned to the ground. We had enough mouths to feed; we didn't need any more."

Well, if anything, that puts my mind at rest. If Sin is amassing an army, he's got a long way to go. But that doesn't mean he can't hurt Denver now.

"What if I just go to Sin?" I ask. I've spent a lot of time the past few hours thinking about that. "I know he would probably turn me, but maybe I could use it to our advantage."

"Don't be ridiculous," Victor says. "I'd walk eighteen miles in the sun before I let that happen."

"I have to think about Denver," I say.

"Let me do that," Clive interrupts. "Eris says she'll spare Denver if you surrender yourself. The very fact that she's giving us that offer reveals a great deal."

"You're right," I say, the lightbulb going off. "If Sin could take Denver, he would have done it by now."

"Precisely," Clive says. "It's a bluff."

From his office we have the view of a good portion of the city and its wall, which suddenly seems so fragile. Before, the sun was the greatest deterrent to vampires. Even Victor couldn't come to this emergency session until it had set. But now, with Day Walkers a reality, it makes little difference.

"What do you think, Victor?" I ask. "Is it all a bluff?"

Victor twirls the liquid in his glass, takes a sip. "Sin wouldn't waste time with deals if he didn't have to. His big plan was to start a revolution within the city. He was hoping all the teens at the Teen Initiative party would join him."

"But they didn't," I say, pride in my voice.

"Now he's desperate. The bigger question is, why does he want you?"

"I don't know. He doesn't want me dead; he had plenty of opportunities when he was dating Tegan, when we all thought he was human. I had my back turned the whole time."

Victor's silent for a moment. I can tell he's holding something in.

"What are you thinking?" I prod.

"My father was obsessed with your family," he says slowly, contemplatively. "I think he was afraid of the influence your name had. I mean, your father wrote most of VampHu. Montgomery is a household name among humans and vampires. Maybe . . . maybe Sin wants you on his side. Maybe he thinks you can convince people to become Day Walkers."

"That's insane," I say. "I'd never do that. What kind of sense does that make?"

"Sin isn't exactly sane," he says.

"That means Sin is after me," I say. "But the city is safe."

"For now," Victor says, standing up. "Although the city is in a danger of a different kind. Sin may not be able to topple the walls, but even a handful of Day Walkers can cause enough fear to throw the city into chaos. Look what he's accomplished so far with his pranks."

"Pranks!" I shout. "People have died."

Victor's face becomes still, unreadable.

"You're right," he says, emotionless, unapologetic.

"People have died. As a result, they're frightened. Already we have fewer donations. Which means less blood for me."

The line of reasoning, from the safety of humans to blood donations, worries me. It's a stark reminder that Victor is a vampire, and his concern must always be for obtaining blood for the Lessers beneath him.

"I guess Victor has a point," I say begrudgingly. "After all, without blood, the vampires will start feeding on themselves, and then we'll have the Thirst to contend with right here."

"What is this 'Thirst'? Eris mentioned it, too," Clive says. "How does that play into everything? It was in Dawn's initial report about Hell Night, and her encounter with Brady, but I'm still not sure I understand it."

Victor offers the explanation: "When vampires are starving and they begin feeding on one another, it changes them. They become ravenous, addicted to vampire blood. They are incredibly violent, rabid, and beyond all reason."

"Everyone is in danger from it," I say. "Humans and vampires."

"It's true," Victor says. "But it's nothing to be concerned with at this moment."

My jaw almost drops at those words.

"It sounds pretty serious to me," Clive says questioningly.

"It's out west right now," Victor says. "My associates and I thought that it might reach Denver eventually, but I'm not so sure now."

"What!" I say, trying desperately to stay diplomatic.

"The Thirst is *everything*! It's the reason you overthrew your father. He wasn't taking it seriously. Now it sounds like you're not, either."

"Dawn, your judgment is clouded. Don't let the Thirst . . . don't let it control you."

"What are you saying?"

"Don't make this into something personal."

Victor's right: It is personal, because I've seen its power, and those Day Walkers confronting me this afternoon were *nothing* compared to the monster Brady became.

"Your focus, Clive, should be the Day Walkers," Victor says, turning away from me. "They pose the largest threat to the stability of the city. Find them. I suspect they will hunt during the day and hide at night. Take the few Night Watchmen you still trust and tell them to search during the day. The Day Walkers were probably turned recently. It takes time for a Lesser to be able to control himself around fresh blood. They'll be clumsy, easy to spot when they strike. Look at the Sunshine Carnival. They're enjoying themselves and their new abilities too much. Exposing themselves too readily. They shouldn't be hard to find and stake."

"And what do you propose I do when Eris returns looking for Dawn?"

"Stake her, too."

Clive finishes his drink, seemingly satisfied with that answer.

I'm still in shock with Victor's dismissal of the Thirst, but then—

"And Dawn needs to be secured at all times," Victor

says. "I suggest you make a safe room here at the Agency, where Dawn can stay twenty-four hours a day. Only Jeff and Rachel can go in and out."

"Why?" Clive asks.

"I suspect she was the impetus behind the Day Walkers' strike at the carnival. Sin has probably given specific instructions to all his underlings to capture Dawn. They want to please their master."

"No way am I being locked up."

"Dawn's good at taking care of herself, and I don't like the thought of putting her in isolation," Clive announces.

"You like the thought of her falling into Sin's hands better?" Victor demands.

Clive pours himself a drink, downs it. He points at the window. "I sent her out there, beyond the wall, to see your father. Her parents died out there, but still I sent her because your father demanded it. Now I've got another vampire demanding I turn her over and you demanding I practically imprison her. Quite honestly, I'm getting tired of vampire demands. We thank you for your counsel, Lord Valentine. We'll take it all under advisement."

I'm acutely aware of Victor bristling. I can't blame him. I want to step in, but Clive is my boss.

"My apologies if I overstepped," Victor says, adopting the formality of Old Family vampires. "I want only what is best for Dawn."

"That's all any of us want," Clive assures him. "Goodnight, m'lord."

Victor bows formally. "Director." Then he turns to me.

"It's late. I'll see you home, Dawn."

"Actually, I need a private moment with Dawn," Clive says.

"I see . . ." Victor says, eyeing Clive suspiciously.

"If you would be so kind as to wait outside," Clive says. "I'll send Dawn out."

"Very good."

Victor is heading for the door when Clive says, "Outside the building, not my office. Vampire ears and all."

A corner of Victor's mouth quirks up, and I know he was hoping to eavesdrop.

I wait a few minutes after Victor leaves, and Clive stands at his window, looking down until Victor is outside and beyond hearing distance.

"Tell me honestly," Clive begins, turning back toward me, "what are your thoughts on the Thirst?"

"It's a problem. A very serious one."

"I thought so," Clive says. "I could tell from your reaction when I brought it up, and when I read your report, it certainly seemed to warrant more concern than what Lord Valentine was giving it just now."

"Well, I *was* surprised by his casual response."

"Don't be," Clive says quickly. "Always remember that he is a vampire first and foremost. I think he's hiding something from us."

I should have known Clive's earlier friendliness was an act. He knows how the dealing-with-vampires game is played.

"The Old Family fears the Thirst, right?" Clive asks.

"Yes. It's the only thing that, arguably, is more powerful

than they are. Apparently most think it's just an urban legend, but if they saw it in the flesh . . ."

"Which you've done."

I nod, swallow hard. I told him about Brady when he debriefed me. "Yeah."

"I don't know this new Lord Valentine, and on the surface he seems much kinder than his father. In fact, I'm sure he is. But that doesn't mean he sees humans and vampires as equals. That doesn't mean he trusts us completely. If the Thirst could conceivably be used against him, he would *never* want us to learn more about it."

Taking a mental step back, I put myself in Victor's shoes and see the image unfolding through his eyes. What if news spread that there was this thing called the Thirst that could overthrow the Old Families? If the humans learned about it, would they try to harness it, try to start another war with it somehow? What if the humans allied themselves with the Thirst-infected vampires?

That would be insane. It wouldn't work. Not for us humans, anyway. Then again, we are notoriously shortsighted. I think of Roland Hursch, a man who would do *anything* to get rid of vampires. Would he join hands with an even more powerful monster, in hopes of being able to control that one? VampHu's chains are so heavy that many would risk everything to throw them off, even unleashing a powerful force like the Thirst.

"Victor might have a very good reason for keeping us in the dark," I say.

"Yes. But his reasons are not our reasons." Clive takes a deep breath. "When I think about the war, all I can think about is how ignorant we were. I keep thinking that if we'd only known more about the enemy, we could have won. It's as if all we were missing was one crucial element, one piece of intelligence that would have given us the edge. We were so close to winning, but it slipped away from us."

"And you think this is it?"

"No. I don't think that at all. The war is over. We lost. I accept that because I must. But having more information is much better than having less."

I couldn't agree more. That's one of the basic rules in negotiation—learn everything you can about your opponent and his motivations. Clive is once again in deep thought. He looks up at me and I expect him to speak, but he slowly turns his gaze downward again.

"The city faces many problems," he says. "Eris's threats. The Day Walkers. And now this Thirst. While it seems the most distant, it could be the wave that becomes a tsunami."

"Knowing what it did to my brother, I agree."

"Then I want you to find out everything you can about it."

"How?"

"Take the Night Train out to Los Angeles."

"Los Angeles?" I've never been beyond the Denver walls, except to visit Valentine Manor. To travel on the Night Train, to head west to the coast—I don't know whether to be terrified or excited by the prospect.

"Sin mentioned that he came from there," Clive says.

"It could've been a lie."

"And it might not have been. All of this is tied together

somehow. I want you to find the threads. In Los Angeles, you'll learn about the Thirst, learn how they've dealt with it—because the few reports we get from the LA Agency don't mention any rampaging vampires—and bring that information back. And if it's true that Sin came from out there, you may learn something about him and his Day Walkers."

"What about Eris's threats? What will she do when she discovers I've left the city?"

"If you're not here, she gains nothing by attacking the city."

"She might do it out of spite. I don't think it's worth it." Enough people have died because of me.

"I won't hand you over," Clive says, his voice stern. "I'll tell Eris that you snuck out of the city without my knowledge after she made those threats. If anyone is to blame, it's her. Trust me, Dawn, dealing with vamps isn't new to me."

He takes another sip of his drink.

"No one can know about this mission," he says. "Not Rachel or Michael or Jeff. When Eris finds out you've disappeared, she may begin questioning them. I want them to have plausible deniability. Just leave Rachel a note telling her you've left town."

I gnaw on my lower lip, thinking this all the way through. I understand the need for caution, but—

"They'll be worried about me."

"I know," he says, as if realizing how many people this will affect, how many sleepless nights this will cause. "They won't be the only ones."

I know he's referring to himself. He's always treated me like a daughter, and now he's sending me away. For my own safety, yes, but maybe into even greater danger as I investigate the Thirst.

"I'd send someone else if I could," he says, as if reading my mind. "But even if Eris never came, I wouldn't let anyone else go out there but you. Because I don't trust anyone as much as I trust you, Dawn."

Tears sting the backs of my eyes, but Clive's stoic demeanor inspires me to put up a brave front.

"I have some arrangements to make," he says. "I'll come to your apartment when the Night Train comes in and explain how we'll handle getting you to LA without anyone knowing. I want you to be like a ghost."

Chapter 10

By the time I hit the lobby, I've shored myself up not to reveal anything to Victor. He's always been able to sense when things are going on with me, and I need to make sure that he doesn't suspect that I'm about to leave town. My best defense is a heated offense, so I draw on the anger that hit me when we were in Clive's office.

I push my way through the door to the outside. He's leaning against the side of the building. When he sees me, his face lights up and I almost lose my resolve. But I hold firm.

"Lock me in a room? Seriously? You thought I would go for that?"

He grimaces. "I can't stand the thought of anything happening to you."

"How about my going insane? Because I would do that

if I was contained. I nearly went crazy in the hospital."

"Sin is a danger."

"Then catch him." I know it's unfair to lash out about that, because he's doing everything he can. My words are meant to distract, so he doesn't ask about the conversation I had with Clive after he left.

"Vampires can sense other vampires," he says, "but we can't sense the Day Walkers. My hunters are frustrated. They don't know what to look for, how to track them."

Parked on the street is a familiar car: a black Mustang. I don't know where he gets the gasoline for it, but if I've learned one thing about Victor, it's that he has a way of getting what he wants.

He opens the door for me and I slide in. The car is pre-war, from a time when automobile factories still existed. But the interior carries the scent of new leather—and Victor. I inhale deeply as he gets behind the wheel. With the turn of a key, the car hums. I've never considered how he keeps the thing running, and I wonder if he works on it himself. Most Old Family vampires are above doing anything that resembles labor, but I can imagine Victor getting his hands dirty.

"Do you ever wish you were human?" I ask.

With a squeal of tires, we're roaring up the street.

"It's pointless to wish for things that can't be." After a few quiet moments he says, "But I do wonder what it would be like to feel the warmth of the sun instead of its burn."

I study his profile, occasionally illuminated by a random light. The shadows move in and out, revealing different things. His concentration. His exhaustion. I can almost see the burdens weighing him down. How much has he been doing behind the scenes that I'm not even aware of? How many other Valentines has he been fending off, each one wanting his throne? Who are his allies? How many foes does he have? I want to stay irritated at him for downplaying the dangers of the Thirst, for suggesting that I be locked away, but it's a battle I'm quickly losing. "In the hospital, I walked to the window and let the sunlight touch my skin. I was glad that it could."

He jerks his head toward me, our eyes lock, and knowledge shatters the tension between us. He could have taken the sun from me. But he didn't.

I tear my gaze away and watch the scenery flash by, every now and then catching sight of someone slipping into the shadows. A Night Watchman? A vampire? A citizen just wanting the right to visit the night?

"Why did you act like the Thirst wasn't a big deal?" I ask.

"I'm sorry I said those things," he says. "But right now, Dawn, the Day Walkers are more of a concern to Clive and the citizens of Denver. None of them have seen the Thirst except you and Michael; none of them can even begin to imagine its horrors. But Day Walkers? That's something they understand and fear. If you tell them about vampires killing other vampires, do you know what the average citizen will say? 'Let them go at each other's throats.' They won't care, and why would they? They aren't seeing the big picture."

"Not all of us are shortsighted," I say.

"Enough of you are." Victor immediately closes his eyes,

maybe wishing he could take that back. It's a reminder that he's immortal and I'm not. Shortsighted for him can be measured in decades instead of weeks.

"I'm sorry," he says. "The Thirst is an issue, but it's a vampire issue. The citizens won't support me, and I need their blood to keep the Thirst at bay. If I can keep Clive focused on the Day Walkers, then he can rid the city of them. With that, the citizens will feel safe; they'll start giving blood again."

A part of me agrees with him, but if we're not prepared for the Thirst, how can we defeat it when it gets here? How can we worry about the rain when the tidal wave is right outside our door? We should be building sand barriers, not patching holes in our roof. I guess that's why I'm heading out west.

"Are you still having those nightmares?" he asks, maybe attempting to change the subject.

"I don't know that I'd really call it a nightmare. It's just kind of creepy. But yeah, it seems to be the only thing I dream about these days." *That and you.* I twist around in my seat so I can see him more clearly. "I went through my father's things at the Agency archives and snuck a few of them out. I found the symbol."

He perks up at that. "What does it mean?"

"He wasn't sure. Some sort of name, maybe. Or it symbolized all the families. I've got his stuff stashed in my room. It'd be great if you'd come look at it. Maybe you can figure it out."

"I told you. I don't know Ancient Vampiric."

I hear his words, but I know what he's really saying is that he doesn't trust himself to be alone with me in my bedroom.

"You know, you're not as irresistible as you think," I say, crossing my arms over my chest.

A corner of his mouth quirks up. "Is that a challenge?"

"I'm just trying to figure out this stupid dream, Victor, so it'll go away. Do you know how boring it is to dream the same thing over and over?"

"Vampires don't dream."

"But you told me you do."

His grin widens. I've always loved his smiles. They don't appear very often, but when they do, they're incredible. "All I dream about is you. Over and over. And it's not boring at all."

I feel the warmth of a blush creeping over my face and down my neck. With my blood rising to the surface, his smile diminishes.

"Please, Victor, just take a look. I promise to keep my hands to myself."

"Unfortunately, I can't make the same promise."

"You won't hear me complaining." I can't believe that when I left the Agency I was angry with him and now I'm flirting with him. Could our relationship be any more complex?

"Bad idea," he mutters under his breath as he pulls the car to a stop outside my apartment building. He turns off the car and faces me, studies me, and I know a battle is raging within him.

"Five minutes," he finally snaps. "That's all I can spare."

I grin in triumph. "That's all I need."

The apartment has that quiet, empty feeling when we step into it. "I guess Rachel is still at the Agency," I say. Just in case she returns before Victor leaves in *five minutes*, I write her a note and stick it on the fridge: *I'm home, safe, sound, asleep.*

"Why the note?" Victor asks.

"A precaution. She wouldn't be happy to discover a vampire in my bedroom."

"I told you—"

"I know. Five minutes. Come on."

In my bedroom, I close the door and turn on a lamp. I always feel a need for low lighting when Victor is around, a way to make him feel more comfortable. Vampires live in the shadows. Well, except for Sin and his newly minted minions.

I go to my closet, move a few things around, and pull out the box that I hid in the back. I don't know why I felt such a strong need to keep the contents secret. It's not just because I took them without permission. Something about my father's findings bother me. I think they may be more important than he realized.

By the time I turn back to the room, Victor has removed his jacket and tie, unbuttoned the top two buttons on his shirt, and rolled up his sleeves to reveal his amazing forearms. He's slender but powerful. Instead of sifting through these aging documents, I want to brush my fingers over his hair, his jaw, his shoulders. I'm already regretting my promise to keep my hands to myself, but I'm not going to break it. Clearing my throat, I carry the box to my desk. "Okay."

I lift the lid, acutely aware of him standing behind me, so close that I can feel the warmth of his body, his breath wafting across my neck. I force myself to concentrate on the reason I wanted him here so I don't spin around into his embrace. I've never understood this immense attraction between us, but it's been there from the beginning. Even when I was with Michael, something about Victor called to me. It filled me with guilt at the time, and that aspect hasn't diminished. He's pure temptation, an apple I shouldn't bite.

I force my fingers not to tremble as I locate the document that my father thought was a contract. I spread it on the desk and iron it out with my palms, realizing that's a bad idea because they've become damp. I don't want to ruin or compromise his work. "See these fourteen symbols over here? My dad thought they represented the Fourteen Families."

"He's right."

I glance over my shoulder to see Victor's brow furrowed in concentration. "I didn't think you read Ancient Vampiric."

"But I know my family's name when I see it." He places his finger beneath the first symbol. "That's Valentine."

A strum of excitement goes through me. It's a beginning. "Are you sure?"

Holding my gaze, he issues a challenge and starts unbuttoning his shirt. I watch as his fingers nimbly release each pearl disc. He shrugs out of his shirt and my breath hitches. I've never seen his bare chest, but my imagination envisioned him with uncanny accuracy. Although he can't bask in the sunlight, he's not milky white. His skin has a natural bronze tint to it. Most Old Family do. It made it easier for them to blend in with us, to camouflage their presence. When he presents his back to me, I see the symbol he pointed to inked on his left shoulder.

"All Old Family vampires carry the mark of their origins," he says.

I can't stop my fingers from touching him. They outline the Ancient Vampiric symbol. Valentine. His skin is like warm silk. So much for the smug promise I made in the car. "What about the other symbol? My father thought it stood for all the families."

I'm embarrassed that I sound so breathless, as though I just ran here from the Agency building.

"I don't think so," he says, his voice rough, and I know my touch is having an effect on him.

"What then?"

"Maybe the lost family."

"The lost family?" Every time I think I know everything about vampires . . .

"Legend has it that originally there were fifteen families. One became extinct."

"How could that even happen?"

Slowly he faces me, but I don't remove my fingers from

his skin. I just allow them to trail a path to his chest, then I flatten my palm against him and feel the powerful thudding of his heart.

"A vampire might fall in love with a human. If he were the last of the family"—he cradles my cheek, strokes his thumb over my lower lip—"he would doom his clan to extinction. Humans and vampires can't produce offspring."

"What if he turned her?" It's a stupid question. Lessers can't breed.

"Maybe he loved her too much to turn her into what she never wanted to be."

Victor's eyes darken as he lowers his mouth to mine, and I realize we're no longer talking about ancient vampires. Maybe we never were. I welcome his deepening kiss and wrap my arms around his neck. Suddenly I'm aware of my feet leaving the ground as he lifts me into his arms and carries me to the bed, the mysteries of the symbols forgotten. All that matters right now is us.

Without breaking from the kiss he lays me on the bed and stretches out beside me. Our hands eagerly explore the various contours that shape us. I hear numerous sighs and moans echoing around us and realize we're creating a symphony of soft sounds. I want so much, but I also know that I'm not ready to take it. I'll tiptoe to the edge and hover—

Because we can't be forever. And I want forever.

But a taste. His tongue dancing with mine, his hand slipping beneath my shirt, his mouth now trailing along my throat, his fangs scraping my skin, my pulse throbbing, the press—

"Dammit," Victor growls and rolls off the bed so fast that I'm surprised he comes up standing instead of hitting the floor. He snatches up his shirt and thrusts his arm into one sleeve.

I'm breathing hard, my body tingling with awareness. "It's okay."

"It's not okay, Dawn." He spins around and I see what his restraint is costing him. Vampires contain an animalism that allows them to do what must be needed to take blood. I see it in Victor now. But I see more. "I want you. I want your body, your blood. You. All of you. You affect me as no one else ever has. No vampire. No human. Sometimes I think I'll go mad with wanting. But I know if I give into my desires, it'll destroy what you are, and being responsible for that will destroy me, too."

He buttoned his shirt while he talked, but it's off-kilter. He reaches the end and he has a button left over and no hole through which to put it. To see him so flustered when he's always so put together touches me in a way his words couldn't.

"Please don't go," I say.

"I can't stay."

"Just hold me."

I don't think I've ever seen him look so sad, so defeated. I wasn't even certain vampires could hold such strong emotions. "I can't."

He grabs his jacket and heads for the balcony.

"You can use the front door," I tell him.

He stops, looks back. "No, I can't. Rachel's home."

I jerk my gaze to the door as though I expect to see her standing there in judgment. "I didn't hear her."

"I did. She's not alone. What do you think brought me back to my senses?"

He opens the balcony door.

"How can you walk away?" I ask.

"Because I love you."

His words merely waft in on the breeze that stirs the curtains, because he is already gone.

Chapter 11

The next morning, I reach over, wanting Victor to be beside me in bed. But of course he isn't. Still, I can't help but remember how close we came to total commitment. We both walked to the ledge and peered down. I saw what could have been, and I was happy. But what did he see? Love is supposed to make you feel wonderful and alive. Victor's parting words, his conviction that he loves me, did make me feel all those things. But it also left me with a sadness because he *had* walked away from it. I don't know if I can.

Hearing Rachel clanging pans in the kitchen, I clamber out of bed and pad out of my bedroom to discover Jeff sitting at the island counter sipping coffee, watching as Rachel is flipping an omelet. This is the kind of morning scene that I'll never have with Victor. I don't resent that

Rachel finally has it, but I long for it, too.

"Morning," I say.

"Hey, sunshine," Jeff says.

I open the fridge, get some juice, and join him. The TV is on but muted and Roland Hursch's face fills the screen. I grab the remote, press a button—

"—for the first time Tuesday night. Victor Valentine will learn that I'm not like my predecessor. I hold the power. He'll give in to my demands or there will be no blood."

I hit the button again and he falls into silence. "I never wanted to be a delegate, you know."

Rachel looks back at me. "I know, but if you ask me, Hursch is a little too eager and that's going to cause problems."

"Do you think he's prepared for his first meeting?" I ask.

"He could use a reality check. He thinks he already knows everything and doesn't listen to anything Clive or I say. I'm telling you right now, he's lucky it's Victor he's dealing with. Murdoch would have killed him within ten seconds of meeting such arrogance. Instead, it's Victor, a vampire who's been around for centuries but doesn't look much older than you. That won't work in his favor."

"Don't be so sure. Hursch is going to underestimate him. Victor will capitalize on that." I sneak a piece of bacon from Jeff's plate. "Rachel, have you ever heard about there being fifteen Old Families in the beginning?"

"No. Why?"

"Oh, just something I ran across."

She sets an omelet in front of me. "Why do I think you're keeping secrets?"

"It's nothing, really. Yesterday when I was going through my father's archives, I discovered a carefully preserved document. It's in Ancient Vampiric, signed by the Fourteen Families. But there's another symbol that looks like a name. I don't know what it means. Do you know anything about my dad's work during the war?"

"I know he was trying to figure out the origins of vampires. Some thought it might hold a clue to defeating them. His work brought him to the attention of the Agency and eventually Valentine. Your father was a renowned scholar. I don't think anyone knew more about vampires than he did."

"He didn't know anything about the Thirst."

"I think that's a relatively new phenomenon."

"I'm not so sure. I think it's been around but the vamps kept it a secret."

"I guess I can see that, but I see it as a vampire problem."

Most people will, and that's my fear.

"But if we ignore it, it's going to bite us in the butt."

"Better than the neck," Jeff says with a grin.

"Not funny," I scold. "This is serious."

"We've encountered one case," Jeff says. "That's hardly a world-ending epidemic."

I'm glad I convinced Clive of the importance of the Thirst. It's amazing that Jeff doesn't see the danger just over the horizon. Then again, he's never seen it in person like I have. One look at Brady and—

Damn. Whenever I see him in my mind, all I can see is the Thirst-infected vampire he became. Those frightening images—the gaping maw, the pitch-black eyes—have slowly eroded away the brother I knew and loved.

"Dawn, are you all right?" Rachel asks, snapping me back to the present.

"Oh, yeah. Just thinking of Roland Hursch as delegate." *Brady—I'm sorry.*

After breakfast I head out of the apartment. I need to see Tegan.

I catch the trolley and am outside Tegan's building in fifteen minutes. Her place isn't as nice as mine; then again, it isn't paid for by the Agency. It's one of the few perks that keeps people working for them—nice digs. I know she's a little jealous of that sometimes, and it doesn't help that her one-bedroom apartment is crammed with four siblings and two parents. But there's a life in those walls, one that I want so badly, one that disappeared once my parents died.

I use the call box and she buzzes me in. I start climbing the stairs, the banisters on the sides eaten away by time and oily fingerprints. Halfway down her hall, I see her door open and she meets me.

"What's up?" she asks, concern on her face. I don't come around here too often, and considering what's been going on, she's probably expecting bad news.

So I put on a smile. "I just wanted to make sure you were okay after everything that happened yesterday."

She leans against the doorjamb. "Michael stayed with me for a while. I cried all over his shirt. He didn't seem to mind."

"He's good at giving comfort."

"Yeah." She studies me for a minute. "There's something else you need to talk about."

I nod. She looks over her shoulder. Even from here I can hear her siblings fighting inside. She sighs heavily.

"We can go somewhere else," I say.

"I have an idea."

Tegan takes my hand and we continue up the stairs. I've never been this high up in her building. We head down a hall until we reach a very slender door. She opens it and I see a narrow set of stairs heading up. They don't look particularly safe, but I simply follow Tegan's lead, hoping I don't fall through and wind up in someone's living room.

At the top, she pushes open another door and sunlight bathes me. It hurts my eyes, and a little warning would have been appreciated. But when we step outside, all is forgiven.

"How come I've never been up here?" I ask, staring at the rows of flowers that pack the rooftop garden.

"Do you like them? I just finished picking a few to take to the memorial outside the Daylight Grill. I wanted to do something."

"That's good," I say. "We don't want to forget."

"No, we don't."

I study the arrangement of riotous colors, the delicate petals that must feel so soft, like silk, like that nightgown

Faith gave me. "Did you grow these?"

"Yeah."

"I never knew," I say.

"We all have little secrets," Tegan says. She's right about that. "My grandma started the garden, actually. But now she can't make it up the stairs, so I took over. I thought it would be a chore. But I love it."

"I can see why," I say, closing in on a rose.

I kneel down and look at it, seeing the city just above its red-lipped horizon. How could something so beautiful survive in a place so harsh?

"You can have that one if you want," Tegan says. "I was going to give it to you as a gift, but since you're here . . ."

"I didn't mean to ruin your surprise," I say, reaching out and gently stroking the petals, afraid they might wilt under my rough fingertips.

"To be honest, I'm glad I got to show you my garden. But I know that's not why you came here. So what's up?"

I almost forgot why I needed to talk to Tegan in the first place, this array of vibrant colors stealing my memory for a second. But, unfortunately, it's back to business.

I begin walking around the other rows of flowers, taking them in, each one so unique, so beautiful. I know Clive wouldn't want me out by myself, and I know he especially wouldn't want me to tell Tegan what I'm about to tell her. But the thing is, I have to. She's been through too much, and I can't just disappear on her.

"Clive is sending me out west," I say. "I'm going to investigate the Thirst."

"Dawn, that's insane," Tegan says with a measured calm. Maybe it's the beauty of the garden keeping her levelheaded.

"There isn't any choice. The Agency agrees that Day Walkers are bad, but we can handle them. The Thirst-infected are more dangerous, and far more mysterious. We just don't know enough about them to defend ourselves."

"But they're way out there."

"For now," I say. "But if people don't donate blood, then Victor's vampires may resort to feeding on one another, and then . . ."

"They're right outside the walls," she finishes for me, seeing the dire situation unfolding.

I give her a moment longer to think about it, to draw the inevitable conclusion that I *have* to go out there.

"No one else knows about this," I say. "Clive wants my mission to be top secret."

"Then why are you telling me?"

I take a deep breath, unsure if the reasons are enough. But I hope she understands. The Tegan months ago wouldn't have, when we were just kids who let the world do what it wanted. I mean, I always knew monsters were out there, but I guess I wished it wasn't true. I'm older and wiser now, and it feels like we've both aged years in a span of weeks.

"If something happens to me on the Night Train or in Los Angeles, I need someone to know why I went out there. Clive will no doubt eventually tell Rachel and Jeff and everybody why I truly disappeared. But how much of the truth will he reveal? I hate the thought of my legacy being that I ran away because I was scared. I hate the thought of no one knowing I *tried* to stop the Thirst, that my final actions were in defense of not just the city, but all of humanity. I guess . . . I guess I just want people to be proud of me."

There it is. Laid out on the table for her psychological mind to dissect. I expect distance, her sharp intellect working through all the hidden meanings. Instead, when I look up, she hugs me.

"We're all proud of you, Dawn," she says. "We almost lost you, and when we stood over you in the hospital, watching the heart-rate monitor beat so slowly, all we could think about was the sacrifice you made. The sacrifices you always seem to make."

I hug her back, feeling the tears start to build up as my best friend tells me what I need to hear.

"Come back," she whispers. "Please just come back."

"I will," I tell her, knowing it's a promise I might not be able to keep.

Chapter 12

Because of the attacks at the carnival, school is cancelled on Monday. I spend the day preparing for my trip: packing, writing letters to those closest to me, putting the sealed envelopes away in a desk drawer to be found later and distributed if I don't return, napping so I'm rested. After darkness descends, Rachel calls to let me know that Clive has her working on an extra project that will probably keep her in the office all night. I'm sure that's part of his plan. He doesn't want her interfering with my departure. After I get off the phone, I write her a note.

> Dear Rachel,
>   I'm fine and safe. I've left the city on the Night Train.
> Tell Eris that if she wants me, she'll have to find me.
>   You've always been more than my mentor and guardian.

You've been my friend. Be my friend now and understand
that I had to do this. I'll see you soon. I promise.
Love,
Dawn

I've just secured it to the fridge with a magnet when
a knock sounds at the door. My heart gives a little lurch,
because I know who's waiting in the hallway and what it
means—no turning back.

When I open the door, Clive strides in. He's followed
by a figure shrouded in black—cargo pants, turtleneck
sweater, black leather duster, his face hidden behind the
balaclava. Around his neck is a medallion that identifies
him as a Night Watchman. The design is so complex, weav-
ing different metals in and out of its shape, that it can't
simply be copied.

"This is the Night Watchman who'll be traveling with
you on the train," Clive says.

"Wait a minute. You didn't say anything about anyone
going with me."

"I'm not letting you go alone."

"But, Clive, you need all the Night Watchmen here,
guarding the city—"

"Dawn," he interrupts. "This is nonnegotiable."

"But the danger you're putting him in—"

"All the Night Watchmen understand when they sign up
that their life expectancy is shortened. Ian Hightower will
be watching over you, too, but he'll be distracted because
of his duty to watch the whole train. I want someone with

you who is dedicated to watching only you."

During the war Ian Hightower was a legend, the deadliest vampire hunter in the world. To vampires he was a walking nightmare who plagued them during the day just as they plagued us at night. He was the only human to ever kill an Old Family vampire single-handedly. Now he guards the Night Train.

I know Clive is right—Ian won't be able to watch me all the time, but I hate the thought of someone else being placed in danger because of me.

"It'll make it easier for me to sleep at night, Dawn," Clive says quietly.

I nod. "Okay."

"Good. Now, here's your ticket, a letter for Ian explaining who you are, and one for the Los Angeles Agency director. Just before the train leaves, I'll contact Ian so he knows to expect you, but I won't give him any details regarding why you're onboard." He holds up a key. "This will get you into the last car. I've ensured that it's reserved for you. But I don't want anyone to see you getting onboard, so . . ." He picks up a duffel bag from the floor. "You'll go dressed as a Night Watchman."

It takes me a long time to get dressed, and Clive definitely doesn't know the first thing about women's sizing. Though I doubt the Night Watchman uniform comes in teenage-girl sizes. Nonetheless, I put on the black cargo pants, black sweater, dark coat, and thick boots that are way too big. I look like a kid wearing her dad's clothes for Halloween, and the end result is a giant black tent hanging from my shoulders.

The final piece is the balaclava. I put my hair up and slide it over my head, covering my face. It's tight and constricting. It takes me a moment to calm my breathing, to recognize that I won't suffocate. I feel self-conscious when I step out of my bedroom.

My Night Watchman looks at me and even his mask can't hide his eye roll. He walks over to me, kneels down, and begins shoving my pant legs into my boots, then rolls up my sleeves, tightens the belt that holds my stakes across my chest. He then plays with my black hood, fixing the fabric, before finally handing me my medallion.

It's just like his, and the intricate scrollwork and mixing of metals makes me wonder how long it took to make. I put it over my neck and then study my reflection in the entry-way mirror. The illusion is complete. The Watchman, with a few simple adjustments, made me look passable.

"Thanks," I say.

He shakes his head and puts his finger to his lips.

Right. No talking.

I glance over at Clive. He gives me a solemn nod. "You'll do."

It's nearly dawn when my guard and I head out, walking to the train station. He hasn't spoken a word. Not even after Clive left. He just stood with his back to the door, arms crossed, waiting.

I'm traveling light, carrying a duffle bag with a few

changes of clothes, toiletries, and some of my dad's writings. Maybe I can discover more about the symbol that's
haunting my dreams. My silent companion has a bag as
well, but his probably contains an arsenal of stakes.

I've heard that before the war people used to leave
their cities all the time, would go on something called a
vacation. But leaving the city now requires a lot of money.
Walking through the streets I can't help but feel kind of
badass in these clothes. The anonymity, the stakes, the cool
medallion. While I have some fighting skills, they aren't
up to the standards of our elite guards, but right now, I just
need to convince people I'm a Night Watchman, not actually be one.

As the station comes into view, a bit of nostalgia hits
me. Michael and I had a tradition of watching the train
roll into town. Crowds always gather for its arrival. Not so
much for its departure. For many, the Night Train is a symbol that we aren't alone. We're isolated but still connected
to something beyond us. Twenty other cities, populated by
humans. It gives us hope.

The massive train, forty cars in total, is waiting patiently.
The blackened steel is covered with claw marks from vampires trying to get to the passengers. Even the iron wheels
look oddly menacing, as if they have crushed plenty of
bone and muscle underneath them in their time. Or maybe
they're just weary from carrying across the country the
hopes and dreams of the human race. Smoke rises casually
from the engine.

A few passengers are waiting on the station platform,

along with several Night Watchmen. Most of those holding tickets look surprisingly young and I wonder if their parents are sending them off to another city, some place that doesn't have Day Walkers.

My partner holds up a gloved hand, extending his first and fourth fingers. The guards nod, we move past them without anyone stopping us, and I wonder if he gave them a coded signal. I've heard Night Watchmen have ways to communicate without talking.

Only the door on the first car is open, admitting passengers. The attendant, dressed to the nines, begins looking at each ticket before waving the passenger through. A Night Watchman stands next to him scrutinizing every passenger and looking out for those subtle nervous tics that give away vampires in search of blood. There's a door on every fourth car, but since it's still dark, they want to be extra cautious with any vampires who are thinking about hopping on for a snack. Now they also have to worry about the Day Walkers.

My heart races as my guard skirts the passengers and leads me through the doorway. He slaps the Night Watchman three times on the shoulder as we pass, and I wonder if it's another signal.

The inside of the train isn't exactly what I expected. I can see the potential for beauty that it might have once had, but now the wood is warped in places, discolored in others. Oil lamps secured to the walls remind me of Valentine Manor.

As we hustle down the narrow aisle from car to car,

I don't have much time to notice the surroundings. My guard is moving with purpose and people duck into their private rooms, giving us space to pass. I peer quickly inside one and see sparse furnishings. A bench seat that probably folds out into a bed. A very small table. No windows. In fact, there aren't any windows at all in this train, except for the glassed-in observation deck. As we pass by the circular stairs leading to it, I'd love to detour up them, but there will be plenty of time to check out that level once the train leaves the station and no one can order me off.

My escort stops at a steel door, which must lead into the last car. He holds out his hand and I drop the key into it. He glances back. No one is behind us. No one is watching. He slides in the key, unlocks the door, shoves it open, and ushers me in. He closes the door and snaps the dead bolt into place.

As my guard begins checking possible hiding places, I stare in disbelief around the room. It's bigger than my bedroom, and more ornate than any room in Valentine Manor. A huge four-poster bed dominates one side, paintings line every wall, a chandelier hangs from the ceiling, and a fireplace at the very back warms a sitting area. Shelves are filled with books, tables stacked with fresh fruit, chairs complete with plush cushions. Hardwood floors glisten from being freshly waxed. A gigantic bear rug sits in the middle of it all, its pure white fur sticking up.

"Nice digs, huh?" I ask, but my guard doesn't say anything.

Seemingly satisfied that we're safe, he comes to stand in front of the door.

I remove my balaclava. "I don't know how you guys can spend so much time completely covered like this," I say as I shake out my black hair.

Silence. This is going to be a long trip.

I hear one short burst of the train's whistle. I've watched the Night Train arrive and leave enough times to know that's the signal that departure is imminent. Five minutes at most. Time to deliver the little speech I've been preparing during the entire walk here.

"Look, if you want to get off the train, now's the time. No one is going to blame you. I don't know what I'll be facing out there. Okay, that's not exactly true. I know there will be a lot of badass vamps and I have no idea how many allies I'll find, but I'd prefer to go by myself. I don't want to feel guilty if something happens to you. I already live with enough guilt to last me a lifetime."

It's like he's turned into a statue.

"All right," I say, accepting the inevitable. "So you're here to stay."

Still nothing. The hood casts his eyes in shadows. I can't tell what he's thinking.

"Well, if you're not in the mood for conversation, then I'm going up to the observation deck once the train starts. I want to watch as we leave Denver. You're going to have to lose the hood if you plan on following me because if it's obvious I have a Night Watchman with me, I'm not going to blend in."

He gives a little twitch, like maybe he hadn't considered that, that he hadn't expected he'd have to expose himself. I wonder if he's horribly scarred or if being hidden beneath the Watchman trappings makes him feel safe. The stories he could tell—

If I can get him to loosen up, at least until we get to Los Angeles, I might have a fairly entertaining trip.

"Might as well do it now," I prod. I smile, trying to be encouraging. For all I know he may never show his face anywhere.

I watch his chest expand as he takes a deep breath. Slowly, he raises an arm, grabs the bottom of the balaclava, and in one swift motion yanks it up and over his face.

Michael!

Chapter 13

I stare at him in stunned disbelief.

"Surprise," he finally says, wadding up his balaclava and tossing it onto a nearby chair. But he doesn't smile, and he doesn't seem particularly happy to be here—but then I'm not particularly happy about it, either.

"You can't come with me," I say.

"Not your call."

"No, no, no. You don't understand . . ." I rush over to him, wrap my fingers around his duster, try to get him away from the door so I can open it, shove him out into the hallway, and find a way to get him off the train. "Brady, what he was, it's rampant out there. I couldn't live with myself if you got hurt or worse."

It would be hard enough to deal with it if something happened to someone I didn't know, but for it to happen to Michael—

"I'm not leaving, Dawn."

The train lurches, and I stagger. Michael grabs me, steadies me, our eyes lock, and I see absolute conviction in his. My feeble attempts to get him off the train are nothing compared to his determination to remain. I sag against him. "Michael."

His arms close around me, and I feel the awkwardness in them. We're not what we once were. We're no longer a couple. But still—I was scared before. Now I'm terrified.

"How long have you been a Night Watchman?" I ask.

"Can we save the questions for later? I've got a slew of my own, too—but I really like your idea of watching us roll out of Denver."

Michael's never been beyond the wall—except for one night when we went wall-walking with Sin and found a way out of the city, but we didn't go far. The city's shadow still touched us.

I work my way out of his embrace, still in disbelief that he's here. I give him a wobbly smile. *Get it together, Dawn. You'll figure out how to ditch him when you get to Los Angeles. A way to keep him safe while still doing what you need to do.*

"Yeah, sure," I say. I can give him this, at least, a view of Denver that most people never see.

Michael quickly takes off his heavy coat, sweater, and bandolier, leaving only his dark pants and undershirt. He opens his duffel bag, shoves the clothes inside, and pulls out a dirt-brown shirt. Putting that on, he buckles the stake-filled belt around his chest and throws a casual jacket over it. His weapons are hidden, and he looks like any other passenger.

I follow suit, stripping away the heavy Night Watchman's disguise and revealing the simple civilian's clothes underneath.

We head into the passageway, our steps a little unsteady with the rocking of the train. We reach the metal curving stairs and ascend them to the observation deck. Its walls are made of thick, shatterproof glass. Chairs are dotted throughout but no one is using them. Everyone is standing, as though what they are seeing deserves that sort of respect. Michael takes my hand and wedges me between two people until I'm right next to the window. He puts his arms on either side of me, pressing his palms to the glass, creating a buffer between me and everyone else—just like he used to do back when we were a couple standing at the barricade watching the Night Train roll in.

"You're getting your wish of going beyond the wall," I whisper, trying to pretend everything is normal, trying to ignore the danger he's placed himself in by coming with me.

He gives me a small smile, and for a moment, I catch a glimpse of the old Michael, the one who could make me laugh, the one with whom I used to share my dreams. "Pretty exciting."

"Not too exciting, I hope," I tease. "A dull, boring ride to Los Angeles would make me much happier."

The city is rushing past us and the sun is rising higher to reveal that we've slipped beyond the part that has been rebuilt. From here, it looks like the destruction of the war was only last week.

"There's the wall," Michael says quietly. "Too late to turn back."

It was too late when the train started. I just wish I could have convinced him to get off.

"Did Clive know it was you?" I ask.

"No."

Does his mother know what he is? When he doesn't come home will she think he's just out protecting the city? I try not to think about how worried she'll be. How upset Rachel will be when she finds my note. What I'm doing is important. I have to remain focused on that.

The sun's heat is intensified by the glass, and I feel like we're all ants under a gigantic magnifier. There was a time when all passengers were ushered up here to face the sun. It ensured no vampires were onboard. It's a policy they've obviously stopped.

The train barrels through the open gate so fast that the edge of the wall is just a concrete blur. Then we're out in the open.

"It's so . . . barren," Michael whispers.

Spreading out before us are the charred and desolate remains of war. Even after all this time, ten long years, the earth is still struggling to recover. When we went wall-walking, we saw this same wasteland. But for Michael, who'd never been outside the walls, I guess there was still hope that it would look different in daylight, or that something beautiful lay just over the hill. But it's all the same gray and colorless landscape.

Everyone is silent. Some of these people are old enough to remember what it was like before the war. Out of the corner of my eye, I see an older gentleman wiping a tear from his cheek. *What does he see?* I wonder. *The trees that once grew? The green grass that flourished within his lifetime? Or does he see the horror of the fires created by all the bombs we dropped in an attempt to rid ourselves of vampires?*

Slowly, one by one, people begin to leave. But Michael and I remain. Maybe because for us, we're still fighting a war.

Eventually it's only the two of us, standing there, gazing out. Denver is quickly becoming a speck on the horizon.

"All right," Michael says. "I think we've seen enough. We're going back to our room and we're staying there until we get to Los Angeles."

"Okay, we obviously need to set up some ground rules here," I say, "because you're not in charge."

"No, he's not. But I am," a deep stern voice announces.

I spin around to find myself staring at the deadliest vampire hunter to ever live. The last person on earth I'd ever want to see angry.

Ian Hightower.

And he's definitely not happy.

I've seen Ian before—one of the reasons Michael always wanted to see the Night Train was to catch a glimpse of his hero. But even when we stood close to him, Ian never seemed real. He was more like an urban legend. He's wearing a black shirt, pants, and duster. Across his chest is a bandolier with metal stakes woven through, each one ready for easy access. His black hair is short. His five-o'clock shadow shows little hints of gray, caused by the premature aging that comes from staring into the eyes of an Old Family vamp and thinking your life is over. Not many walk away from that. I have. And so has Ian. The difference? Ian's Old Family vamp *didn't* walk away. Lord Percy died with a stake through his heart.

Ian strides toward us and I can't help but compare him to Victor. He's just as deadly, just as dangerous. Instead of the refined tastes of a vampire, he reflects the survivalist instincts of a human—the unending desire to see just one more sunrise, and never knowing if you will. That mentality breeds a state of mind unique to warriors. Ian has spent more time outside of city walls than in them. He has to rely on his wits and strength for protection. No one does it for him.

He glares at us. Across his cheeks, I can see the faint traces of old wounds, each one a close call, each one a near-death encounter. A man this young shouldn't look this old.

"Dawn Montgomery," Ian Hightower says, his voice deep and ragged, as if scars line his throat as well. It's not a question, it's a statement, and I can't imagine that he ever asks anyone anything. Everything that comes out of his mouth would be said with certainty.

I'm actually surprised that Michael hasn't dropped to one knee and offered Ian his fealty, because even I feel a need to bow before him. He's been our hero forever.

I swallow hard, force myself not to be rattled by his sudden appearance. "Yes, Mr. Hightower?"

"I see you know who I am."

"Everyone knows who you are," Michael says, and I

hear the hero worship in his voice.

"And you would be?"

"Michael Colt."

"You're the one the Agency sent along to keep her company?"

"To protect her, yes, sir."

Approval lights Ian's dark eyes. "I was about your age when I went to war. You'll do."

He shifts his attention back to me. "I don't like trouble, Miss Montgomery."

"I'm not here to cause trouble, Mr. Hightower."

"Well, you're already doing it. I found something hidden in the one of the cargo cars that apparently belongs to you."

What? "I don't know what you're—"

"Christopher!"

With perfectly styled blond hair, a young guy not much older than Michael steps into the area. He's dragging someone behind him—

"Tegan!"

"Dawn!" She breaks free of his hold, runs over, and wraps her arms tightly around me. I can feel her trembling. "I didn't know they checked every inch of the train. I nearly got staked."

Rubbing her back, I glower at Christopher.

He begins using a stake to clean beneath his fingernails. "She could have been a bloodsucker for all I knew."

"So is she with you?" Ian asks.

"Yes." Placing my hands on her shoulders, I ease her

back a little so I can look into her eyes. "Are you crazy? What are you doing here?"

"I was afraid for you. I didn't want you to be by yourself." She pouts a little. "You let Michael come."

"I didn't *let* him come. The Agency sent him. How did you sneak onboard?"

She shrugs. "Flirted with a Night Watchman."

Tegan, with her cute pixielike features, has always had guys stumbling over themselves to be around her. I'm not surprised that she was able to convince someone, even a Night Watchman—maybe he was new and near our age— to help her get on the train undetected. Now two people I care about are in the path of danger. I wonder if I can convince Ian to back the train up and return them to Denver. But when I lift my gaze to his, I can tell that he's not going to welcome any suggestions from me.

"Enough with the happy reunion," Ian says. "Clive gave me a call just before I got out of cell-phone range. Told me you were onboard and that you had something for me."

He doesn't sound pleased at all, like someone learning his burdens just doubled. Which I guess in a way they have. I pull out the letter and hand it to him. Never taking his eyes off me, he tears it open and unfolds the parchment. His face is impossible to read as he glances down at it. But his voice isn't . . .

"You do everything I say," he commands. "If you step out of line, I won't hesitate to shove you back in, clear?"

"Yes, sir."

"Your director didn't go into details, but they never do. I don't like secrets."

I dart a quick glance at Michael and Tegan. "Neither do I."

"Sounds like we'll get along, then."

"Believe me, Mr. Hightower, I want this trip to be as painless as possible for everyone involved."

His gaze travels over me, recalculating as he realizes that I'm not some spoiled kid simply looking for a bit of excitement. He jerks his thumb behind him. "Christopher, my protégé, will be responsible for your protection while you're on the train. Now if you don't mind, let's return to your quarters."

Christopher steps aside and Ian heads down the stairs. I follow, with Tegan so close on my heels that she keeps stepping on them. At the bottom, we begin making our way down the narrow passageway. When we reach the last car, I withdraw the key, unlock the door, and enter, with everyone following me inside.

"This is amazing," Tegan whispers.

"Don't be fooled by the luxury." Ian knocks on a wall, and the tinny echo reverberates around us. "The Agency reserves this car for those on official business. It's the safest place on the train."

"Am I confined to this room?" I ask.

He turns to look at me, his brow furrowed. I'm not sure if he's surprised that I spoke or if he's surprised to find me here, as though he almost forgot about me. "I prefer that you stay here, but I'm already getting a sense that you and your friend"—he points to Tegan—"aren't exactly rule followers. If you leave the car at night, you make absolutely sure at least one of these guys is with you." He studies

Michael. "Ever kill a vampire?"

"Yes, sir," Michael says sharply.

Ian nods. "Just be sure that you understand this assignment isn't about killing vamps. It's about keeping Miss Montgomery alive—at any cost. While you're on my train, you answer to me, not her. You're expendable. I'm expendable. She isn't. Are we clear on that?"

Michael nods. I start to say that Michael isn't expendable, that none of them is less important than me, but Ian's presence commands the room, seems to command the very air we breathe.

In his line of work, he's seen more death than most will ever see in ten lifetimes. During the war, he moved from city to city, killing vampires while those around him were slaughtered. I look into his dark brown eyes and I swear scars run across those, too.

"We're heading into the heart of rogue vampire country," he says. "The vampires out here are desperate for blood. They will attack. They may even penetrate our defenses and get on the train. You have to stay alert. That means no booze, no partying, no sex. Nothing to distract you. Do I make myself clear?"

"Yes, sir," Michael says crisply.

"Make no mistake, if anything happens to her, you will deal with me. And I'll make you wish the vampires had gotten to you first. Any questions?"

Silence reigns and he gives a nod. "I'll check back later."

He marches from the room, closing the door with a thunk in his wake.

"I can't believe I was breathing the same air as Ian Hightower," Tegan says.

"He's not such a god," Christopher says as he moves to a table adorned with decanters and bottles. He grabs the whiskey.

"He said no drinking," Tegan reminds him.

"He didn't mean it. You gonna tell on me? Be a snitch?" He gives her a once-over. "Nah, you don't look the type."

Christopher brings four glasses over to the table and pours a drink for himself.

"We're on duty," Michael tells him.

"Relax, Colt." Christopher tosses back the amber liquid and pours another. "You're taking the job way too seriously. Ian and I already established there aren't any vampires around—just one very loud stowaway."

"I wasn't loud!" Tegan shouts.

"Ah!" Christopher says, putting his hands over his ears. "I never thought I'd get my hearing back once you stopped squealing."

Michael storms across the room, and Christopher stupidly pours a drink, expecting Michael to join him. Instead, Michael snatches the decanter, the whiskey sloshing around, some of it spilling onto the floor.

"You're wasting good stuff, man," Christopher says.

"No drinking," Michael orders.

"Oh. My. God." Christopher laughs. "You're playing Night Watchman, aren't you? Hoping to impress Ian. That's all right, you'll get the hang of it eventually. Once you stake a few more vampires, watch a few more people get their throats ripped open, all that pretty idealism will fly out the window."

"And then what, I'll become you?"

I'm impressed that Michael didn't confess to being a Night Watchman, but then that's rule number one. Never admit that you are. Right now, all Ian and Christopher know is that Michael was sent to guard me. They don't know he's one of our elite.

Christopher scoffs. "If you're lucky you'll become me. You can take first watch."

He swaggers out of the room. I'm glad for the privacy.

"This place is amazing," Tegan says, going over to the bookshelf and pulling one of the massive volumes out. "These are real leather-bound editions. Not too many people can afford this kind of stuff."

"Tegan, what were you thinking?" I ask.

With a sigh, she puts the book back. "I told you. I didn't want you going alone. Besides, if there's any chance at all that we'll run into Sin, I want to be there to shove a stake through his treacherous heart."

"Tegan, this is so dangerous. In ways you can't even imagine." She's never seen a vampire infected by the Thirst up close. "When we get to LA, I want you to stay on the train."

"No way. Not gonna happen."

"Tegan—"

"I can have that Christopher guy wrapped around my little finger with two bats of my eyelashes. You know that. He'll help me get off the train, just like a Night

Watchman helped me get on."

"Fine. But if we cross paths with Sin, we run."

"I'm sick of running! I know you are, too."

"If anything happens to you—"

"Hey, you're always getting me out of trouble. Maybe this time, I'll save your ass."

I sigh heavily, acknowledging that I've lost the battle. I walk over and give her a fierce hug. "I know I shouldn't be, but I'm glad you're here. I was already missing you."

"Same goes. If anything happened to you, Dawn, I'd never forgive myself for not being there." She eases out of my embrace and looks over at Michael, who is staring at the floor, arms crossed as though he's not comfortable with all the emotion in the room. "But I might not have come if I'd known you were going to be here to watch over her."

He lifts his gaze, gives her a crooked smile, shrugs.

"Why would the Agency send you, anyway—oh my God! You're a Night Watchman!"

Michael can't say anything to that, because it's the only answer and Tegan isn't stupid.

"And you didn't tell us?" she asks with indignation that matches my earlier reaction.

"At some point if you want to become a Night Watchman, you have to stop telling people about it."

"You could have put Christopher in his place by telling him," she says.

Michael simply shakes his head. "I really don't care what he thinks about me or my abilities."

I think about the times we were together, and the

secrets he was holding from me then. Then I realize the secret I kept from him. Victor. I guess, in some ways, we didn't really know each other. But now that the conversation has shifted off Tegan to Michael, I ask, "How long have you been one?"

"Not that long. I was recruited a couple of days after Hell Night. The Day Walkers infiltrated the organization, and after they were dealt with, positions . . . opened up."

"I'm so glad you're here to watch over us," Tegan says.

"I'm *not* glad you're here," Michael responds. "What you did was reckless. It puts you in danger—"

"Okay, I get it. I'm an unexpected complication and no one is thrilled I'm here. But I've had enough scolding so I'm going to go explore the train. I didn't get to see much when the Night Watchman snuck me into the cargo car."

Michael narrows his eyes. "What was his name?"

"I didn't even ask, and he probably wouldn't have told me if I did." She strides up to him and punches his shoulder. "Step aside."

He scowls at her. "I don't think that's a good idea."

"What can happen on the train?"

With a grunt of agreement, he opens the door. Christopher is standing there. Maybe he takes the job more seriously than he lets on.

"Come on," Tegan says to him. "I need to check something out."

He looks back at me.

"I'll be fine," I assure him. "Just watch out for her."

He grins. "It will be my pleasure."

Michael watches them walking away before closing the door and turning back to me. "So you want to tell me what this is all about?" he asks. "What we're doing here?"

"Didn't Clive tell you?"

"All he did was ask for a volunteer for a special mission. Said it involved leaving Denver. He sure didn't say it involved you, but I guess I should have figured it out."

"Michael, can we call a truce?" I glance around. "I mean, we're really going to be in close quarters here. I know you're still upset about Victor and me—and I don't blame you—but what I have to do is going to be hard enough without having to deal with a guard who hates me."

"I don't hate you."

"Why did you volunteer to leave Denver, then?"

He sighs heavily.

I know him well enough to fill in the silence. "You wanted to get away from me. How's that working for you?"

He gives me a small grin. "Not as well as I'd hoped."

Walking over to him, I flatten my hand against his chest, feel his heart pounding. "Can we please be friends?"

"It's hard, Dawn."

"I know. I care for you . . . a lot. I still want—*need*—you in my life. And I need something else from you. I need you to give me your word that if a choice has to be made between saving Tegan or me that you'll save her."

I see the depth of his feelings for me in his eyes.

"I can't promise that, Dawn," he says quietly.

"Please, Michael, if you care for me at all, you'll put her first."

He sighs heavily. "I never could tell you no. Now why are we here?"

His response isn't really an answer, but I have to hope if it comes down to it, he'll do what I want. "You've seen the Thirst, interacted with it firsthand."

He absently rubs a small scar on his cheek, a scar he has courtesy of his encounter with Brady. "Yeah."

"Well, Clive and I are worried about it. He's sending me out west to investigate it. I know that it's rampant out there. But if the people of Los Angeles have found a way to protect themselves, then we need to learn it. Before it's too late."

He nods, taking it in. "Sin came from Los Angeles."

"Maybe. He could have been lying. But it's not inconceivable that we'd find something there to lead us to him."

"How does your vampire feel about all this?"

"Victor doesn't know."

"Makes me feel better knowing you keep secrets from him, too."

I wish I hadn't been forced to. I always thought we'd fight for the same thing, be on the same side. Now I'm not so sure anymore.

Chapter 14

"Okay, so the word is that tonight there is going to be a party in the lounge car," Tegan says when she returns, obviously pleased that her little outing discovered some information that she considers vital.

Michael and I put down our books—we've been passing the time reading since books are such a luxury nowadays.

Tegan plops down in a chair beside me. "So we're going, right?"

I grimace. "Actually, I'm having dinner with Ian." He stopped by a few minutes before Tegan's arrival to inform me of this fact.

"So tell him you have plans."

"It wasn't exactly an invitation."

She groans. "Well, Michael and I are going, right, Michael?"

He looks at me, then Tegan. "We'll go when Dawn gets back."

"Okay, fine. And Christopher's not such a bad guy after all. He convinced me to forgive him for almost staking me." She tucks her feet beneath her. "Quite honestly, I think Michael's confidence intimidated him a little. Besides, he's kind of cute."

"I'll take your word for it." I stand up. "If we're going to a party after dinner, I'm going to take a little nap. I didn't sleep any last night." Besides, I wasn't in the mood to be haunted by the dream that won't leave me alone.

"Yeah, neither did I," Tegan says. "Think I'll join you."

Michael sets his book aside. "I'll keep watch in the hallway."

"Okay," I say. "Come back before I go to dinner so you can keep Tegan company."

He understands my real message: *Watch over her, just like you would me.*

"I will. Sweet dreams."

He walks out. The door is too thick to hear what he might be saying to Christopher. I'm suddenly so tired that I just crawl into bed in my clothes. After dousing all the lamps, Tegan joins me. Because there are no windows, the place is pitch black. It's a little intimidating at first, with no soft light streaming through to outline the shape of the room. But it doesn't take long before I feel at home, enveloped in the darkness. Soon, it just feels like another blanket of protection.

The last words Brady spoke to me when he was hiding

me in a closet before he was turned into a vampire were, "Don't be afraid of the dark." It looks like it finally happened. I'm not afraid anymore.

"I'm glad Michael's here," Tegan says into the empty space around us.

"Yeah, me too."

"He still"—she yawns—"loves you, you know."

I swallow hard. "Things will never be the same between us."

"But you can be . . . friends," she murmurs, then I hear her light snore.

I smile. We've had enough sleepovers that I know she often goes to sleep while talking. "Yeah, we can be friends," I whisper.

I roll over and close my eyes, hoping that the mountain will leave me in peace.

I'm walking through Valentine Manor. My feet are bare. The stone is cold against my soles and my toes curl. The residence has an abundance of windows but thick curtains have been drawn in front of each one to ward off the sun. A few oil lamps have been left burning.

Vampires detest technology, although I suspect in time that Victor will have electricity installed out here.

Outside the building there will be guards, humans paid exorbitant amounts to watch over vampires during the day. So I know Victor is safe. That I'm safe.

I lift a lamp from the table in the massive foyer. I used to hate coming here to meet with Lord Valentine, but it seems different without him. Not so intimidating. I wonder if Roland Hursch will be impressed.

I wander over to the grand sweeping staircase that leads to the second floor, to the bedchambers, to the place where Victor is sleeping. I've been there before. He was wounded during the battle with his father. I slept in his arms while he healed.

I touch the banister, surprised by how smooth the wood feels beneath my fingers. Surprised by how solid everything seems, even though it's a dream. I know I'm on the train, heading for Los Angeles, sleeping.

But like the mountain dream, this one seems so real. I start up the stairs slowly, but then realize that I might be awakened at any moment for my dinner with Ian. I don't know how time moves in this world. It already feels as though I've been here forever.

I hurry up the stairs, my feet slapping against the marble. At the top, I almost fly down the hall to Victor's room. I open the door and see him lying in bed. On his back. Shirtless. The blankets are drawn up to his waist. He appears so peaceful. So young.

I tiptoe across the room, even knowing that I won't disturb him. Vampires sleep the sleep of the dead.

I set the lamp on the table beside his bed. Lifting the covers, I slip beneath them until I'm nestled against him. He feels so warm, so solid, so real. I can smell his tart, rich scent. I can hear his slow, even breathing. Still asleep, he lifts his arm, brings it around me, and draws me in even nearer. I close my eyes. I could stay here forever. I could—

"Dawn?"

I open my eyes to find Victor hovering over me, concern in his eyes. Still, I can't help but smile.

"What are you doing here, Dawn?"

"I wanted to see you."

"But you're on the train."

"How do you know?"

"I had someone keeping an eye on you."

"How many spies do you have in the city?"

"Enough." He combs his fingers through my hair. "So I don't understand how you're here."

I laugh. "It's just a dream."

His brow furrows. "No, it's more than that. It's not just a dream."

"Of course it is," I say, but then he touches my shoulder lightly, and it feels electrifying. I shudder, beginning to believe him.

"See," he says. "Everything is so . . ."

"Clear," I finish for him.

He simply nods. "Are all dreams like this?" he asks.

"Do I know something the mighty Lord Victor Valentine doesn't?" I ask, unable to help my smile.

"I'm serious, Dawn. I've only begun dreaming since I met you, but . . . but it was never like this. It always felt like you were my own private thought, a secret only for me. This feels . . ."

"Real," I finish for him again, then answer his earlier question. "It's never like this."

I place my hand beneath his head and pull him down for a kiss. His flavor is so rich, his tongue questing, his—

"Wake up! Dawn, for God's sake, wake up!"

My teeth are clicking together, I'm being shaken so hard. Tegan is standing beside the bed, both her hands on my shoulders, jerking me up and down like a rag doll.

"Tegan!" I roll away from her and sit up. "Remind me not to use you as an alarm clock ever again."

"You wouldn't wake up."

I realize then that Michael and Christopher are both standing at the foot of the bed, worried expressions on their faces—well, on Michael's, at least.

"I was just in a deep sleep, that's all."

"I tried calling, then nudging—I thought maybe you'd slipped into a coma again."

"No. I was dreaming—" I feel my face turning hot, especially because Michael is here. "It was nothing."

"See, it was nothing," Christopher says. "You guys get worried about everything, even someone sleeping."

Michael just studies me like I'm a new specimen of some undiscovered species. I don't like it. His look is too distant, too foreign.

"Well, I'm okay now." I scoot across the bed and clamber out. "You guys need to leave so I can get ready for my dinner with Ian."

"I hope you brought something fancy to wear," Christopher says. "He likes to eat in the main dining car."

"Thanks for the tip. Now leave."

The guys walk out and I grab my duffel bag. Anticipating a meeting with the Agency director in Los Angeles, I'd packed one nice black dress and heels. I pull them out.

"Are you sure you're okay?" Tegan asks.

"I'm fine." I try not to think about how real the dream was. Or that my lips are tingling as though they've just been kissed.

After I change my clothes and pin up my hair, I head out. Christopher escorts me to the main dining car. All along the way, it's impossible for me to tell whether it's night outside. I have to rely on my watch and internal clock to tell me the moon is rising.

I quickly spot Ian at a far table. He isn't as polished as the other diners, but he doesn't need to be. Everyone knows who he is; everyone knows his job is to protect the train, not look good. Then again, he looks good anyway. Not in a well-dressed, well-mannered way; but what he lacks in clothes he more than makes up for in confidence. And not the kind that boys fake just to impress; it's the kind that gets things done.

"I'm glad you could join me," Ian says as I take the seat opposite him.

"I didn't realize it was an option not to."

He gives a small concession—a slight turning up of his lips. "I'm not Valentine. We're not adversaries."

"Sorry. I sort of automatically go into delegate mode when I'm not sure what to expect of a situation."

"I've heard a lot about you. You're very good at what you do."

"I could say the same about you."

That makes his smile grow.

A waiter comes by and we both order steaks. I know all my expenses will be handled by the Agency and I figure I may as well enjoy what perks I can.

"How far are we from the city?" I ask, trying to take this conversation into friendlier, nonpersonal territory.

"Far enough to put me on edge. Vampires like to attack

in this area, knowing that we're a full day and night's ride from the next major city."

"But how likely is that? I mean, a vampire can't exactly walk through this steel wall."

"They can find a way. Even a rolling fortress like this has its weak points. I've known vampires to crawl along the undercarriage, inches away from the tracks below, searching for a single piece of wood not covered by steel." He stamps his foot, drawing my attention to the hardwood floor. I suppose with enough time and determination, and raw strength, a vampire could get through it if he found the right spot.

"Once, a vampire climbed through the smoke stacks and emerged blackened and near death, only to kill an engineer before making his way toward the passenger cars."

"God!"

"Don't worry. He never reached his target. In fact, since I've guarded the Night Train, we've only lost four passengers: two heart attacks, one accident, and one suicide."

"How many vamps have you staked onboard?"

Ian smiles. It's different from Victor's. It carries more secrets, something I didn't think was possible. It also reveals Ian's macabre sense of humor, like the only way to deal with everything is to find laughter in the blackness of the world. "More than I tell people."

That confidence again. I can't help but smile back.

The steaks arrive and are *amazing*. They are much thicker and moister than the steaks I shared with my family when we were celebrating my father being named the delegate. I close my eyes with every bite, just savoring the juices and flavors.

While we eat, I can't help but study the hunter across from me. His hands are lined with scars and misshapen joints. At a distance, he's gorgeous; but up close, everything is off, everything is ugly. Each scar is a little triumph over the reaper once again. Of course, the wounds on his skin are obvious, superficial. I imagine the worst scars are those that wounded his soul. How many friends has he buried? How many have died in his arms?

"You aren't impressed?" he asks.

"What are you talking about?"

"With me. The way I look. You haven't peered in my eyes for five minutes; you've just studied my face, the scars, my hands, wondering, analyzing."

"No, it's not that, it's . . ."

"I look better from far away."

What's wrong with me tonight? I can't think of lies quickly enough. Normally I'd be deflecting this kind of thing left and right. Is it the train? Is it Ian? Is it the dream that seemed so real?

"When I did my first interview, after killing Lord Percy, they spent three hours on my makeup. And then they demanded the lights be lowered, and lowered, and lowered, until I was in pitch black. They told the audience it was to protect my identity. Really, they just wanted a pretty face to represent humanity's best chance and I couldn't give it to them."

I've seen that interview before. It's a classic, one of the few victories we had in that war. He's right, of course: They portrayed him as their secret weapon, the ultimate warrior against the vampires. Anything to keep our hopes up at the end. And it's funny, because the dim lights worked. I always imagined he was some beautiful demigod, a vampire-slaying angel who came to save us all. With the lights on, the makeup off, he was just a man. Is just a man.

"That was twelve years ago," he says. "And I've only gotten uglier."

"You're not ugly," I say.

He laughs at my little attempt to make him feel better.

"I'm not trying to win a beauty contest," he says.

"You could probably win the talent portion," I say.

There's a tense moment; then he smiles with me and we both laugh.

"You're right. Not many people can do what I do."

He taps his fingers on the metal stakes lined in the bandolier across his body. I count six. I imagine in a good fight that would mean six dead vampires.

"I knew your father, you know," he says quietly.

My eyes nearly bug out of my head. My father knew the great Ian Hightower?

"It was after I'd killed Lord Percy. Your father was sent in to go through Percy's manor. I don't know what he was searching for—or even if he found it. There was probably no one who understood vampires more than your old man. But even all the knowledge he gained couldn't help us defeat those bloodsuckers. I'm sorry he and your mother were killed."

The words aren't just rhetoric. I know he means them. "I still miss them."

"That'll never go away. Just don't become like me."

"A vampire hunter?"

One side of his mouth goes up in a grin. "No. Don't stop getting close to people. But then you have loyal friends—they probably won't let you go the lone-wolf path."

There's lightness in the air as we move on to dessert: a creamy coffee for me and brandy for him.

"So where does the train go after Los Angeles?" I ask.

"Normally up to Seattle, but this time we'll be going straight back to Denver."

"That's not fair to Seattle."

"Not much is fair anymore."

I can tell the detour my mission will cause annoys him. After all, a train is supposed to run on schedule, and this drastic change will shift everything. It may take months to get all the deliveries lined up again. I wish it didn't have to be that way.

He leans forward, crossing his arms on the table. "Okay, Dawn, enough games. Why is Clive sending the city's delegate to Los Angeles?"

"I'm not the delegate anymore."

He looks surprised at that.

"Roland Hursch is."

"That bag of wind?"

I laugh. "You've met him?"

"Oh, yeah, he's always telling me how awful I am at managing the train, the 'lifeblood of the country,' as he calls it. So if you're not going as the delegate, are you following in your father's footsteps, getting into intelligence work?"

In a way I suppose I am. Clive wanted my mission to be kept a secret, but not from Ian. We need his help and cooperation. "Are you familiar with the Thirst?"

He ponders my question for a moment, shakes his head. "Can't say that I am."

I remember Richard telling me that it was the vampires' dirty little secret. "Do you ever run into vampires that seem completely out of control?"

"The Starving? At least that's what I call them. It's obvious they're desperate for blood, and it isn't pretty. The area around Los Angeles is rife with them. We make a point to arrive during daylight to avoid the rampaging hordes."

"They're not starving so much as infected." I explain how the Infected become addicted to vampire blood. "Clive sent me to investigate what's happening in Los Angeles. The city is safe, right?"

Ian thinks about it, nods.

"Then I need to learn how they've protected themselves, so if we're confronted by the Thirst, we'll be prepared."

"The solution is more blood. That's all."

"But if the citizens refuse to donate, then . . ."

"Why would they do that? I mean, Denver has it the worst of any of the cities. You're controlled by Lord Valen— ah, wait. The stationmaster mentioned that the Bloody

Valentine was overthrown. His son is now holding the reins."

I nod. "Victor."

"I take it he isn't as vicious as his father."

"He wants cooperation," I say. "Or, he did. I think he's seeing things differently now that he's actually Lord Valentine, instead of just Victor."

"The idealism found in youth can quickly fade once power is obtained. Even for a vampire."

"Yeah. Sadly, it can." But Victor will be different. I believe in him with all my heart.

We always met our blood quotas, but only just. And we met them out of fear. Murdoch Valentine's shadow fell across the city even when the sun was up, one that chilled the bone, froze the heart. People felt his presence at all times, even if no one spoke his name.

Victor and I used to talk on my balcony about a better world, and the one thing we could agree on was that fear was no way to control a city. We were convinced that cooperation between humans and vampires would achieve so much more. We were convinced it would encourage people to donate. I hate to think that we were wrong this whole time, and that Murdoch Valentine was right: Fear rules above all else.

Chapter 15

When I enter my VIP room—Christopher right on my heels because he was waiting for me outside the dining car—Tegan hops out of her chair. "How was dinner with Ian?"

"Fine," I say, not wanting to go into details with Christopher here. I may have let Ian in on my mission, but that doesn't mean his protégé needs to know.

"Then let's go party!" Tegan says cheerfully.

"I want to change—"

"You look fantastic," she says, grabbing my arm. "We're already going to be late enough as it is."

I want to tell her that I'm not here to have a good time, but where's the harm in a little innocent fun? Besides, it'll be nice to forget everything for a while, to pretend that we're on an exciting adventure, exploring the world.

"Let's go."

I look over at Christopher as he holds the door open.

"I'm surprised you're okay with us doing this," I say.

He just shrugs. "It's a party; the kids here have all the time in the world and little to do, so they need to fight the boredom. Besides, it's safe. It isn't like a party in one of your cities, where vampires show up every time and kill half the people."

We pass through a few cars of sleeper berths. No one's walking the hallways. It must be really late, most everyone asleep. As we approach the lounge car, I can hear the music thumping through the metal door. When I open it, the sound blasting into me almost rattles my teeth.

It's dark inside, flashing strobe lights giving it a surreal feel. It's also crowded with a lot of young people.

"Hey! You made it," a guy says as he comes up to us. As far as I can tell he has short-cropped blond hair.

Tegan greets him with a hug and introduces him as Jake. Beside him is a guy with dark hair and rings piercing each eyebrow.

"This is my friend Doug," Jake says. "So y'all got on in Denver, right?"

"That's right," Tegan says, smiling brightly.

"Y'all part of the redistribution process?" Doug asks.

The VampHu treaty stated that the vampires would strive to keep the population in the cities balanced, but I've never known anyone who was identified for "redistribution" from Denver. The old Valentine wasn't concerned with the other cities. He was powerful enough that he wasn't intimidated by the Vampire Council that oversees the fourteen Old Families and the management of our country.

"No," Tegan says. "We're just going to Los Angeles for a few days. Don't know that I've ever heard of redistribution."

"Dallas has a lot of people," Jake says. "Apparently Los Angeles is in short supply, so they asked for volunteers. We decided we wanted to see what other parts of the country looked like."

I'm wondering if the people in Los Angeles have decided to start donating blood again—or are these guys going to be delivered straight to Lord Carrollton, kicked off the train right outside his manor?

"Booze is free. Help yourself," Doug says.

We head over to the bar. Michael gets us each a beer. Tegan grabs hers, then joins Jake and Doug on the dance floor. Christopher starts talking to a tall brunette. Michael and I back away into a corner. He takes a chug of beer while I slowly sip mine.

"'Redistribution'—that word always bugged me," he says after a while. "It's like vampires just see us as commodities."

"Yeah, unfortunately, most do."

"All of them do."

"Victor isn't like other vampires." I'm watching the people gyrating on the dance floor. The slowly flashing lights are starting to give me a headache. I see flaming red hair—

It can't be. But the next moment it's gone before I can

be sure. I search the crowd. I catch a glimpse of a guy, a narrow braid of hair hanging down one side of his face.

Crap!

"Want to dance?" Michael asks.

"Sure," I say automatically, still wondering if the impossible really followed me onto this train.

We both finish off our beers and grab another before we wind our way toward a small empty space between people. I see Tegan smiling brightly, laughing, and I'm glad she seems more like her pre-Sin self. I turn my attention to the rest of the room, looking—

"You okay?" Michael asks.

"Oh, yeah." *Gotcha!* I think when I see the couple who caught my attention earlier standing against a far wall. "I'll be right back."

I've barely taken a step away when another girl wiggles in front of Michael. I can't blame her for her interest and realize that she'll keep him distracted for a moment.

I march over to the brown-haired guy and the red-headed girl. They don't look surprised to see me, but then vampires aren't known for giving away their emotions.

"What are you guys doing here?" I whisper, grateful vampires have such keen hearing so I don't have to yell to be heard above the music.

"Heading home," Richard says, leaning in so I can hear him.

"Sightseeing," Faith says.

Yeah, right. Do they really think I'm that stupid? I give them a pointed glare.

"Victor's orders," Richard admits. "Faith and I are to protect you."

But even with his spies Victor didn't have time—

And then it hits me. "How long have you been following me?"

"Ever since you left the hospital."

I should've known Victor wouldn't let me out of his sights that easily.

"How did you even get tickets?" I ask.

"It's amazing what large sums of cash can buy at a moment's notice," Richard says.

"Why didn't you try to stop me?"

"Our orders were not to interfere with your life. Just follow and protect."

"What about Sin?" I ask. "With him running free, causing havoc, shouldn't you two be protecting Victor?"

"If Sin comes after you," Richard says, "he *is* going after Victor. Nothing will bring Victor out faster than you being in danger."

I feel like a pawn being moved across the board. It's always the vampires' game; I'm just a piece in it. Or worse, a bargaining chip.

"Do you know how dangerous it is for you to be here?" I ask.

Faith scoffs. "Please, the most dangerous thing so far is this outdated décor."

"Ian Hightower is dangerous."

"No, he *was* dangerous. He's a washed-up alcoholic now, probably hasn't staked a vamp in years. The guy's thirty-eight years old and he looks sixty—talk about letting yourself go."

A vampire's arrogance, always her greatest weakness. I look over at Richard. He's at least a little more humble than Faith, but he doesn't seem very concerned, either.

"Ian wants the train to arrive without any incidents," Richard says. "So do we. Really, we're on the same side."

I don't know if I buy his logic, but so long as I have them here, something has been bothering me.

"Listen, I have a puzzle for you," I say to Richard.

He grins, shifts his gaze to Faith. "I love puzzles."

"Some of these people, the young ones," I begin, "are being moved from Dallas to Los Angeles."

"Yeah," Richard says slowly, "I overheard a few of them talking about that."

"Why? If Los Angeles isn't giving blood to the vamps, why would they put in a request for donors?"

"I've been wondering the same thing. The last time I checked, Los Angeles had more people than any other city."

"Maybe your father grew a pair and reestablished control over the Agency and city," Faith suggests.

"Could be," Richard says. "But it's doubtful." I know he and his father, Lord Carrollton, are not on the best of terms.

"So maybe they eradicated the Thirst?" I ask. It was rampant there because the citizens weren't giving blood. Maybe seeing the rampage made them realize giving blood wasn't such a bad trade-off. If I can bring back that kind of news to Denver, then our own citizens might start donating, too. At least, I can hope for that.

But instead of answering me, he says, "We're looking forward to seeing Los Angeles."

I furrow my brow in confusion just as a hand lands on the small of my back, and then I get it. I look over to see Michael.

"Thought I lost you for a minute there," he says.

"No, I was just talking with—"

"Faith Fitzgerald," Faith says. "And my . . . boyfriend, Richard Young."

If I didn't already know her, I might not have caught her slight stumble over the word "boyfriend." I also can't miss the irony of the name she chose for him. He's not young. He's almost as old as Victor.

"I don't recognize you from school," Michael says, and I can sense his suspicions.

"We attended another school," Richard says, "but we were at the Teen Initiative party. We were just telling Dawn how unfair it is that her wonderful plan was tainted by what that guy Sin did."

"Well, I'm glad we had a chance to talk. Maybe later—"

My sentence is cut off when the wheels howl and squeal beneath us. And then a half second later, a terrible crashing sound echoes through the compartments of this long steel can. It sounds like the tracks split, and the train is tearing itself apart. The car stops violently. With the sudden jolt, I'm lifted off the floor. The momentum throws me forward and I cringe, afraid of where I'll land, and who will end up on top of me as all the kids fly through the air.

But Richard, with his vampire speed, catches me before I hit the floor. Faith's right there, too, her arms wrapped around me.

The music has screeched to a halt. The macabre lights are still flashing, in an odd way camouflaging Richard's and Faith's actions because only a few movements are seen.

"What the hell was that?" Faith asks.

"I think we crashed," Richard says.

What did Ian say? This was the most desolate part of the journey. A full day and night's ride from any other city. A wasteland. Dead space. A void.

And we're in the middle of it.

Chapter 16

Michael pulls me out of their embrace and snakes an arm around me. "I need to get you back to your car."

"Where's Tegan?" I glance frantically around. People are scurrying out. "Tegan!"

I can't see her anywhere.

"We can't wait on her."

"Michael, we have to find her! I won't leave her behind again."

I try to fight my way out of Michael's hold knowing I'll lose, but I have to make a point.

"Dawn, we don't have time."

Richard steps up beside me and puts a comforting hand on my shoulder. "I'll find Tegan, you get back to your room."

"No," Faith says, pulling Richard away. "I don't trust

you with a damsel in distress. *I'll* find Tegan, you follow Dawn back."

"Fine."

Maybe I'd laugh at this squabbling if everything weren't so serious.

Michael, still holding my arm, lets Richard lead the way through the crowd of people. Most of them have scurried into their assigned bedrooms, and the hallways are clearing out. Too bad we're at the far end of the train, nearly twenty cars away.

Suddenly we see Ian coming down the narrow corridor.

"Dawn, go to your compartment," he orders, never losing step. He passes us and then turns toward Michael. "Stick close to her. And lose the jacket."

Michael nods and begins ushering me through the dining car. Along the way, he takes off his jacket and I see the stakes strapped to his body, hanging from bandoliers and belts. I try to imagine this as no different from the walks we used to share in school, holding hands as we strolled down the hallways to our next class. But this is nothing like that; his grip is so tight around my wrist that it hurts.

As we pass through a berth car, one of the doors opens and Christopher steps out. He quickly begins buttoning up his shirt and jacket.

"What were you doing?" Michael asks.

"Come on, Colt. What do you think? Girls find me irresistible."

Richard is still far up ahead, keeping a lookout.

"Have you seen Tegan?" I ask, as we begin moving

again and Christopher falls into step behind us.

"She was with that Jake guy."

"Did they go somewhere?"

"I'm not her mother."

This is awful. I have no way to find her, no way to know if she's okay. All I can do is trust that Faith has found her.

We finally reach my car. Michael takes the key from me and unlocks the door. He enters first, checks to make sure it's clear, and then signals us in. Richard immediately scopes the place out, too, using his vampire senses to detect any unwanted intruders. He checks every nook and cranny carefully.

"The place is clear," Michael says, not bothering to disguise his irritation that someone he's just met seems to think he's in charge.

But Richard takes his time, and when he's satisfied he makes a move for the door.

"We should stay here," Michael says.

"No, I have to check the rest of the cars, make sure everyone's okay."

"Are you crazy? What if there are vamps out there? They'll tear you apart. Have you ever even seen a vampire up close?"

"No, but I've heard they aren't pretty."

Somehow I keep a straight face. If only Michael knew.

"Just let him go," Christopher says, already sitting down in a chair and kicking his feet up onto a table.

I rush over to Richard as he stands by the doorway.

"You're going after Faith, aren't you?" I ask.

He nods.

I squeeze his hand, give him a slight shove out, and then lock the door behind him.

Now it's just the three of us, and I feel much better knowing that two Old Family vampires will be protecting Tegan. If they find her.

"You should take off your jacket," Michael tells Christopher, pacing the room.

"Why? So we have 'easier access' to our weapons?" he asks, complete with air quotes. "This isn't the war, you know? Times have changed."

"The vampires haven't."

Christopher waves Michael off, like he doesn't know what he's talking about.

"You might as well settle in, Dawn," Christopher says. "We're going to be here awhile."

Taking that as his own signal, he does the settling down by pouring himself a drink from a crystal decanter.

"Why do you think we stopped?" I ask Michael.

"I don't know."

"Does this happen often?" I ask Christopher.

He just shakes his head.

"How can you be so nonchalant about it?"

"What do you want me to do?" he asks. "Get out and push?"

He's impossible!

"What does Ian even see in you?" I ask. "I mean, there are hundreds of hunters—why you?"

"Don't let the good looks fool you," he says, a tad more

serious, finally. "I'm fast with a stake. Vamps knew not to mess with me. I was a professional hunter for a while, made my living selling fangs."

"That's barbaric."

"That's reality. That's money. But this gig paid more. Though I'm starting to regret it."

"How long have you been doing this?" Michael asks.

"A few years. But I've never been out this way. I usually work with Ian whenever the train is on the east coast, making the trip from New York to Miami. He picks up another guard there to make the trip out west."

"Why stay in Miami? Why not ride the whole way?"

"Like you have to ask? Sunny beaches, beautiful women, why would I leave? Of course, by the time Ian comes back I've always blown all my money and need the job again. This time I decided to stick with him for the whole route. That won't be happening again. It's so boring."

Only now that the train is completely still do I realize how strange the lack of motion feels. The slow rocking of the carriages had brought a strange peace, and without it, I'm aware of every little sound, every little creak. The night outside seems so much larger now that we aren't moving through it.

The time passes slowly, and while Michael is like a statue, Christopher keeps lolling his head around as though he's bored. Finally, he pulls out a pocket watch and checks the time.

"It's been thirty minutes," he says, for the first time

showing a hint of worry. "That's way too long. Something is going on. I'll go find Ian."

"He told us to stay here," Michael says.

"Well, either he's dead and won't come relieve us, or it's nothing and he just forgot about us. Come on, man, we can't stay cooped up in here until sunrise."

"Why not?" I ask. "That seems like the best thing to do."

"You two stay, then. I'll do some 'reconnaissance,'" he says, pulling out the air quotes again. I'm not sure if he's mocking our concern or trying to mask his own.

"Don't open that door, Christopher!" Michael says. "You don't know what's on the other side."

Christopher puts his ear to the door and listens. "Oh my God. You're right. Vampires are everywhere. They've somehow made it through ten inches of solid steel, past Ian, and are slowly killing everyone onboard. Oh, the humanity!"

"That's enough . . ."

"We have to save them!"

He puts his hand on the lock and turns it, the metal bolt moving out of the way.

"Christopher, don't!"

He slides the door open and steps out into the calm hallway. It looks no different than it did an hour ago.

"You're never going to make it as a hunter," Christopher tells Michael, probably the greatest insult he could deliver. "You're too jumpy; you take it all too seriously."

"And you don't take it seriously enough," Michael says.

"Maybe you've been on this train too long and haven't had to deal with vampires in a while."

"Whatever." Christopher walks away, stakes not even drawn.

"Hello!" I hear him yelling from farther down the hallway. "Is anyone alive? No? Oh well."

Michael goes to the door. I can see him hesitate, wondering if he should shut it.

The train jumps as if the lead engine had rocked heavily and the wave traveled through each compartment before colliding with ours. I hear the metalworks underneath twisting and turning with the tension.

I expect us to start up again, but we don't. I join Michael at the door. "What do you think that was?"

"I don't know, but I don't like it," Michael says, his voice measured. "Christopher, get back here."

The entrance to the next car is open and I can see Christopher standing still, his head cocked, clearly listening.

A thunderous sound shakes the entire train and I imagine a giant stepping on the track just outside. Then I hear the deep scratching and twisting of metal. I don't know where it's coming from, but it sounds close.

I see Christopher turn sharply, looking farther down the hall, into the other cars. He sees something we don't, something that worries him, because he pivots and begins running toward us.

"Shut the door!" he yells.

But we can't leave him outside to face alone whatever it is he's running from.

"Shut it!" he screams again, fumbling to unbutton his jacket and pulling out two stakes, gripping one in each hand.

Behind him, I see a vampire leap into the hallway and, like some deranged animal, bound off the walls with ease, closing in on his prey.

Michael curses, yanks out a stake, and sprints forward to help Christopher.

"Michael!" I yell.

He doesn't turn back, simply shouts, "Close the door!"

Not going to happen. I won't hide when he's facing danger.

I kick off my heels, rush to my duffle, and jerk out a stake. Running out into the hallway, I size up the situation, trying to determine how I can be the most help.

Any other night, the odds would favor the hunters. Trained just for the killing of vamps, they stake hearts for a living. And with two of them working together in perfect sync, I wouldn't be worried. But this vampire isn't like the ones they're used to.

He's been infected by the Thirst.

He looks just like Brady: eyes blackened, muscles unstable and twitching as if trying to flee their owner's skin. And instead of a single pair of fangs, his entire mouth has been transformed into a maw lined with teeth that take on the form of shattered glass.

For all of Christopher's arrogance, he backs it up with skill. His stakes seem like natural extensions of his body, and he moves them with finesse. But the monster coming at him strikes with more strength and as Christopher tries to bring down a stake, the vampire catches his arm and throws the seasoned hunter across the room with ferocious power.

Michael wastes no time, unable to even register shock in the heat of battle. He rushes in, slams his stake into the beast's chest, but he is off his mark. The creature howls in outrage before delivering a kick that sends Michael back and into the wall. A cracking sound follows. I can only pray it wasn't his ribs breaking. Just in time, Christopher is up again and charges. The distracted vampire can't catch the stake, but deflects its deadly trajectory—it lands solidly in the vampire's shoulder, just missing the heart.

The raging beast is stunned, and Michael comes up, his stake finding a weak point just below the monster's rib cage. The stake slides in so cleanly, it's hard to reconcile the violence with the precision of Michael's movements.

Each of the hunters, still holding a stake inside of their prey, pulls out another and delivers the final killing blows deep into the chest—one from the front, one from the back.

The vampire's blackened eyes don't change, only the face surrounding them. It moves from anger, to defeat, and finally to fear of what's to come when his life slips away.

Michael and Christopher step back and the vampire falls to the floor. Dead.

Breathing heavily, Christopher stares down at the sprawled vampire. "That's one ugly mother—"

His words are drowned out by a long whistle sound, and I hope that means we're about to start moving again.

"I need a drink," Christopher says, brushing past me as

he heads down the hallway to my car.

In spite of the strenuous battle, Michael is barely out of breath as he puts his hand on my back and urges me to follow Christopher. We step into the compartment in time to see Christopher walk over to the bar, reach into it, and pull out a bottle along with three glasses. He pours amber liquid into each one.

"See," Christopher says, finally catching his breath, "I killed one, and still managed to look good." He straightens his jacket and runs his fingers through his hair.

Before I can scoff at his arrogance, a vampire suddenly jumps onto him from behind the bar, his glistening fangs tearing into Christopher's neck.

Chapter 17

"No!" I scream as blood spews from the ravaged artery. This vampire, just like the one before him, has been taken by the Thirst. Christopher's blood won't give him any sustenance, but the thrill of the kill may put a fanged smile on his face all the same.

Taking a running leap, I slam into the vampire's back and bring my stake down with force, but I must have missed the heart, because he throws me off like I weigh nothing, his strength not diminished at all.

I land with a thud, stunned, watching through a haze of dizziness. At least he released his hold on Christopher, who struggles to his feet and puts a hand to his neck to stop the flow of blood. With the other hand, he pulls out a stake.

Michael rushes in and delivers a clumsy strike that only grazes his opponent. He's pushed back violently, his head banging into the train wall, the tinny vibration echoing around us. Christopher takes a step forward, but quickly stumbles, drops to one knee, and opens his palm. His stake rolls out with a clatter. I've never seen so much blood.

Laughing manically, the creature darts around the room. Shaking my head, I force myself to focus. I tighten my grip on my stake, determined to do whatever I can, to go down fighting. Pushing myself to my feet, screaming with anger and frustration, I charge—

The shining metal tip of a stake bursts through the vampire's chest. I stagger to a stop as he blinks in muted surprise before falling forward, dead. Ian stands behind him.

Turning my attention to Christopher, I grab a blanket from the bed, hurry over, and kneel beside him. I press a corner of the soft material against the gaping wound. "Just hold on."

Ian drops down beside us. "Hang in there, kid." He places his hand over mine, but it's not enough to stop the flow of blood.

"Oh, Ian, you've joined us just in time for drinks." Christopher coughs up blood.

"Stop talking."

Reaching down, I wrap my hand around Christopher's. His fingers respond, squeezing mine tightly.

"Looks like I should've stayed on those sunny beaches," Christopher croaks.

"We'll get you back there," Ian assures him.

"I can already hear the waves crashing against the rocks. What about you, Ian? Can you hear them?"

"Yes . . ."

"They sound . . . beautiful . . ."

His fingers go lax in mine and I know he's gone. Tears burn my eyes, clog my throat. I stand up. I don't want to leave him, but I can't bear his stilled expression. So final. So permanent.

Ian reaches down, grabs a small leather necklace Christopher wore, and yanks it off, then places it in his pocket before shooting to his feet. "Let's go, Michael. I rushed here when I heard your screams, but I'm pretty sure I spotted a vampire moving through one of the cars. Maybe even Old Family by the looks of him." He heads for the door, Michael in his wake.

"Old Family?" I call out.

"Yeah. He brushed by me. When I looked back, he was gone. No one moves that fast," he says, a flash of uncontrolled anger in his voice.

"Brown hair, a braid on one side?" I ask, rushing after him because he's almost through the door.

"That's him."

"Ian, he's a friend! And there's another one."

That stops him dead in his tracks. It doesn't help that Michael is staring at me, an incredulous look on his face, and I know what he's thinking: *More vampires, Dawn? Really?*

But when Ian turns around slowly and glares at me, I have a sense of how Lord Percy may have felt when he found himself face to face with Ian Hightower: terrified.

Chapter 18

Half an hour later, the train is lumbering along and everyone is in my bedroom, the luxury of it all feeling more like a prison now. After Ian gave me the death stare, we went searching and found Richard and Faith with Tegan in one of the sleeper cars, along with a dozen other teenagers. I gave her a big hug and said I'd explain everything.

Ian said, "You will. Right now."

So here we are. Michael, Tegan, Ian, Faith, Richard, and myself, all sitting around in various chairs near the fireplace. Ian had the train staff remove all evidence that any violence occurred here, but I'm still chilled and wish we had a fire going.

"Did you two have anything to do with this attack?" Ian asks immediately, eyeing their hearts.

"No," Richard says, not intimidated. But then why should he be? He's Old Family. Even with four stake holders in the room, the odds are still in his favor. Faith is no slouch when it comes to defending herself, either. "We were with Dawn when the attack occurred. Faith grabbed Tegan, along with a number of other kids, and got them to safety. I found them shortly after. Along with a Thirst-infected."

"Yes, I saw the body," Ian says. "I wondered who killed him."

"He put up quite a fight. He probably scented Faith. Not that he wasn't looking for humans as well. The Infected need vampire blood, but they'll take any blood that's available."

"They saved us," Tegan says, her words cautious and slow as though she's having a difficult time believing that she's saying them. She's always been fascinated by Old Family vampires, but now that she's sitting in a room with two of them, she seems uncertain. Should she be curious or afraid? After all, Sin was the last Old Family vamp she spent time with, and that didn't turn out too well. "If Faith hadn't been there, we would've been running around aimlessly, just waiting to get pounced on. And even when we were all huddled in that room, she had her stake out, ear at the door, waiting."

I look over at Faith, and can tell she doesn't like the thought of being a heroine. Still . . . she can't hide her smile completely.

"Did the passengers see your fangs?" Ian asks.

"No," Faith says. "They didn't see Richard's, either. As far as they're concerned, we're good hunters who just happened to be at the right place, at the right time."

"Good. Let's keep it that way. And . . . thank you. It would've been a lot worse if you hadn't been there."

I breathe a little easier. Things aren't so bad. But then again, Michael hasn't spoken. At least not with words. His eyes convey betrayal, a look I'm painfully familiar with. Because I introduced them right before the attack. I deliberately let him think they were human. It's Victor all over again.

"How many vampires are you going to keep from us, Dawn?" Michael asks.

"They're the last."

"Wish that were *literally* true," Michael mumbles, glaring at them.

"How do we know that we got them all?" Tegan asks, glancing around warily. "I mean, how did the one who killed Christopher get in here? Maybe there are others."

"He must have been hiding beneath a seat in the next car," Michaels says. "When we all rushed to fight the first Infected, he snuck in here."

"Why didn't he just join the fight with his friend?"

"Who knows why vampires do the things they do?" He slides his gaze over to Richard.

"If you expect me to be offended . . ." Richard smiles. "We often say the same thing about humans. As for the Infected who surprised your comrade-in-arms—I agree that it's impossible to determine his reasoning. The Thirst eats away at all rational thought."

"But there could be more hiding on the train," Tegan insists.

"I truly doubt it," Ian assures her. "Several former soldiers are onboard. They took on the task of sweeping through the cars and making sure no vampire remained unstaked. Except for Dawn's two friends here."

"Do you know how the Thirst-infected got onboard?" Richards asks.

"They put boulders on the track," Ian explains. "Fortunately, the engineer saw them and was able to stop before we smashed at full speed into them. Don't get me wrong, this train can deal with some rocks, but only at slow speeds. Hitting them going full blast might derail us. That's probably what the vamps wanted. By the time the engineer assessed the situation and determined he could plow through without causing much damage to the train, the vamps had already gotten through a weak point. An old plate had been welded over a hole in the floor. It had come loose. They crawled along the bottom, found it, and tore it off. Along with Christopher, eleven were killed tonight."

"Oh my God," I whisper. Eleven. I knew the dead humans and vampires had been left beside the tracks. I hated that, but Ian had no way to preserve them. "Have you ever been attacked by these Infected before?"

"No. I've seen them on the outskirts of Los Angeles, but not out here. Only unaffected vampires, Lessers, come this far away from the cities. At least, they used to. I'm afraid, Dawn, that your little trip to Los Angeles may have come too late."

"I'm sure I can still discover something to help us. But I'm also hoping I might learn something more about the Day Walkers or get a lead on where we might find Sin. He said he came from Los Angeles."

"That's probably a lie," Faith says. "He's too cunning to make such a stupid slip."

"Besides," Richard adds, "Los Angeles doesn't have any Day Walkers. Sin certainly never created any havoc there."

"But you haven't been back in two years," I remind him. "Would you hear if he'd done anything?"

"Humans are isolated; vampires aren't. We have ways of communicating, and we travel more freely than you might think. Old Family, anyway."

I reluctantly admit that Richard is probably right. I won't find out anything about Day Walkers in Los Angeles. Sin kept his abilities a secret until Hell Night.

"In his letter Clive said you needed three days in Los Angeles," Ian says. "Is that going to be enough time?"

I don't want to stay away from Denver too long. The last thing I want to do is return to find that its walls have already crumbled. I grit my teeth. "I'll make it enough."

Chapter 19

It is late in the night when Ian, Faith, and Richard leave. I am certain that Ian is going to check on the passengers and scour the train for any other dangers. Faith and Richard—well, I wonder if they might try to find a cozy little corner. Facing death has a way of putting things into perspective, making you realize who is important in your life.

Tegan is obviously exhausted. We prepare for bed as though we're moving through molasses. When we're both in flannel pants and tanks, I invite Michael back in from the hallway where he's been waiting. He leans against the entrance.

"You should try to get some sleep," I tell him.

"I'll keep watch."

I know it's pointless to argue. I head for the bed, then

turn to face him. "I didn't know Faith and Richard were onboard until I saw them at the party. If I'd told you right then and there that they were vampires, would you have kept your stake holstered?"

He looks down at his feet. That's answer enough.

"Who are they?" Tegan asks quietly. "I mean, it's obvious that they're Old Family. They're too beautiful to be Lessers."

I join her on the bed. "Faith is Victor's half sister. Richard is his friend. He's a Carrollton. His father is the overlord of Los Angeles."

"Are you going to meet with his father?"

"That's the plan. He might know something about Sin or Day Walkers that can help us. At the very least he's familiar with the Thirst. The Infected have been there for a while."

She shivers, and I suspect it's not because she's cold.

"You don't have to go with me," I assure her. As a matter of fact, I'm going to make certain she doesn't. Michael, though—unfortunately I'm probably going to need him.

Drawing her knees up, she wraps her arms around her legs. "I don't know what I thought we'd find outside of Denver's walls. I just know this isn't it."

No, I think as the train hurtles over the tracks, *I don't think anything could have prepared us for all this.*

Hours later, as hard as I try, I can't sleep. I hear Tegan snoring softly beside me. I can't believe she fell asleep so easily. But then, she didn't see the horror and carnage that I did.

I'm glad that being with Faith spared her that. Although maybe not entirely. She did ask that we keep one lamp on, its light dim.

Michael is stretched out on the couch, his eyes closed. I'm not sure if he's asleep, or just thinking. I guess we all need those quiet moments to ourselves, where the world is shut out.

I slip out of bed. Tegan murmurs. Michael doesn't move. I grab my hoodie and the holster with the stake. Not bothering to slip on shoes, I creep across the room, glance back once. No one has stirred. Quietly I unlock the door and step into the hallway. I lock up, draw on my hoodie, and strap on the holster. I'm actually a little sad Christopher isn't outside waiting. I'm hoping he's with the crashing waves now.

I walk through the cars, noting the stillness around me. No one is in the passageway. I'm surprised Richard and Faith weren't outside my door, but they knew Michael was taking a turn at watching me. They'll be mad if they discover that I snuck out without an escort, but I'm feeling hemmed in again. I need something. I'm just not sure what it is. I reach the winding stairs that lead up to the observation deck. When I get there, a sense of relief washes over me at the sight of the night sky. Without any windows, time acts strangely. I had no idea whether it was really day or night until I came up top.

For some reason I needed to see the moon and the stars; I needed to be lost in the vastness of the night sky.

I'm happy up here; I needed my own quiet moment.

The moon isn't quite full yet, but it's bright enough to illuminate the countryside. Taking a seat, I watch the scenery
roll past. Mostly desert with tiny patches of dying vegetation, yellowed from the heat and drought. Mountains rise
in the distance, so far away they seem like pieces of art,
only there to be looked upon, and forever beyond reality. I
figure this must be the safest area. Without any forests or
caves to offer shelter, where could the Infected hide when
the sun is out? I guess there could be small towns off in
the distance, just beyond those hills, their citizens once
human, now turned. The vampires may stay locked away,
resting inside shacks made from old cardboard and whatever scraps of wood they can find, anything to keep the
sun out. The idea of an ornate coffin, varnished and clean,
with velvet lining in which Dracula sleeps, is fiction. Even
the Old Families wouldn't touch that: They sleep in comfortable beds in elaborate manors.

The scenery is repetitive; the train rocks me back and
forth, making me drowsy. I lie down on the bench. And
before long, I nod off to sleep.

*I'm in Valentine Manor again, walking down a familiar hallway.
I come to the room where Valentine and I discussed abductions
and blood supply. The door is open.*

*When I peer inside, I see the huge table that stretches from
one end of the room to the other. Victor is reclining on the massive
throne where his father once sat. Waiting. I can sense the tension
in him. His breathing is long and shallow, but his hands are gripping the armrests and I think that if he were suddenly startled he*

would rip them free of their mooring.

I hear footsteps echoing along the hallway. I glance over my shoulder and see the ancient vampire servant who always escorted me to this room. He was once elegant and regal, forever polite. Now he just seems harried. He's walking fast as though he's afraid the lumbering man behind him will step on his heels.

Roland Hursch.

So much has happened, I feel disoriented and realize that this is the night that he was boasting about when I saw him on TV. This was the night that he was first meeting with the new Lord Valentine.

The servant enters the room and bows. "My lord—"

"I don't need an introduction," Roland Hursch says as he storms through the doorway, brushing past me as though I don't exist. Maybe for them I don't.

The servant is obviously upset and confused. Protocol wasn't followed. He doesn't know what to do and is afraid that he'll pay for it. With the old Valentine he would have. With the new—

Victor simply nods. "Thank you, Eustace. You may leave us."

Eustace. During all my visits to the manor, I never knew his name. Was I any better than Valentine, seeing only the shell instead of a man with burdens and a desire to please?

He closes the door with a click, and I'm inside the room. A ghost in the shadows. Observing but not really here. If I yelled, would Hursch hear me? Would I want him to?

He's dressed in a black suit with a blood-red tie. It's the only color on him. I wonder if he chose it as a symbolic representation of the thing Victor and his vampires need so desperately, a kind of underhanded jab.

The entire scene is shaky, like a picture moving just a little in front of me. I have to concentrate to hold it still, to keep the voices clear.

Victor waves his hand toward a chair. "Please sit, Delegate Hursch."

"Look here, young pup, I have no interest in games. The power is going to shift. You need our blood. There's nothing we need from you. Nothing. You'll get your damn minions out of the city, every last one—"

In the blink of an eye, Victor is out of the chair and slamming Hursch against the wall. His hand is wrapped around Hursch's throat. His fangs are extended, glistening and close to his captive's throat. Hursch's dark eyes are so wide that I can see the whites of them. At any moment I expect them to roll back in his head.

"What I did, Mr. Hursch," Victor says, "was dispense with the need for etiquette. I did not dispense with the need for manners."

Releasing his hold, he steps back. Breathing harshly, Hursch slumps against the wall, deep white marks on his throat from where Victor's hand had been wrapped around it in a death grip. I almost feel sorry for Hursch. He just got an unpleasant reality check. He's lucky it came from Victor. Murdoch Valentine would have simply snapped his neck.

Victor tugs on the cuffs of his suit jacket. "Shall we start again?" He walks to his massive chair, sits, and indicates the one opposite him for Hursch.

Hesitantly, Hursch wanders over and drops onto the leather seat.

"Now," Victor says, "before we discuss blood donations, I want to know what happened when Eris returned for Dawn today."

Hursch's eyes widen. "You know about that?"

"I know everything, Hursch. What happened when Clive didn't turn Dawn over to Eris?"

"She had a fit, because no one seems to know where Dawn is. The little coward apparently went into hiding."

Victor's voice cuts through the air like a knife, aiming for Roland's heart. "You're the last one to speak of bravery, Hursch. Where were you during the war? Where were you while your brethren fought and died in trenches in lands they never heard of? Hmmm . . ."

"I was . . . I was fighting a different war. Behind the curtains, in the shadows."

"You were hiding in the darkness. You took refuge with all your money and all your influence and you ran far, far away until the war was finally over. Dawn's brother fought. Dawn's father negotiated VampHu when no one else would. And Dawn herself faced my father, something you always claimed you wanted. But you would not have survived. Trust me."

Hursch's fists tighten, but he can't think of anything to say and lets the silence linger for as long as Victor likes.

"What of Clive? What did he say to Eris?"

"Clive assured her that he has people out searching for her. She gave him three more days to find Dawn before she unleashes hell."

"Our meeting is over." Victor rises and turns his back on him.

"But the blood—"

"You've already said you won't deliver it. I'd strongly recon-sider that if I were you; otherwise I cannot guarantee the safety of your city or its citizens."

His father once said the same thing to me . . .

The door opens, and Eustace steps into the room. He always had the uncanny ability to know when the meeting was over.

"Eustace will see you out," Victor says.

I can tell that Hursch is conflicted. He wants a confrontation, but one that he'll win. He hasn't yet learned that with vampires that seldom happens.

When the room is empty, Victor sits in the large padded chair, leans his head back, and closes his eyes. I move forward. I just want to touch him, to brush his hair off his brow, to comfort—

"You came back."

I spin around and stare in shock at Victor standing there. I jerk my attention back to the chair. He's still sitting there, eyes closed.

"That's me sleeping," he says as he comes up behind me.

I turn to face him, touch him. He seems so real. "And you?"

"Me dreaming."

"I don't understand."

He skims his knuckles along my cheek. "I'm not sure I do, either. You're warm. You're . . . solid."

A snore startles me into a little jump. "The sleeping you is kind of creeping me out."

He flashes a grin and takes my hand. "Come on."

I follow him down a hallway that I've never traveled before. Statues of mythical creatures stand on pedestals—or at least as far as I know, they're mythical. We used to think the same about vampires.

He leads me into a smaller room. A fire is already burning in a hearth. In here paintings of sunrises adorn the walls.

Victor releases my hand and walks to a table. "A little brandy?"

"Sure." I don't know if I can get drunk in a dream.

He returns to my side and hands me a snifter. Then he taps his against it. "To knowing that you're safe."

He takes a long swallow, while I take a small sip. The fumes burn the inside of my nose; the liquid pricks at my throat.

"Are you?" I ask. "Safe?"

He turns away from me and walks to the fireplace. He stares into the flames. "I think things would be easier if we could just find Sin."

"Have there been any more attacks by Day Walkers?"

"No."

I breathe a sigh of relief. I almost tell him about the attack on the train, but he has enough to worry over. This is all just a dream. Do I really want to spend it talking about Sin and Day Walkers and the Thirst? I stroke my hand over his back, can feel the contours of his shoulders. "I can't believe how real you feel."

He takes my snifter, places it on the mantel beside his. He cradles my face. "I can scent your blood, but it's not calling to me as strongly as it was. I'm not sure if it's the passage of time or because we're dreaming together. I've never craved human blood like that before, but then I've never had to take so much. At first I thought I might go insane with the need."

"And now?"

"Now, I'm back to just wanting you."

"But you walked away."

"And I should again. I would never turn you, Dawn, and that condemns me to someday losing you."

"Did it never occur to you that without immortality, it means I'll lose you, too?"

"But that's the way it is with humans. You accept it."

"Doesn't make it easy. And do we really want to spend this dream talking philosophy?"

He grins. "No."

He's still smiling when his lips touch mine. I don't know if it's because of the weird state of this dream but everything seems more intense. I press myself against him. I never want to wake up. I just want—

"Dawn, please, please wake up."

It's a rude awakening, the sunlight harsh in my eyes. I raise a hand to shield myself from the glare. Michael, crouched in front of me, hands me his sunglasses.

"Thanks," I murmur, even though I want to slip back into the dream. "The sun seems so much brighter out here."

"Yeah, I was noticing that. No smoke from the Works blocking out the sky."

My body aching, I shove myself into a sitting position. "Tegan—"

"Is fine. Still sleeping."

"She shouldn't be alone."

"Neither should you." He can't see me rolling my eyes behind the sunglasses.

I stretch, trying to work out the kinks.

"Here, turn around," Michael orders.

I shift around slightly. He sits down on the bench and begins kneading the muscles in my shoulders. He has such large, strong hands.

"Oh, that feels good," I murmur. Really good.

"You have a nice, comfortable bed and you sleep on a

bench," he chastises.

"I needed a little time alone."

"Not wise, Dawn."

He presses his thumb on either side of my spine and I arch my back like a cat getting up from a long nap in the sun.

"Are you okay after last night?" I ask.

"Yes."

"If you need to talk, you can tell me. What you went through was brutal."

"That's the thing," he says, stopping the wonderful massage. "I *am* fine. It was violent, but that's what I signed up for. I take no joy in it, nor do I feel any remorse. It simply . . . is."

Michael's shedding his youth just like I have. It's as if the farther we move from Denver, the older we become.

"A month ago, you and Tegan were complaining because you'd never been beyond the wall. Is it all you thought it would be?"

"Not exactly." He starts the massage again.

"I'm sure you impressed Ian. I don't mean to sound cold, but he'll need a new protégé. You could work alongside your hero."

My shoulders have relaxed. His kneading has softened until it's more caressing than working out knots in my muscles.

"I'm doing what I want to be doing. The only thing that matters, the only thing that has ever mattered to me is you, Dawn. Even if we aren't . . . together. I've always considered myself your guardian. When I was training, I wasn't fantasizing about protecting the city; I was fantasizing about protecting you. Before you were ever a delegate. Before we even started dating. Throughout training, when they asked me to visualize the person I was meant to protect, I always thought of you."

This entire train seems to be empty, and it's just us and that vast space. Somehow, though, the distance from here to those mountains seems shorter than the one between both of us on this bench.

He eases up and I can feel his breath whispering along the back of my neck. "I miss you, Dawn."

I slam my eyes closed. I miss him, too, but it's his friendship I long for.

His hands cup my shoulders and he turns me to face him. His eyes are the color of rich chocolate, and they hold so much emotion. My life would be easier if I could simply fall into his arms and be content there. I can see how badly he wants to kiss me. And I know how great his kisses can be, but they aren't enough. What we had before isn't enough.

"You deserve someone who thinks about only you," I say in a low voice, as though that will lessen the sting.

"How can you want a vampire?" he grounds out.

"It's complicated."

"You know a time will come when he'll dig his fangs into you again, but this time he won't stop. He'll either kill you or turn you into a monster."

"No, last night he said the craving has lessened."

Michael stiffens, going into full hunter-alert mode. "He's on the train?"

"No." I press my hands on either side of my face, rub my temples. Suddenly I have the mother of all headaches. "No. I don't know why I said that. It was in my dream, but it was so real."

"You're not fully recovered from your coma. You should never have left Denver. Maybe three days in Los Angeles isn't such a good idea. We should probably turn around as soon as we arrive."

"No. I'm fine, Michael. Things just get mixed up sometimes. That's all." I stand up. "I'm hungry. Let's go eat. Then I want to read my dad's journal." Until nightfall. At which point, I want to talk with Faith and Richard.

Chapter 20

*L*ord Percy's demise has rallied the troops. Lieutenant Ian Hightower is being heralded a hero for taking down an Old Family vampire single-handedly. I celebrate his success but I also mourn the loss of an opportunity to speak with an ancient soul, with someone who might have been able to provide answers to the questions that haunt me.

The vampires are hoarding secrets, dark secrets. Deep in the catacombs beneath Lord Percy's manor, I found a vault with more writings in Ancient Vampiric. It's not just the complex writing that creates a barrier to the knowledge that I seek. It's the cryptic messages—half-formed thoughts, random musings, words that seem out of place. I find a reference to a plague and a mention that blood must be kept pure. Can vampires contract disease from us? Are they not *immune to the Black Death? Or is this something else?*

Of note, within the vault was a painting. Fifteen male vampires standing behind a table. I recognize several as the heads of the Old Families. But who is the fifteenth man? I feel as though I am playing a game similar to one I've played with my daughter—what is wrong with this picture? Who does not belong? Why is he there?

Is he the man of whom my father spoke? My father threw away his entire academic career looking for proof, always searching for the legendary lost family.

Have I found it?

Absorbed in my father's writings, I barely hear the knock on the door. I can't help but think that he is as cryptic as the vampires. What was my grandfather searching for? I never knew him—he died before I was born.

I want to puzzle out what my father was referring to, to delve deeper into his writings, but as Michael gets off the bed where he's been playing cards with Tegan, I have a feeling that I'll be closing the book for the night. When Faith and Richard stride into the room I know I have more important things to address—like making sure Michael doesn't try to stake them.

He's been moody and unnaturally quiet since we returned from the observation deck. Even with her blatant cheating at the game in order to win, Tegan hasn't been able to get much reaction out of him.

Despite Faith and Richard being on our side and the fact that I trust them, Tegan scoots back against the headboard, grabs a book she left on the bedside table, and pretends to read. Warily she watches them over the edge of the spine.

Michael isn't happy, either. He's standing nearby, his arms crossed in such a way that he could grab two stakes and jerk them free as he's unfolding his arms.

Faith saunters over to the liquor cabinet and opens a bottle of wine.

"Why don't you just make yourself at home?" Michael says.

Faith smiles and winks at him. "I will, thank you." She grabs three glasses between her fingers and comes over to the sitting area, where Richard has joined me. She pours the deep red wine into the glasses. "Vintage cabernet, 1855. You simply must have a sip. And don't use your age as an excuse not to indulge. You're old in soul, that's all that matters. Not what some, oh . . . identification card says."

A chill goes through me at the thought of being an old soul. I'm not sure why it bothers me. Maybe because Father referred to Lord Percy as an ancient soul. I guess sometimes he got tired of writing "vampire."

Richard doesn't hesitate to take a glass and clink it against hers. In spite of Michael glaring at me and Tegan studying me with curiosity, I lift a glass and salute the vampires before sipping the wine. To my surprise, it goes down smoothly. I don't choke or cough. If I didn't know better, I would think I'd been drinking wine since I was born instead of only since I've become friends with vampires.

After we exchange pleasantries—everyone slept well,

no evidence of other vamps onboard, lovely moon out—I retrieve the document, unfold it, and flatten it on the coffee table.

"Can you tell me which symbol represents the Carrolltons?" I ask Richard.

Without hesitation, he places a finger beneath a symbol right beside the Valentines'.

"So you have that inked on your shoulder?"

He studies me for a minute, maybe wondering how I know about that. Then he figures out that Victor must have told me. Vampires try to stay so mysterious and, as my father noted, tend to guard their secrets. He finally nods.

"And Faith, you have this one?" I ask, pointing to the one Victor has.

"Yes. What is that document anyway?"

"I'm not sure. But there are fourteen names clustered together; then we have this one over here. My father thought it represented all the families, and so far, I've had no luck discovering more by reading his journal. I don't suppose either of you read Ancient Vampiric."

"It's a dead language for a reason," Richard says. "Vampires have a way of overcomplicating everything, including their own language."

"So that's a no. Do you think your father can read it?"

"Probably not. But if old father Carrollton is anything, he's eccentric."

"Probably" gives me some hope. I'll take this with me when I meet with him.

"Is that the symbol you're dreaming about?" Tegan

asks. She's moved to the foot of the bed, her feet tucked beneath her as though fearful that if she places them on the floor she'll be connected to the vampires.

"Yeah."

"You're dreaming about it?" Richard asks.

"This one that's off by itself. The dream is so freaking real. But then all my dreams are, recently." I decide to ask Faith about something that's been nagging me all day and ease to the edge of my seat. "Speaking of dreams that seem really freakishly real, last night I dreamed I was at Valentine Manor."

"With Victor?" she asks.

I was going to keep the Victor part of the dream private, and can feel the heat of embarrassment rushing into my face. I wish I'd asked Michael to leave.

"We walked into a part of the manor I'd never been in before. I'm sure that it's just what I imagine that part of the manor would be like, but as I said, it's so real. I can feel things, smell fragrances, hear sounds . . . I sound crazy. Never mind."

She lifts a shoulder. "So what did you see in this 'never-before-visited' part of the manor?"

I can tell by her tone that she's just humoring me, but I decide no harm can come from telling her.

"It's a hallway. Pedestals line both sides and on each one is a mythical creature."

"What kind of mythical creatures?"

Humoring me again.

"Oh, I don't know. Werewolves, dragons, goblins. A

woman with snakes growing out of her head."

"That hallway is in the manor. Maybe you saw it at some point and just don't remember."

I know I've never seen it. I would have remembered it. Whenever I saw Valentine, I was on a very strict path, where any deviation would've meant death. With Victor, the few times I was there with him . . . I never saw this place. I saw other parts of the manor, but never this room. Never.

"We went into a small room with comfortable chairs. A fire was burning in the fireplace. On the wall were paintings of the sun over the horizon."

If vampires could go pale, I think she might have. "Okay, you couldn't have seen that room before. Victor had that room redone after Father died. He refers to it as his dawn room, because each painting is the sun rising. I think it's an homage to you."

"How could I dream about it, then?"

"Have you ever dreamed about Victor before? Like this, in the manor?" Faith asks.

How do I answer that? Dreams that include Victor began the night I met him, before I ever realized he was a vampire. They made me feel guilty because Michael and I were together then. But I knew they were dreams. What happened last night has happened only once before. "I've had one more."

"After you let Victor take your blood?"

"Yeah," I say. "I mean, I've always, you know, had dreams about him. But now they're powerful. More intense. It's like I'm actually there."

Faith looks at Richard, who quickly finishes his wine and refills his glass.

"Why?" I ask. "What's going on?"

"It's just very unusual," Faith says. "Vampires never dream. Except . . . well, sometimes, if they have a very strong connection with someone, they do dream, but only about that person."

"That's what Victor told me," I say. "He said that he never dreamed until he met me."

"And I believe him," she says. "The thing is, sometimes both people can share these dreams, and it forms a link between them. They can still communicate, be it in a strange sort of way."

"Victor wasn't asleep, at least not at first. I saw his meeting with Roland Hursch."

"Very strange," Faith says. "That sort of thing doesn't happen unless you're a vampire."

"I knew it!" Michael yells. "He's turning you into a vampire!"

I glare at him. "Don't be ridiculous. You were on the observation deck with me, sun streaming in. I didn't go up in flames."

"Maybe you're a Day Walker," Tegan suggests faintly.

I give her a pointed look. "That's even more ludicrous. Michael, I'd like you to take Tegan into the hallway so I can have a little more privacy, and a little less hysteria, to finish this conversation."

"You can't possibly think I'm leaving you alone with

two vampires."

"They watched over me in the hospital. If they wanted me dead, they would have done it then."

"Come on, Michael," Tegan says, hopping off the bed. "As much as I'm fascinated by the vamp psyche, this conversation is starting to make me feel icky."

She gives me a little wink he can't see, and I know she's encouraging him to leave because she realizes that I may need to say things I'd rather he not hear.

"I'm leaving the door partly open," he says as he follows Tegan. "You scream if you need me."

Once he's outside, Richard says, "He does realize that if he hears your scream, it's already too late."

"You're not going to give me any reason to scream. So tell me, have you ever heard of what Faith is talking about?"

"It happens," he says. "But she hasn't told you the key detail: It only happens with Old Family vampires. And both have to be Old Family vampires."

"It's a rare phenomenon," Faith says. "Very, very rare. My mother supposedly had it with my father. It's like a defense mechanism, a way for the Old Family to watch out for one another. No one's ever been able to explain it."

"We don't like studying these things," Richard says. "Vampires aren't concerned with understanding how the world works and nature's strange nuances. We just take things as they are. I mean, if you understood every mystery of life, what fun would it be? And we vampires become bored very quickly. So the more mystery, the better."

"And without Victor here it's impossible to know," Faith offers. "Which has always been part of the problem. The only time you ever hear about this connection is when the vampires are far away, a great distance between them."

"*And* when strong emotions are involved," Richard says, which immediately gets a scoff from Faith.

"Don't go on about that," she says.

"It's true. A blood connection only exists when there's love between vampires."

"We *can't* love."

"We can!" Richard stares at her and I realize I'm no longer part of the conversation, and this is more about them. I watch as Richard contemplates going further, but Faith breaks away from his powerful gaze. After a moment, Richard turns back toward me, as if just remembering I was sitting across from him.

"True vampire love comes along only once in a few thousand years," he says. "Some think it doesn't exist, but I disagree."

He chances another look at Faith, but she simply rolls her eyes at his effort.

"Now isn't the time to be wooing me," she says. "But he's right; *if* vampiric love exists, it's extremely unusual. We vampires just don't have those powerful emotions. It's the reason we've always been better than you humans. Sorry, but it's true. We aren't tied up with feelings and passions."

"What if Victor feels that way about me, though?"

"Even if he did, Dawn, just as you reminded your

overprotective friends, you aren't a vampire."

"But you just said yourself: This 'blood connection' is mysterious. Isn't it possible that it could exist between a human and an Old Family vampire?"

"If there's one thing I've learned in three hundred years," Richard says, "it's that anything is possible. Especially when humans are involved. Unlike Faith, I give them more credit. Yes, your emotions are ridiculous. Yes, they often cause more harm than good. But there's a beauty to them, one that I see, even if Faith doesn't. Could you and Victor be experiencing a blood connection? I doubt it. But who's to say? Even after all this time, the world is still a mystery to me."

"Yeah . . . I seem to know less and less every day."

Richard seems to believe, even if Faith is skeptical.

But I did describe a room I couldn't have possibly known about—the dawn room. Somehow, I can connect with Victor even though I'm on a train hurtling away from him.

Chapter 21

After the revelations about my dreams, I feel as though the walls of my room are closing in on me. I suggest we all go to the lounge car as a distraction from the thoughts thundering through my head. I doubt a party will be going on tonight, but it had a large bar and tables where we can take in the atmosphere.

When we step out into the passageway, panic slams into me. Tegan and Michael are gone!

A thousand atrocious possibilities dash through my mind before Faith says calmly, "They're in the observation deck."

I jerk my head around to study her. She shrugs. "Vampire hearing."

"Do you know what they're saying?"

"No, they're mumbling, and at this distance it's like

listening with water in my ears, but I recognize their voices."

I consider waiting for them to return, but I'm anxious to move around, so I take the lead and head to the stairs. A few people are in the seating cars, but I can tell that they're jumpy. After all, it's night again. When we reach the spiral staircase, I say, "Wait here. I'll get them."

I'm not sure why I issued that order. Maybe because I suspect they won't be happy that I'm asking Faith and Richard to join us for the evening, and I'm anticipating having to do some preemptive convincing that they need to accept these guys as part of our group now. I'm nearly to the top when I hear Michael's voice.

"—stupid. I practically poured my heart out to her this morning, told her I missed her. Such a fool."

My own heart feels like he's punched his fist into it. I didn't want to hurt him. I ease down onto the step and bury my face in my hands. I don't know how to make things easier for him.

"You have to let her go," Tegan says kindly, and I can imagine her taking his hand or rubbing his shoulder. While she's studied vampire psychology, she's good at applying her knowledge to humans, to figuring us out, to knowing what we need.

"I know, but it's hard. I love her," Michael says.

I'm crushed. I still love Michael, but it's not the same as the way that I love Victor.

"I can't believe Dawn—of all people—would fall for a vampire," he continues.

"She didn't know he was a vampire when we met him. He saved our lives."

"I've saved your lives."

Tegan releases a very tiny laugh. "That's not the only reason. And for what it's worth, I know she was conflicted about it. It wasn't easy for her to admit she loved him. She barely talked to me about him, and I thought she shared everything with me."

But not Victor. She's right about that. For so many reasons. That it would place her in jeopardy. That it would place *him* in danger.

"But then I haven't shared everything with her, either," Tegan says quietly. "Sometimes I feel so broken. I want to move on, but it's like there's this wall in front of me and I can't get through it. Like that Jake guy. I was talking with him, but I kept expecting him to sprout fangs and tear into my neck. I look at people—even kids I know at school—and I think, *You could be a vampire and I won't know until it's too late.*"

"Ah, Tegan." I hear the bench seat moan, like someone is shifting around on it, and I picture Michael wrapping his arms around Tegan, holding her close. I should be doing that. I should be there for her more. I wonder if that's part of the reason that she snuck on the train—not so much to be here for me but because she needs me to be there for her.

"I can't sleep," she says. "I keep seeing him, every time I close my eyes. I see his triumph—"

"And he'll see yours when we find him and stake him."

"Oh, Michael, do you really think we will?"

"Absolutely. He's too conceited to live his life in the shadows. I don't know what he has planned, but he'll show his face again and when he does, we'll be ready."

"I hope you're right."

"Trust me. Dawn isn't going to stop searching until she finds him. Neither will I. She might be saying this trip is about the Thirst, but it's about Sin. We're going to get him."

Only as I lift my head at his words do I realize I've been staring at my shoes, trying to come up with my own answers and consoling words for Tegan—and for Michael. They're on this crazy journey with me because of loyalty and love. Michael might not have known what he was volunteering for, but as soon as he and Clive arrived at my apartment building, Michael could have announced that he wasn't the best choice for this assignment. If Clive had known who he was, he would have understood. I feel the burden of their friendship in ways that I never have before. Maybe this is why Ian is such a loner. It's easier when you don't have to think about anyone except yourself.

I don't have that luxury. I love Michael and Tegan, but if anything happens to them—

"It can't make things any easier for you now that Dawn has these two vamps hanging around," Michael says, his voice oozing disgust, and a fissure of irritation slices through me. Have they not learned anything? Not all vampires are like Sin.

"I don't know," Tegan says, and the slowness of her words alerts me that she's considering her answer. "Victor . . . Faith . . . Richard—they don't seem that different from us."

"They'd take our blood in a heartbeat if they needed it."

"Would they?"

I shove myself to my feet and lunge into the observation deck. I don't want to hear where Michael's going, or maybe I just don't want him to say it.

"Oh, there you are," I say, acting like I've just walked in, rather than eavesdropped this whole time. "I was looking for you two."

I was right. Michael did take Tegan into his arms. What strikes me is how right they look together. Tiny Tegan curled up against powerfully built Michael. It doesn't last long. She jumps up guiltily.

"We were just, uh, you know, enjoying the view," Tegan stammers.

I look over at Michael, who is quickly straightening his jacket, but leaving it unbuttoned, as always.

"We were also talking about your new friends," he says, a hint of revulsion in his voice, which Tegan quickly overcompensates for.

"Yeah, and how great they are. I mean, if we're going up against Sin we could really use all the help we can get."

"He's an enemy to all of us," I say. "And when Victor finally confronts him . . ."

"Victor," Michael snorts.

"Stop judging him because of what he means to me, Michael." I turn back to Tegan. "When Victor finally confronts him, he'll be the last thing Sin ever sees. He's no match for all of us. And like it or not, Richard and Faith are stuck with us, so we better start trusting them more."

Tegan's mouth twitches, then settles into a straight line. "I like Richard, but I'm not so sure about Faith."

"She's a—" Is she even a friend? "Look, I haven't known her all that long, but I trust her. And Richard. I'm not saying that you have to like them, but consider this as an opportunity to study Old Family vampires up close. You were always begging me to take you to Valentine Manor. Believe me, they are much nicer than Valentine."

She rubs her neck, then shrugs. "Well, they did save me from the Uglies."

"I think they call them the Infected."

"But they're not really infected, are they?"

"Not like a virus, not like when we get sick, but I guess it's the closest they have to an illness. My father may have made a reference to it in his journal. They need to keep their blood pure. Vamps aren't known for their creativity. Maybe 'Infected' made sense to them."

"Really makes them dependent on our blood, doesn't it?" she asks.

"Yeah."

"Puts the situation in a different perspective."

"What about Faith and Richard? What are they doing for blood while they're on the train?" Michael asks, his voice rife with suspicions.

"Vampires can go a week between feedings before they begin to weaken."

"Well, then let's hope they fed before they got onboard."

I don't bother to tell him that they wouldn't just take the blood. If they discovered that they needed it, they would pay someone—very handsomely.

"So are we good with Faith and Richard?"

"Sure," Tegan says, and I can tell she's willing to give them a chance to prove themselves.

"Michael?" I ask pointedly.

He shakes his head. "I'm never going to like them, Dawn, but I'll tolerate them until they give me a reason to stake them."

I realize that's the best I can hope for from him, for now.

"Okay then. Faith, Richard, and I are going to see what was happening in the lounge car tonight. Thought you might want to come with us."

"Nothing better to do," Michael says.

Chapter 22

The atmosphere is way different tonight. The lighting is low, but at least it's not pulsing. The music isn't so loud. People aren't dancing. Tables and chairs are scattered throughout. The bar is open.

Tegan, Faith, and I grab an empty table while the guys fetch us drinks. I can't help but notice the way Faith watches Richard walking away from us. She's totally focused on him.

"You love him, don't you?" I ask quietly.

She knits her eyebrows together to form a tiny furrow. "Don't be ridiculous. I just appreciate a nice male form."

"Where's the harm in admitting your feelings?" Tegan asks.

"Vampires don't love."

"So when Sin told me he loved me, it was all just part of his con?"

Richard and Michael become lost in the crowd. Faith shifts her attention to Tegan. "Not necessarily. I really don't know enough about Day Walkers to know how they function. They could love. My brother certainly seems to understand the emotion of revenge."

I'm pretty sure that's her attempt to console Tegan. Richard has told me before that Faith isn't as cold as she appears. Of course, if my father had been Lord Valentine, then I might have locked my heart away as well.

"But you do care about Richard," I persist.

She scratches a perfectly manicured nail over the table-top, as though something she can't scrape free is stuck to it. She suddenly appears young, vulnerable, more my age than two hundred. "It's—it's complicated."

"You think he'll hurt you."

"I know he has the power to."

"He loves you. He wouldn't hurt you."

She pierces me with her blue gaze. "How do you humans do it? How do you take that chance?"

"Because we don't want to be alone. And because the rewards are worth the risk."

"I don't even regret falling for Sin," Tegan says quietly. "While we were together, it was the best part of my life. I just wish he hadn't turned out to be the bad guy."

"The notion of giving someone that much control over you—"

"If it's real, it's not about control," I interrupt quickly. "It's about sharing, helping, being there for each other. Maybe you could try letting some of your defenses down."

She shakes her head. "That's the most frightening thing one can do."

"Start small. With Tegan and me."

She wrinkles her nose, so un-Old-Familylike. "Are you saying I should fall in love with you?"

I laugh, and Tegan just stares at Faith as though she can't believe what just came out of her mouth. For all her vamp psych courses, I imagine she's learning more about vamps while we're on this train than she has in any book she's ever read. "No. But you can trust us to be your friends."

I don't know how she might have responded to that offer, because the guys return and set strawberry margaritas in front of us.

"You okay?" Richard asks solicitously as he takes a chair beside Faith.

"Fine."

Michael sits between Tegan and me, watches the exchange between the vamps, then looks over at me. I just give him a nod and soft smile before reaching for my drink.

"Old Family females are so lucky," Tegan says after slurping on hers for a few minutes. "I bet you never go long without a date."

"Why? Because we're rare? Because we can only produce one offspring and then we go sterile? Don't you see how careful we have to be that we don't make a mistake when selecting our mate? We may be precious commodities, but that's only until we have a child. Once we reproduce, we're often cast aside. My mother was. So was Victor's."

"And Sin's?"

"I'm not really sure of Sin's mother. Her name was Esmerelda, but that's all I know. I'm not even sure which family she came from. Father never spoke of her. For all I know, he may have killed her for creating the abomination—as Father liked to call Sin."

"Here's something I don't understand," I say, leaning forward, crossing my arms on the table. "Sin claims to be the first Day Walker. Why didn't your father consider him a miracle? Why didn't he embrace him, flaunt him—"

"Announce to the world that he had a child who could bridge both worlds: the one of light and the one of darkness?"

"Yeah, something like that. It would be like discovering your child was a baby Einstein. Wouldn't you be proud of what he could accomplish?"

"Just because he hid him away doesn't mean he wasn't proud," Tegan says, kicking into psychoanalyzing mode.

"Keeping him hidden made him a weapon Valentine could use at his discretion," Richard explains. "If you're planning a war, you don't tell your enemies that you've created a more powerful bomb."

"You think that's what this is all about? Another war?"

"I think Valentine wanted absolute control over all humans and the blood supply. If he controlled that, he could control the vampires."

"But what does Sin want?"

"I suspect he wants the same thing."

"Those had better be virgin drinks," a deep voice booms.

I glance back to see Ian standing there. I'm wondering if he's worried about us getting drunk or reducing his liquor supply. "We're cool."

"You'll want to get some sleep tonight. We arrive in Los Angeles shortly after dawn. You'll have three days. No more, no less. Per Clive's orders, I intend to stick close the entire time. The good news: Los Angeles is one of the safest cities. Still, we do have to follow some protocols."

He tells me that our first stop will be the Agency, where I'll be introduced to the director who runs the city, and from there we'll go to our hotel. *Straight* to the hotel.

Three days. It doesn't seem like enough time anymore, but I'll make it work.

Chapter 23

I fall asleep, hoping against hope that I see Victor again. Instead . . .

Blackness.

But there's something here. All around me. I can feel it. I want to call out, but I'm afraid. I can't explain why. I take a step forward, feeling the solid ground, so real, so cold. Clean and sterile. Clinical.

Crying. Ahead of me.

"Victor?" I bravely call out.

The crying grows in response, nearly stopping my heart, and I think I'll wake up from the jolt it causes. But I don't; instead I slip further into this dark world.

The crying echoes off of unseen walls, unseen ceilings.

I take another step, and another. I begin to run as the crying grows, unsure if I'm heading toward it or running from it. In my peripheral vision I see the darkness changing; I see shapes forming. Shapes that are my own. Reflections of me, ghostly and hollow, as though mirrors surround me, closing in, showing me running.

Only something is within these glass walls. And its hands make streaks along the corridor, following me, so my reflection is never whole, never perfect, always filled with the black claws of some monster that can't escape.

The crying pierces me and I'm seized with the strange fear that if it grows any louder, it will shatter the fragile walls and the monsters within the cages will escape and devour me, unsatisfied with merely feasting on my reflection as I run past them.

Then I see him. The crying . . . thing. He's kneeling in front of a glass chamber, looking in, but there's not enough light for me to pick out details.

I slow to a walk.

"Hello?" I call.

The crying stops. But the thing doesn't turn toward me. Is he a child? Is he a man who has succumbed to the weight of the terrors surrounding him? The terrors that lurk behind these walls of glass, their darkness ever-reaching?

I approach the crying thing, wanting him to move, to recognize my presence. I don't want to scare him, but maybe I'm the one who should be afraid. I sense some power within his fragile shell, some darkness that matches this world, a darkness that has bled into it.

A few more steps and I'll be near. A few more steps and I can . . .

"Dawn."

I turn around and see the outline of Victor, distant but recognizable in the shadows.

"Victor!" I shout.

"Dawn, you have to go."

"What?"

"You can't be here, Dawn."

"Victor, what are you—"

"Dawn, run!"

Over his scream, the shattering of glass reverberates around me. Behind him, I see the rain of reflection, giant shards that fall to the ground, and the smaller fragments scattering as they explode on the hardened floor. Victor's right—I shouldn't be here. All I know is that I can't stay in this place. I wasn't meant for it. This isn't a dream.

It's a nightmare. I'm trapped in Victor's nightmare.

Victor turns away and heads toward the darkness, toward the raining glass and the monsters that have been released. He's buying me time. Time that isn't real in this place. But the fear is. Whether it's my own, or Victor's, it's palpable and genuine.

So I run. I run through the darkness, away from the screams, but they're always around me. I run and run and run. And then the darkness becomes something else. The glass walls that hold my reflection become like stone, and the moon rises above me. And the mountain calls.

The mountain of my own dreams. My own nightmares.

"Find me."

I don't want to listen; I don't want to be drawn toward it.

"Find me."

But what choice do I have? What choice do any of us have against the nightmares that haunt us?

"Find me!"

I awake in a cold sweat. The terror of *what was* still thundering in my heart. And the terror of *the unknown* growing greater.

As I get dressed in jeans and a red sweater, the nightmare lingers in my mind. What did it mean? What was that place? Why would Victor visit it in his dreams? If vampires don't dream, did I conjure it up? Or did we both fall deep into his subconscious, to places he'd rather keep hidden?

"You're awfully quiet this morning," Tegan says. She's also wearing jeans, but she's layered on a white T-shirt, a green tank top, and a yellow one. "Were you with Victor again, in your dreams?"

I strap on my holster and slip the stake into it. "Sorta. It's hard to explain. It's more like I was in his nightmare."

Placing her duffle bag on the bed, she starts stuffing her clothes into it. "Can you control what happens when you're there?"

"Not really." I stop zipping my duffle and look at her. "I don't think so, anyway. I haven't really experimented with it."

She sits on the edge of the bed. "What if you are transforming into a vampire?"

"It's not a gradual process. They drain your blood, you die, they give you their blood, and then you're—according to Victor—awakened."

"Then why are you able to do something that Faith says only vampires can do?"

I shrug, trying to make light of it. But I'm just frustrated because I've never felt so in the dark about something. "Sometimes I think vamps know less about themselves than what we know about them. They didn't even know a Day Walker was possible."

"You're probably right. How many times do Old Family fall in love with humans anyway? It probably has more to do with the power of your love for Victor."

I move over, sit beside her, and take her hand. "I heard what you said to Michael in the observation deck. I'm sorry if I haven't been here for you, Tegan."

"You've been there, Dawn. It's just going to take time. That's all." She gives me a wicked smile. "What will really help is when we find Sin. What if he's here, Dawn? What if he's in the city?"

"It doesn't make sense that he would come back here. He wants to destroy Victor. He wants Denver—"

"He wants *you*. And you're here."

"But he doesn't know that." Her face falls. I can't leave her with no hope. "But maybe we'll discover something here that will help us find him."

She perks back up at that, jumps to her feet, and grabs her duffle bag. "Then let's go."

We step out in the hallway. Michael is waiting for us, his bag clutched in one hand, his stakes at the ready.

"Ian stopped by just a few minutes ago," he says. "He wants us in the observation deck."

"Okay, I know we're here for some serious business," Tegan says, "but it is so exciting to have the chance to see another city."

"According to Richard, it's very different from Denver," I tell her.

When we get to the observation deck, we discover that many of the other passengers have crammed into the confined quarters, wanting a glimpse of the city. But Ian has saved us a spot near the front, and we have nothing to block our view as we approach Los Angeles.

It's amazing. The desert has continued all the way here, and the roads that would normally come out of the walled city are nonexistent. And then I remember Richard's description, that it was the opposite of my city. The walls are so thick, and so high, that the Carrollton family has no influence, can issue only idle threats. Even if they want to attack, they can't. As a result, the vampires fed off of one another and the Thirst set in. But because the sun is out, the Infected are hidden away for now.

"Oh, man," Michael says in awe. "Have you ever imagined anything like that?"

The walls are absolutely massive! I thought they were a small mountain at first, a geological oddity, before I saw the tracks running right into them. As the metal gate slowly retracts to allow our passing, Ian tells us that this is the only entrance into the city.

We speed along the tracks as if chased by demons, and they need to close the doors quickly to keep them out. As we enter the narrow passageway, I see that we barely fit, the designers of the wall wanting the smallest entry possible in order to safeguard their city. And the walls, which seemed tall from afar, are even more impressive as we move through them. They must be a mile thick, all stone masonry intricately laid to make them as strong as possible, and they are higher than the train itself.

When we emerge on the other side of the wall, I catch my breath. Shock ripples through me. The city is in absolute decay. It's as though we're going through an old battlefield, blocks of buildings that have been bombed so only their shells remain. Their clothes little more than rags, people walk the streets like the dead looking for the graves from which they escaped.

"This is the Outer Ring. Most of the poorer population lives here. And those deemed less than beautiful," Ian says, surely noticing my surprise. "They're as close to death as you can be while your heart still beats. They no longer fear vampires, only starvation."

"I didn't know."

"Not many people do."

"Why didn't you tell Clive?"

"What could he do, Dawn, from so far away? He has enough on his plate worrying about his own city."

The realist, once again. He's right. I'll put it in my report, and Clive will read it, but what can he do to help a city beyond his reach?

"I hate this city," Ian mutters. "It's rotting from the inside."

I realize that he is one of the few who has seen the full

devastation of our world. Even knowing that Los Angeles wasn't like Denver didn't prepare me for this. But I'm left to wonder what the other cities might be like.

A group of children are chasing a rat, and I hope that they aren't grocery shopping. Men and women, their arms thin and their stomachs bloated from malnutrition, let the flies converge over their bodies, too tired to swat them away. It's hell. There's no other way to describe this place. It is hell.

Something grabs Ian's attention. A man running toward the train makes a desperate leap onto the speeding machine and latches on to the front car. I don't know what he's hanging by, but it isn't much, and his face contorts with pain as he struggles to hold on.

"Get off," Ian mutters. "Get off, you idiot."

It's a cold thing to say. But then I realize Ian's trying to save the man.

Up ahead, another wall, as large as the first, looms. I suspect we're about to enter the Inner Ring of the city. And the man, clinging on for dear life, isn't invited. On top of the wall is a guard tower, much like the ones around Denver. But the guardian at the top, rifle in hand, isn't after vampires. He's after trespassers.

He takes aim. I turn my head, hearing only the cracking report echoing in the distance. When I look back, the man who was holding on to the train is gone.

Tegan's face is buried against Michael's chest. He's holding her tightly, and I wish I had Victor to hold me, wish he was here to share these horrors with me. Even though

I'm standing beside Ian, with my friends at my side, I feel alone. There will always be so much that I can't share with Victor. Even if he was onboard the train, he couldn't be up here in the sunlight.

I wonder if he knows about these atrocious conditions. Surely Richard told him.

As discontented as people are in Denver, we've got it pretty good. What I don't understand is how this could have happened.

A metal gate opens, rolling to the side and allowing the train to rush through, before quickly closing. Once again, the wall towers over us and lasts for several lengths of the train. But when we leave the chasm, my mouth drops open.

The Inner Ring is like nothing I've ever seen. It's like the war never happened. It's beautiful. The streets are paved and clean, cars run through them, pedestrians carry shopping bags. Everyone is tall and gorgeous and perfect. The sun itself seems brighter.

"How is this possible?" I ask.

Ian looks across the city. "Money. Privilege. Civilians on the outside willing to work for crumbs of bread."

At an intersection, a guy in a suit chatting on his cell phone is almost run over by a car. A trio of high-school girls smack their gum and text and look at their new manicures. A white convertible pulls up to them, two boys in it, their hair slicked back, shades on. The girls hop in and they ride off.

I notice a group of twenty people standing off to the

side, one of them holding a gigantic camera.

"What's going on?" I ask.

"This is the only place in the world that still films mov-ies," Ian says. "They aren't distributed, not yet, though that's always been their plan. It's Hollywood—I guess they just can't do anything else, you know? It's in the blood of the city."

The white car stops and begins reversing. The girls get out, stand in their places again, and go through the same motions that they did a few minutes earlier.

"We probably blew their shot," Ian says, a bit of hidden laughter in his voice.

I don't get what he's talking about, but I don't under-stand how they can appear so carefree when so much darkness exists in the world. It's like they're so lost in make-believe that they've forgotten what reality is.

"I'm not sure I'm returning to Denver," Tegan whispers beside me. "Have you ever seen anything so sparkly and clean?"

"I don't like it," Michael mutters. "Something about it is . . . wrong."

I agree. It's not right that it's so beautiful here and so ugly on the other side of the wall.

The train eventually comes to a stop inside a gigantic building, complete with glass ceiling and marble floors. It's a train station, one that I imagine gets plenty of scenes filmed inside.

We get our bags and disembark.

I could spend all day at the terminal, looking at the

polished floors and stonework stairs, the ancient gargoyles nestled into the corner of the high ceilings. It's stereotypical Gothic in its ornateness, so much so that it seems fake. Like the architects designed the place to be nothing but a set piece. It's functional only as far as a train can pull through it. Looking around, I can see that winding staircases lead to dead-end walls, and that columns stand tall, only to hold up nothing.

Tegan, Michael, Ian, and I begin walking up the stairs into the sunlight. I suppose Faith and Richard will have to wait until dark to disembark.

Once we leave the station I immediately see the building that Ian told us last night would be our first destination. The Agency, much like the one in Denver, is housed in a tall, glass, reflective building at the heart of the city. But to get there, we have to deal with the people. And the traffic.

"Look at all the cars," Tegan says in awe. "How did they end up with everything here, while we ended up with nothing?"

"I don't know," I admit. I can't imagine that there are any rolling blackouts here. If I hadn't seen the ugliness that existed between the two walls, I might consider never leaving this place.

Of course, the people aren't exactly inviting. They may be gorgeous, but they're rude, seeming to only care about themselves. Talking on their phones, they expect me to get out of their way because the business they're discussing is too important. When one particularly obnoxious man shoulders me, Michael stops him.

"Hey!" the guy yells.

Michael grabs the man's wrist, twists it, and pulls the phone free before launching it into the street, where fast-moving cars smash it.

"Watch where you're going next time," Michael says, before shoving the man away.

"Thanks," I say.

"It's my job," he says, all business.

Ian looks at him. "Normally I'd get onto you for lacking tact. But here, I can forgive you."

After that, Ian takes the front and acts like a wedge, diverting people around us, while Michael stays close by. But eventually, the congestion gets too thick and Ian decides it's time for a cab.

He hails one, a strange ritual in which he holds up his hand until one stops for him. He pops the trunk, and we place our bags inside before climbing into the vehicle. Ian pays the driver to chauffeur us around. We don't have enough working cars—or gasoline—in Denver to allow for this sort of luxury.

The driver takes us to the Agency. Ian instructs him to wait for us. Saves us the trouble of having to cart our bags around with us. We jaunt up the steps, but are stopped at the entrance by several armed guards. They seem like they're playing a part. Their body armor and weapons are cliché. It's just what I'd expect from a props department for one of the *terrible* television shows they put on in Denver.

Ian gives them the proper paperwork, and they call in. Everything checks out and we're waved through.

"Some advice," Ian says. "Everyone here has a huge ego. They're idiots, but they're very powerful. A dangerous combination. Whatever it takes to please them, do it. You were a delegate, so act like this is just another Old Family vamp you have to make happy. Use him to get what you need, but rely on yourself as your ultimate resource."

At the very top of the building, we exit the elevator. Ian tells a receptionist that we're here to see the director. She presses a small intercom button.

"Mr. Matheson, Ian Hightower is here to see you."

"Oh goodness me," the gruff voice comes back. "Send him in right away. Yes, yes, indeed. Right away."

"He has several guests . . ."

"Send them all in!"

She clicks off and points to a heavy hardwood door.

Ian doesn't seem excited when he opens it, and he looks ready to leave this place before he's even stepped foot inside.

"Ian, my good boy, how are you?"

Mr. Matheson, the Agency director, stands up from behind his desk. He's one of the oddest characters I've seen so far. With a large mustache waxed at the ends, a monocle, and coat with tails, all he needs is a top hat and cane to finish the picture of an ancient aristocrat from one of my history books.

"I'm well," Ian says, shaking the man's hand.

Matheson's elaborate office is the opposite of Clive's. Instead of the rustic wooden furniture that was probably dug out of junkyards and revarnished, Matheson's place looks like it was built brand-new yesterday. Once again, it reminds me of a stage set, and he appears to be just an actor in a movie waiting to be produced. It's as if all their history came from the films in their great vaults, and they think this is how life should be lived.

"And the Night Train? How fares it?"

"We were attacked by rogue vampires."

"Really? My, my, what trouble that is. And who has accompanied you today into my fine city? Hello, little ones. I'm James Matheson, director of the Agency and the mayor of this wonderful metropolis."

The news of the attack doesn't seem to faze him in the least, and I'm wondering if this guy is for real, or if he's fake like everything else I've seen so far. Either way, I hand over the letter from Clive. He barely gives it a passing glance before saying, "Dawn Montgomery? Denver's delegate?"

"Yes, sir." I guess Clive thought a little fudging of the truth was in order, or maybe he's reinstated me for the mission.

"Terrible news about your parents. I'm so sorry, my dear."

"Thank you." I say it automatically now; I've heard everyone's sympathy too much to say anything else.

"I've heard Valentine is a tough customer; I do hope he's treating you well. I'm afraid to say that we have it lucky here. Old man Carrollton is merely a nuisance and little else."

"He's had a change of heart recently," I say. Apparently word of Valentine's demise hasn't filtered to the Agency here. Understandable. The vampires have done what they can to limit communication between the isolated cities. "Actually, his son has taken control."

"An ascension? Those are usually so violent and create turmoil within the vampire community. Have things gotten ugly in Denver?"

"They have, but not because of Victor. Are you familiar with a vampire named Sin?"

He looks taken aback. "What an unusual name. I wager that he's a troublemaker."

"That's putting it mildly. He's a Day Walker with an agenda."

"Oh no," he says, chuckling. "Not you, too. Their existence is a myth."

"Believe me, we wish that were true. Sin is trying to take over Denver. We thought you might know something about him because he says he came from here. Do you have any information that might help us defeat him?"

"I'm sorry, but I've never heard of the fellow. And I've certainly never seen a vampire walk in the sun." He twists the end of his mustache. "Although I suppose I wouldn't. We don't allow vampires into our city."

It makes sense that if Sin had been here, he wouldn't have shown his hand. He'd save his unveiling for Denver so it would take us by surprise.

"Then maybe you have information on another problem we're facing: the Thirst."

"Ah, yes, the vampire plague. Trust me, its dangers are vastly exaggerated."

"Not based on what we've seen."

"Well, then, perhaps you simply need to understand it as we do." He presses the intercom button on his desk. "Julie, please send in Simon."

"Yes, Mr. Matheson."

He looks back at me. "Simon is our resident scientist. He's been studying this Thirst for some time now."

He stands up and walks over to the window. "Please, join me while we wait. Take a look at our wonderful, walled sanctuary."

I stand next to him and see little wonderful about it. If this epicenter were all I'd seen, maybe. But the Outer Ring is so rancid, how could anyone describe it as wonderful? And as much as I'd like to say exactly that, I have to put on my delegate hat.

"When we came in, I noticed the Outer Ring wasn't up to the standards I see down below. It seems a shame that so many must live on so little."

"It was their choice. We expect certain behavior here. Those who fail to comply—" He shakes his head. "Consider them the rabble-rousers, the disobedient, the refuse of society. They brought their suffering upon themselves, Miss Montgomery. Life is about choices and they chose . . . poorly."

They've managed to escape the control of vampires, but I'm not sure they've managed to create a Utopia. Denver, somehow, seems better. From up here, the walls are in a clearer perspective and I can see their tops. They stretch to such an amazing width, they could build another city across them.

"It took twenty years to erect those," he says. "That was the benefit of surrendering so early in the war. While the rest of the country was fighting a losing battle, we did the smart thing. We signed an unofficial treaty with the Carrolltons. We started building the wall as a 'defense against the occasional unruly vampire,' as we described it. Really, we were preparing for the inevitable. But Lord Carrollton was so busy with the war and fighting everyone else, he didn't notice until it was too late. The wall, which started a few feet high, grew until it was larger than the city itself. Now look at us. We're free to live our lives without fear. No one else in the country can do that. All their bravery and all their optimism bought them nothing in the end."

"I didn't realize cowardice was a virtue," Ian says.

I see a flash of anger in Matheson's eyes. It quickly disappears, swallowed back inside, which somehow makes it even more frightening. Like it was never meant to surface in the first place.

"You have become a soldier without a war, Mr. Hightower," Matheson says, not even bothering to look at Ian, to give him the courtesy of eye contact. "But we were realistic. The fight couldn't be won. You can talk about cowardice, but my citizens still have their children. In other cities, such as Denver, for example, how many people talk about losing their sons and daughters in the war? How many of them are broken? Look them in the eyes and tell them that their child died for a noble cause, and then have them look at the world they're living in. They died for nothing."

The door to the office opens and someone who is no doubt Simon steps in, tearing us away from a conversation that was only going to serve up hard feelings. He's wearing a lab coat with a pocket protector and pens, thick black-rimmed glasses, and his hair is in desperate need of combing.

"You wanted to see me, sir?" he asks, his voice noticeably wheezy.

"Yes, Simon. Miss Montgomery has been asking about the Thirst. And since you are the expert, I decided you could help clear things up for her."

"Of course," he says. "Come with me."

"It was a pleasure meeting you, Miss Montgomery. I do hope you enjoy your stay and I'm sure we'll cross paths again."

I do little more than give him a nod. I have a feeling that he's dismissing me and my concerns. Fine. I can discover what I need to know without this bloated jester.

Simon takes us to the elevator. We ride down for so long that we must be underground by the time it stops. When it opens, we enter a completely white room with doors branching off, and test tubes and equipment occupying clean, black slab tables.

Simon immediately removes his coat, revealing surprisingly ripped biceps; takes off his glasses; and quickly slicks his hair back. When he turns toward us, he looks nothing like he did. He looks, well, good. Hot, even.

Tegan blinks her eyes as though she's not sure what she's looking at now. "Why would you choose to look so . . . so—"

"Different? Sorry about that," he says, his voice deep and minus the annoying wheeze. "It's all about image here, you know? The closer you are to the center, especially. I applied for this job two years ago and they didn't accept me. I came in looking like a dork and I was immediately hired; they didn't even look at my résumé."

"You have to meet their expectations," Ian says.

"Precisely. We're all movie clichés. Our historical books and documents didn't make it out of the war, but our massive film archives did, and they've served as a crude blueprint. Anyway, we're going this way."

Walking through several doors I see more equipment and have the sneaking suspicion that, like Simon's glasses, it's all fake or at least nonfunctional.

At a strikingly polished metal door, Simon holds up a key card and rubs it against the electronic pad. The light turns green and the door opens.

The room is like all the others: testing equipment, computer monitors, clean and neat surfaces, the smell of sanitizers. But against the wall is a cell containing a monster. I have no doubt that this vampire is one of the Infected. Just like Brady. Just like the ones on the train. And the only thing separating him from us is very thick, clear glass.

Tegan releases a tiny screech, and I realize she has never had a chance to really see an Infected up close. She digs her fingers into Michael's arm.

"Don't worry, the prison is completely impenetrable," Simon says. "Even an Infected vampire doesn't have the strength to break through."

I take a step closer—

"Dawn, don't—"

"I'm fine, Tegan." I can sense that Michael is conflicted. He probably wants a close-up look as well, wants to do his job and guard me, but he can't leave Tegan when she's so obviously frightened. "Michael, stay with her."

I see the relief in his eyes that I've taken charge here, that I've given an order. Ian is beside me, his hand wrapped around a holstered stake.

"The pitch-black eyes," Simon says with a measure of admiration in his voice, like someone commenting on a beautiful butterfly instead of a hideous creature. "The engorged jaw and teeth. The long, tough nails. All clear signs of the Thirst. They go from dangerous as vampires, to absolutely deadly when the Thirst kicks in. It's like they become designed to kill and do nothing else."

"Tell me everything you know," I say, staring at the creature, who surveys the group before focusing his attention solely on me. A chill shivers down my spine. Goose bumps rise on my flesh. If I didn't know better, I would think he knew who I was.

Simon walks very close to the cell, but is completely comfortable, having observed this creature for a long time. He tells us that the Thirst is activated after a vampire drinks too much vampire blood within too short a time span. As

far as he knows, different vampires have different toler-
ances.

"For some it takes only once, for others it takes once
a week over an entire year. It's a lot like an infection in
humans. Some just have stronger immune systems than
others."

"What about Old Family? How long would it take to
affect them?"

"I hadn't even thought about that," he says. "But it
must take ages. I hate to think about an Old Family vampire infected with the Thirst. Imagine how powerful he'd
become."

He's lost in his own thoughts for a moment, his scien-
tific mind maybe crunching numbers, visualizing how it
would be in an advanced calculus equation. But he shakes
out of it.

"Anyway, I've been observing him for some time,
determining what it is about vampire blood that makes
him tick. This one's been denied vampire blood for about
three weeks now. Notice how feral he is. He lost his ability
to communicate just a few days ago."

The vampire screams and spittle flies from his disgust-
ing jaw. He starts clawing at the glass, trying to escape, but
it's useless.

"We were actually able to play a few games of chess
at the start," Simon says. "But when the hunger kicks in,
unlike with regular vampires, the Infected, in one last
desperate bid to get blood, actually grow in strength, it
seems. They become more ferocious, instead of weaker.

They're like stars that burn out quickly right at the end, you know?"

A creature who's even more dangerous when he's near death.

"How many are there?" I ask over the screaming of the deranged vampire.

"Hundreds. Maybe thousands. I can't really get a good estimate and no one's willing to go outside the city and get me a head count. I got some information from this one here, but I'm not sure how reliable it is."

"I'd love to talk to him," I say.

"So would I. Unfortunately, I'm a little short on vampire blood."

"Can't you just send out hunters? I mean, surely there's a village in those hills where vampires live. Or even in the city. It can't be that hard."

"This isn't like Denver," Ian says, stepping into our conversation. "There hasn't been a vampire within these walls for years. And there's fewer and fewer on the outside. The Agency here hasn't sent out blood in, what? Weeks? Months?"

"Six months," Simon says.

"Valentine would've slaughtered the city if we acted that way," I say.

"Well, your city doesn't have a combined thirty miles of thick wall surrounding it. We make our own rules here. And as far as the vampires outside, I think their recent decline is a sign that the Thirst is taking over and they're turning on one another. The guards along the watchtowers report seeing fewer every night. We used to get the occasional vampire, curious about the gigantic city and the fresh blood inside. They never made it to the wall before being hit by flamethrowers, but still, they were out there, looking for a way in. For the past several weeks, it's been completely quiet."

The calm before the storm, maybe.

"So, you don't have any vampire blood to feed this poor guy?" I ask.

"Sorry, nothing. On the upside, I will get to see how long it takes before he's totally incapacitated."

A little too morbid for my taste.

"What if I could get you some vampire blood?" I ask.

Simon raises an eyebrow. "Did you bring some with you? From Denver?"

"Yes," I say. It's still in the bodies, but I have it. "I came here to investigate the Thirst, and knowing how important vampire blood is, I brought a small vial with me, just in case."

"Well, get it to me and I'll feed him. After that, you can talk as long as you want. They aren't always coherent, but they're much easier to deal with when they're satiated."

I take one more look at the Infected. His black eyes are bulging and curious, but I doubt he understood a single word of our conversation. He runs his claws against the glass slowly. His mouth dips open and I can look straight down into his black throat. An odd sympathy, like the one I felt for my brother, envelops me. Whoever this vampire was, he didn't deserve this.

Chapter 24

When we step into the Beaumont Hotel, Tegan's eyes widen. "Wow!"

I have to admit the running fountain in the lobby is impressive. Bellhops wearing little black hats, red jackets, and black pants are assisting guests. Everything is so bright.

Taking it all in, we wander to the registration desk. The clerk, in her navy-blue suit, smiles brightly. "Welcome to the Beaumont."

"Where do all the guests come from?" I ask. They can't all be from the train.

"Different parts of the city. They come here when they want a day away from the drudge. We're known for our pampering. Perhaps I can schedule you for some time at our spa."

"What's that?" Tegan asks.

The clerk's laughter is like tinkling bells. "Massage, facial, all-around spoiling."

"I don't think we'll have time," I tell her. Tegan's face falls. I feel bad, but I can't get distracted from our purpose in being here.

When we finish checking in, the clerk gives me a sealed envelope. Inside is a slip of paper with a room number and "F&R" scrawled on it.

After dropping off our luggage in our suite, we head to the indicated room, which turns out to be the largest one in the hotel. While Michael, Tegan, and Ian explore its luxury, I sit down with Faith and Richard.

"Isn't this hotel lovely?" Faith asks. "It's probably the only human palace I've ever seen."

I know I should admire the wooden décor, the French art on the walls, the TV that plays nonstop Hollywood movies. "It's all fake, though."

"So? Who needs it to be real? We have enough of that every day; it's nice to get lost in fantasy."

"Whatever, I'm not here to talk about the hotel. The sun is still out. How did you get here?"

"Vampires always have ways, Dawn," Richard says.

"So there could be vampires in the city that Matheson doesn't know about."

"Could be, but I haven't sensed any. Although it's still early for them to come out."

"Something about this city seems really off."

"It's just that you're not accustomed to the cleanliness," Faith says.

"Maybe. Matheson thinks Day Walkers are a myth."

"Until my half brother made his ghastly revelation, so did we."

"So what are the plans?" Michael asks, standing a short distance away, arms crossed.

Tegan sits beside me, and Ian drops into a nearby chair, his hard-edged stare focused on the vampires. Fortunately neither Faith nor Richard seems bothered that not everyone is as relaxed around them as I am.

I explain what we encountered when we went to the Agency, about Simon, his ideas on the Thirst, and the Infected he's been studying. And then I ask them, "Can I have a little bit of your blood to feed him?"

"Ewww," Faith says. "For that monster? I don't think so."

Giving her a tolerant smile, Richard simply shakes his head. "I'll offer up my veins," he says. "Does it need to be fresh?"

"No," I say. I dig into the pocket of my hoodie and pull out a test tube that I borrowed from the laboratory, complete with cork stopper.

Richard lets down his fangs and pierces his wrist. He hovers the wound over the glass vial, leading the blood into it.

"I won't need much, I suspect," I say. "I have a feeling Old Family blood will be more potent. What do you think?"

"Probably. But who knows anymore? The world seems to be changing, and all the rules along with it."

The blood runs down the vial, slowly collecting at the bottom, its color pure crimson.

"When was the last time you saw your father?" I ask Richard.

He thinks about it, tilts his head one way, then the other way. "Two years."

"That long ago?" I ask.

He just laughs and Faith can't hide her own little chuckle.

"That's nothing to us, Dawn. It might as well be last week. The last time I spoke with him he was going on about how I was such a disappointment. I took off, traveled a bit. I saw my mother six months ago. But like most wives, she was exiled after she gave birth to me. She's just north of here, living happily in her own manor."

"Are you going to see either of them while we're here?"

"Unfortunately, yes," he says. "Victor wants me to try to smooth things over with Father. After all, if we have any hope at stopping the Thirst, Sin, and the Day Walkers, we'll need every Old Family patriarch we can get to be willing to work with Victor."

"Perfect, then I can join you. I'd love to ask him some questions about the Thirst. And he may have a lead on Sin. Just because the Agency doesn't know about him doesn't mean he wasn't here."

"Leaving the city is not an option for you," Ian says.

"You and Michael can come with me."

"No."

"But you know how bad the Thirst is. It's moving

beyond the Carrollton territory."

"You're not leaving the city."

He's stubborn, opinionated, and accustomed to giving orders. But then I spent a good part of my delegate days doing things I wasn't supposed to do, so I slip into delegate mode and smile sweetly. "You're probably right, Ian. It's not necessary."

I exchange a glance with Tegan. She knows me well enough to know that I will find a way to get out to Carrollton Manor. And if need be, she'll help me do it.

Night has fallen by the time I return to Simon. Michael and Ian escorted me through the city, while Tegan stayed with Richard and Faith. I'm surprised she was so willing to keep two vampires company, but maybe she just sees them as the lesser of the two evils. She really didn't like being in a room with an Infected, even with thick glass separating them.

Once we're in the lab, I present the vial to Simon.

"Excellent, Miss Montgomery. Let me offer him this and we'll . . ."

The vampire begins a new rage, screaming at the top of his lungs, his eyes locked on the tiny vial of crimson. Does he know what's in there? Can he smell it? Can he comprehend what Simon is saying? I'll find out soon enough, I hope.

"Sounds like someone is excited," Simon says, pouring the blood into a small goblet. He then presses a button, opening a tiny compartment next to the cell, just big enough to place the cup in. Once he does, he pushes another button and the tiny door closes, a new one opens in the cell, and the vampire reaches in for his reward.

He drinks the blood, not savoring its smell or taste. He just devours it in greedy gulps, then takes his fingers and wipes any off his chin before suckling them.

It was so little, but I can tell that it is enough. His breathing eases, his chest calms. He looks up, and while his eyes are still pitch-black, they reflect a calmness. He puts his hands on the glass, palms facing us, and leans into it. He takes in deeper and deeper breaths, before saying, "I recognize that."

"The blood?" I ask.

"Oh yes. Old Family."

"Impressive," Simon says. He looks at me with a brow arched in an unspoken question.

I know his question already—where did I get Old Family blood? On the tip of my tongue is "None of your business." But I need the information he's gathered so I sort of lie. "The Denver overlord has a keen interest in the Thirst. He sent some of his blood along in case it was needed."

"How generous of him." He turns back to the Infected. "How does it taste?"

"Marvelous," the creature says, losing more and more of his feral demeanor and becoming something closer to human. "Do you have any more?"

"No," I say.

"No matter. That will keep me satiated for many weeks. Maybe months."

"How do you know? Have you had it before?"

He smiles and that evil returns to his eyes. "You really don't know what's coming, do you? What's just around the corner?"

He slams his hands against the glass and I jump back.

"Don't worry," Simon says. "He can't get through that."

"I won't need to," the vampire says. "They'll come for me. Eventually. Not tonight. Not tomorrow. But I've got all my life to wait."

"Who's coming?" I ask.

"The rest of us."

"How many of you are there?"

"Plenty."

"Is there a cure?" I ask.

He laughs and the victorious guffaw echoes through his little chamber. "Now why would I want to be cured?"

He smiles and slams his hand into the glass again. A tiny fracture appears.

Simon's eyes widen in alarm. Pulling out their stakes, Ian and Michael step forward, pushing Simon and me behind them.

"I'm stronger than a regular vampire," the Infected says. His palm hits the glass again and the fracture grows. "I'm faster." Again, and the hairline crack splits into several more. "I'm the next step in world domination. And our only weakness has finally been absolved. Our savior has come. The Day Walker. And he has blessed us with his ability."

"Sin . . ." I whisper, and chills run up my spine. Sin is

responsible for this creature. He was here.

"You should've taken me into the sun, Simon," the vampire says, his head twitching slightly, the same as Brady but more controlled with the fresh blood running through him. "You would've seen that we no longer fear the day. And our time has come!"

With that, the vampire smashes his fist against the tiny fissures, and the glass explodes. He rushes toward Michael and Ian with blinding speed. With both hands and incredible strength, he ferociously pushes Michael, hurling him off his feet and into the lab equipment, test tubes and beakers shattering around him.

Ian tries to end the vampire's life in one blow, but the creature, imbued with the power of the Thirst, dodges and strikes Ian in the jaw, making him stagger back. He punches him in the stomach, and Ian doubles over, landing in an undignified heap on the floor.

The vampire jumps onto Simon, crashing them both against a table before falling onto the floor. Holding a shrieking Simon in place, the vampire straddles him. "Join us, Simon."

With a yell, I leap up and come down with my stake poised to go through the vamp's back and straight into his heart, but at the last second, he reacts—spiraling around and sending me flying, colliding against what remains of his "invincible" cell.

His attention is focused solely on me now. Out of the corner of my eye, I see Simon crawling away, dragging his broken left arm.

"Dawn Montgomery," the vampire growls.

My heart thunders. "You know who I am."

"All the Day Walkers know who you are. You belong to Sin."

"Like hell I do." I try to stand up, but the room spins and my legs slide out from beneath me. I haven't even regained my breath yet, let alone my ability to fight.

"My God will reward me greatly for delivering you." He reaches for me—

Diving, Michael strikes the vampire in the leg, sending a stake completely through his thigh. The beast howls and then backhands Michael, who skids across the floor. Ian is back in the fray, bringing down a stake. The vampire snags it, ripping it from his grasp, but is vulnerable and unprepared as I go in low and lodge my stake between his ribs, plunging the point through his heart.

The vampire's eyes go wide, his jaw goes slack, and he falls to the floor at my feet.

We all stand tense, waiting for the beast to close his eyes, his breathing to stop, his heart to go still.

We wait until it's finally over.

"Well," says Simon shakily from a corner where he's cowering, "it seems I miscalculated his strength."

Not just his, but all of them. I wonder how much more we've miscalculated—especially when it comes to Sin.

Chapter 25

Simon is taken to a hospital. A bone in his arm apparently snapped when he landed on the table. Workers are cleaning up the mess. No one seems willing to touch the Infected. Matheson just stares at him.

"He said he was a Day Walker," I tell him.

"The Thirst makes them go insane. I wouldn't give much credence to his blabbering."

"He knew about Sin. He knew who I was."

He finally lifts his gaze to me. "Vampire hearing. He could have heard a conversation outside this room. You make too much of a madman's words."

"Why aren't you taking this seriously?"

"Miss Montgomery, we've been safe within our walls for years. Nothing is going to change that."

"Simon thought the Infected was secure behind his cell."

"All right, then. What do you suggest? How do we prove this is a Day Walker?"

"We can't," I reluctantly admit. In death, he's like any other vamp. When the sun hits him, he'll burn up, all except his fangs.

Matheson pats my head and I have to fight myself not to slap his hand away. "When Simon recovers from his injury, I'll see if he wants to try to capture another one. Will that make you happy?" He talks like a father promising to replace his daughter's lost toy.

He doesn't get it. I feel as though I'm banging my head against a wall.

When Ian, Michael, and I return to our hotel room, we find a note from Tegan alerting us that she's in the bar with Richard and Faith. I wonder if she wasn't quite as comfortable with them as she indicated, if she needed to have other humans around her to make her feel safe. Or maybe it was the Old Family boredom kicking in that drove them out of their room to seek entertainment.

We find them easily enough at a table in the corner. I tell them about what happened at the laboratory.

"That's unfortunate," Richard says. "If I'd known my blood would be that potent . . ."

"What?" Faith retorts, wineglass in hand. "You would have watered it down?"

"At least now we know how an Infected reacts with Old Family blood in its veins," I say. "Not a pretty sight." Taking a pen from the pocket of my hoodie and the napkin the waitress brought with my drink, I prepare to take notes as we talk this out.

"That's not all we know," Michael says sourly.

"What else did you learn?" Faith asks.

I see Tegan's anxious expression and I wish she didn't have to hear his. "Sin turned him. There are apparently other Day Walkers infected with the Thirst. More of them, just like Brady."

"Then we have proof that Sin was here," Tegan whispers.

"Not necessarily," Faith says. "A Day Walker can travel with no restrictions."

"But I'd bet a pint of blood that he calls this city home," Richard says.

"What do you think he meant, when he said 'their savior' has come?" I ask.

"Who knows?" Faith responds. She downs her drink, signals for another one. "The Infected aren't exactly stable. They're rarely coherent, and when they are, all they talk about is nonsense. I swear, they try to scare you more than anything else."

"Not this one," I say.

"Fine," she says. "It means Sin has come to wreak havoc on the entire world. It means that my little half brother has somehow managed to outsmart every Old Family leader. It means that the end-times are here. There? Is that what you want to hear?"

"When are you going to take this seriously, Faith?" Richard asks, quick anger running through his words.

"Unfortunately from my observations and what he's managed so far, Sin doesn't appear to be stupid. Whatever he's
planning is apparently well thought out."

"It doesn't mean it'll happen. For all we know, one of
his 'creations' may have killed him already."

But even Faith doesn't sound convinced, and I can tell
her apathy is waning.

"What I don't get," Michael begins, "is why they would
choose the Thirst. I mean, if Sin turned them, and they
became Day Walkers, why not enjoy their life in the city,
with all the humans to feed off of? Why become a monster?"

"You're assuming they had a choice to begin with," Ian
says. "If they can't get into the city, what choice do they
have except to feed off other vampires?"

"I think Ian's right," I tell them. "Sin created Day
Walkers knowing they wouldn't have access to blood here.
He was proud of what Brady had become." I'll never for-
get that night when Sin cornered me in the hallway at the
Daylight Grill and revealed what he was. "He told me that
Brady was his favorite *creation*. Perfection. I think he's try-
ing to use the Thirst to create bigger monsters."

"Jesus," Michael says. "I guess I never thought we'd be
facing a worse enemy than vampires."

We're all quiet for a moment, taking that in.

"I don't mean to appear uncaring," Richard finally says,
"but there's not a lot more that we can do tonight. Besides,
I've planned something special for this evening."

He glances over at Faith. She pretends to be fascinated

with her drink. So they have a date?

Before I can point out that there is a lot more we can do, Ian says, "The rest of us can use the sleep. Let's go."

As Tegan and Michael get up from the table to follow Ian's lead, I call out, "I'll catch up in just a sec."

They all stop to wait. Great. Still, I lean toward Richard and whisper, "What about your father? Can we go talk to him tonight?"

"Unless my father has changed his routine, which is highly unlikely, tonight is the one evening of the week when he always meets with his lieutenants, so he wouldn't agree to see me. Before you suggest that we barge in anyway, let me assure you that interrupting him will only guarantee that he won't cooperate. Tomorrow night would be better." He smiles at Faith. "For all of us."

I reluctantly admit that one more night won't hurt. "Okay, then, tomorrow. Have fun."

He winks at me as he assists Faith from her chair. "We will."

As I start to get up, I glance down at my notes. I didn't write a single word. But I drew the mountain from my dreams. I crumple up the napkin. Why won't it leave me alone?

That night I'm restless. Tegan is sharing the bed with me and simply rolls over to her side and goes to sleep. She wants the light left on, which works for me because I want to read my father's journal. Sitting with my back against a

pillow, I scour quickly through the pages until I find something that catches my attention.

*I have found a reference to Esmerelda. Only Esmerelda.
No last name.*

My heart stops. That was Sin's mother.

*She is Old Family, but I can't determine from which line.
So I have to wonder if she is the missing link that my father
was searching for.*

I look up and my gaze is drawn to the window, where
the night flourishes. What were he and my grandfather
searching for? It feels like I'm carrying on my father's legacy in more ways than one. Not only was I a delegate, but
now I'm seeking the answers he couldn't find. Answers his
own father couldn't locate . . .

But what is the question?

Suddenly exhausted, I sink down in the bed. As I drift
off to sleep, the mountain is calling to me, but I push it
back. I'm beginning to resent it because its pull on me
seems stronger than Victor's. But tonight I need Victor.
More than anything.

I feel as though I'm floating in a void of darkness.

*When I open my eyes, I'm standing in Valentine Manor, in
the room where Victor met with Roland Hursch. He's engaged*

in another meeting tonight, but his guests aren't easily intimidated.

He stands at the head of the table while they sit around it. I had once thought the table was obnoxiously large, but now I see that it was built to accommodate a host of vampires.

"We Lessers are becoming restless, my lord," one of the vampires says. "We are each in charge of a hundred or so vampires, and each one starves. They look to us for answers, but we have none. What are we to tell them? You've forbidden the taking of blood directly from humans—on pain of death. Soon, that threat won't be enough to control them."

"Tell those in your sectors that they must be patient," Victor says. "Ration what you're given so that everyone has at least some blood."

"A few drops, my lord, are hardly satisfying," a woman says. She has flowing white hair. Since Lessers don't age after they're turned, it's impossible to know how old she is, but her calmness indicates she's been around for a while.

"I'm aware of the sacrifices that must be made, Anita. I take no more than you or your Lessers. Remind your minions that Sin and his Day Walkers are responsible for this current famine. If they know where he is, they must tell us. The rewards will be great for all concerned. The humans are afraid. We must convince them we are not the enemy."

"You show them too much mercy," a vampire with silver eyes challenges.

"Careful, Jude, or you may find my mercy doesn't extend to you." He holds the vampire's gaze until the latter looks down in submission.

"See my guards for your rations. We'll meet again in three nights."

I move over to the window where the moonlight filters in. I don't want them brushing by me as they leave. Unlike Hursch, they might have the ability to sense my presence. Vampires are so much more alert to subtleties than humans are.

When they are gone, Victor walks over and closes the doors, pressing his forehead against it. He heaves a deep sigh that seems to reverberate through me. I wish he could be relieved of this burden. I wish I could be there to help him.

I don't remember crossing the room, but suddenly I'm near him. I place my hand on his back.

His head comes up. "Dawn."

"I'm here, Victor. I'm here for you."

I don't think he can hear my voice, but he's gone incredibly still. He moves away from me, stretches out on the couch, and closes his eyes.

"I thought I sensed your presence," Victor says.

I spin around. He's leaning against the door, so incredibly sexy in his jeans and black T-shirt. I guess in dreams, we can choose what we wear. I glance down and I'm wearing a slinky black dress.

"You look so beautiful," he says, as he walks over and cradles my face between his hands.

"I don't know if this is real. I don't understand it. It feels real, but it's a dream."

"I don't understand it completely, either. I only know that at this moment, we are together." He circles his thumbs around my cheeks. "And you're sad."

"We've both had a rough night. Someone got hurt because of me." I tell him about Simon, the infected Day Walker, and Sin being referred to as a savior.

His hold on me tightens. "What is my brother trying to do?"

"I don't know. It makes no sense. You can't control the Infected. And yet after I gave him Richard's blood, he seemed almost rational. Do you think Old Family blood is a possible cure? Sin had told Brady it was."

"Sin lied. He wanted me dead and he was using your brother to accomplish that."

"Have you had any luck discovering where he is?"

"No."

I hear the frustration in his voice.

"At least the vampires here are listening to you."

He releases a dark chuckle. "It's more difficult than I thought it would be, Dawn. My father may have been brutal in his ways, but he kept the vampires in submission."

"You've stopped the Lessers from attacking humans."

"But soon they'll attack one another. Or they'll put me to the test of carrying out my threat to kill them."

I press my face against his chest, inhale his scent, take comfort from it. "I'm so sorry, Victor. I'm not sure I realized how truly awful this is for you."

"It could be worse. I might not have you."

I sink against him.

"Trust me," he whispers.

Everything goes fuzzy, foggy. Shadows rush in. Then retreat. I'm standing in the theater. Victor's theater, where he lived in the city before he overthrew his father and took up permanent residence in the manor. "We can travel in our dreams?"

"Only to places at least one of us has been. And only to places we want to be."

And I so badly want to be here. With him.

I glance at the movie screen. A girl wearing red shoes is following a path of yellow bricks while a beautiful woman holds a wand. "Los Angeles is like this," I say.

"Filled with small people?"

Smiling, I look up at Victor. "No. Too colorful, too bright. Too pristine. It's like something you might visit, but you'd never live there."

"Yet people do."

I shake my head. "I don't like it there."

"But there are no vampires. I would think that would make it Utopia for humans."

He's right and yet—

"It's like everyone's pretending." And I'm already tired of talking about Los Angeles. "How are things in Denver?"

He wraps himself around me and kisses me. There's almost a desperation to his kiss, as though it's the last time he'll ever have my lips pressed to his. I feel that light-headedness again, but then his kisses always steal my breath and make me feel faint. But there's a subtle shift. He draws back and I gasp. We're on the roof of the Agency building, looking out over Denver. The wind is blowing and my hair is flying around me.

I make my way to the edge and glance down. People are walking the streets. Not a lot, but more than I've ever seen here. I smile. "You made the vampires leave the city. The people are feeling safe."

"Too safe."

I jerk around to face him. "What do you mean?"

"No blood was delivered this week. Last week I took no rations for myself because the supply was not as much as we were expecting."

"You're hungry."

"Very. I made a mistake with Hursch. Underestimated his resolve. He is about to discover that he underestimated mine. I'm going to initiate mandatory blood withdrawals for anyone over the age of sixteen."

"That will be impossible to enforce."

"Not when I embed microchips in the citizens. I'll know who has donated and if they don't . . . I can find them."

"Microchips?"

"With tracking. I can monitor and find anyone, anytime. My father abhorred modern conveniences, but I'm not him."

"If you do this, you'll be a worse monster than he was."

"I have no choice."

"You always have a choice!"

I jerk awake, the air strangely disturbed as though I cried out in my sleep. Maybe I really yelled the words. Was I with Victor? Or was it just a nightmare? The Victor I'd fallen for would never be so harsh with humans. He would find a better solution. What's happening to him?

I lie back down, force myself to sleep. I have to see him again. I have to know.

I feel like I'm leaving my body. My breathing becomes clean and full, as if my lungs have grown to twice their size. My body and head are light. I'm not sure whether I'm floating, or the world is floating around me.

But this time, I land right where I started. In the hotel bedroom. Tegan isn't here, but then she wouldn't be. I'm in the dream again. I watch the curtains moving back and forth in front of the open window. I feel someone climb into bed gently, as if not to disturb me. And then his arm slowly reaches around my waist, drawing me up against him.

"Victor . . ." I whisper.

"Dawn, you left me."

It wasn't a nightmare. "Victor, there is blood. I don't know why they aren't giving it to you. Don't do anything until I get back to Denver. Please. I'll talk to Clive and Rachel. We'll get you blood."

"I'll wait. For you, I'll wait."

I don't know if he's agreeing to wait before doing anything drastic or if he means that he's waiting for me personally. He said we can't be together, and yet here in this dream world, it's as though there are no obstacles. We can meet secretly with no one knowing.

As he lowers his mouth hungrily to mine, I hope this means we've found a way to be together.

"Hey, sleepyhead, wake up," Tegan sings.

I force my eyes open when all I want to do is jam my head under the pillow. The dream has left me wanting. It's not enough. It's not solid. It's not real. It's just a pleasant illusion, like this city.

Tegan starts bouncing on the bed. "Come on. We have a surprise waiting for us."

I peer up at her. "I thought we were going to hang loose until tonight when we can go to Carrollton Manor."

"When *you* go," she corrects me. "I'll be distracting Ian from figuring out that you're doing what he doesn't want you to do. Anyway, Matheson showed up at the hotel this morning saying he has something special planned for us."

"That's weird," I say.

"I know. But the guy's like a gigantic, pudgy grandpa. Come on, he's going to buy us breakfast downstairs. Michael and Ian are already there."

"All right," I say. "I'm starving."

By the time we arrive, Michael and Ian have already finished four stacks of pancakes and an entire plate of hash browns. Matheson is next to Ian and demands more food for all of us.

"Not too much," I say. "I don't want to be wasteful." Of course, I'm thinking about the Outer Ring and the people starving there.

"Nonsense," he says. "After that harrowing encounter last night in the laboratory, you deserve everything. Here, more syrup."

"How's Simon?" I ask, refusing the syrup as a kind of protest for those suffering outside.

"With his arm in a cast, he's already back at work as we speak. Perhaps you'll have another opportunity to visit with him—compare notes, as it were."

"I don't know what more I could add," I confess.

"Well, no matter. I heard you were leaving us tonight," he says. "I went to visit the Night Train, and they've already turned it around on the tracks."

"That's right," Ian says. "We're heading back to Denver. Our work here is done."

I jerk my head around to stare at him. "What?"

"I don't see that there's anything else we can accomplish here."

"But—" I stop myself from saying that I haven't been out to Carrollton Manor yet. I need to go there, talk with the Old Family vampire. I have to find a way to manage that before we leave.

"Well then, it seems I've caught you just in time," Matheson says. "I have a very special treat in store for the four of you, something very, very, very few people have ever seen."

He leans in and waits until he has our undivided attention. And then he says the two words that I never thought I'd hear. "The ocean."

We ride with Matheson in his limo to the Agency building. On the rooftop he has prepared a helicopter for us. I am in absolute awe of this thing that I've only ever seen in photos. I look at Michael, whose jaw might be permanently stuck to the ground, and even Ian can't hide his boyish excitement.

"I haven't been on one of these since the war," Ian says. "I thought VampHu made them illegal."

"It did," Matheson says. "But we follow our own rules

here. Now, hop aboard, my lovelies, and enjoy the view."

We step up into the helicopter and strap ourselves in, Ian helping us with the complex X-shaped belts that secure us in place. The pilot is wearing a giant helmet with a microphone, into which he spouts an endless stream of code words. Matheson hands us two large duffel bags.

"You'll need these. Have fun!"

His voice is drowned out by the whirl of the propeller above him and he shuts the door with a big smile.

The blades pick up speed, and just when I think they've reached their maximum and the noise and shaking is deafening, they keep going. And going. And going. I instinctively close my eyes like something bad is about to happen, but force them open when we begin to move.

The ground slowly descends, and we rise into the sky. I can't help but laugh. I never imagined anything like this.

From up here, I look out the windows and see the city and the walls that comprise the double rings, the separating of the haves and have-nots. Then we head off toward the horizon.

"Can you believe this?" Michael yells. "They've done everything right here, Dawn. They kept the vampires in their place and this is their reward."

"But now they have to deal with the Thirst."

"Small price to pay—and it's not in the center of the city. It's not the Thirst we need to be studying. It's how Los Angeles achieved domination over the vampires."

I'd like to argue, but the view is too breathtaking. From here, I can see the vast stretches of empty space and they seem so beautiful from such a distance. I can even see the mountains way, way off in the horizon.

The mountains that feel so familiar . . .

A weird dread falls over me—

Suddenly Tegan is punching my shoulder. I turn away from the mountains and gasp at the magnificence stretching out before me.

The ocean.

It's staggering in size, curving with the earth, so blue that I could stare at it for an entire lifetime and still not find every shade undulating within its folding waves. It's alive. It breathes. It gives me hope for something better far beyond this place, to where the waves crash anew on different shores.

I'd hoped the ocean was some mythical place that we'd never find, and we could simply glide through the air for an eternity, taking in the sights meant for only birds. But we eventually land.

We step out and instantly the air is fresh and pure and somehow salty. It's like nothing I've ever felt before and my lungs suddenly crave it like a new sensation they know will soon be taken away.

The pilot shuts off the propeller. The new smell is overtaken by an incredible sound. A soft crash, but spread wide like it covers the earth. It has a rhythm, a song, a melody all its own. It's heavy and infinite, completely beyond words, and I already know I won't be able to describe it to anyone who hasn't heard the roar of the ocean.

Tegan is next to me, and I dare not look at her, in case

this magnificent place is just a dream and disappears when I turn away. So instead I lace my fingers through hers, and realize that this is a moment I could only ever share with her, and it'll be our moment. Forever.

"I never imagined anything like this," Tegan whispers.

The vampires took this, took so much beauty from us.

"How long do we have?" Michael asks the pilot.

"As long as you want. When you're ready to head back, just join me at the chopper."

Taking off my shoes, I hold them as we scramble over the dunes to get to the water. The sand is warm against my soles and it shifts beneath my feet. Tegan and I are laughing, clinging to each other, struggling to keep our balance. Ian and Michael follow behind us. When I glance back, I see that they're both wearing smiles that are brighter than I've ever seen.

This is what our life should be—smiles and happiness.

We drop the bags that Matheson gave us on a smaller sand drift. Tegan runs ahead, dancing over the beach with wild abandon. Michael, Ian, and I approach the water's edge. Seashells litter the shore. The water rolls in, swirls around our ankles. Our feet sink just a little and I release a startled squeal. Michael laughs.

Seagulls cry out, swoop down gracefully. On sticklike legs, sandpipers race up and down the beach. I only know what they are because of books at school. I never expected to see them.

Tegan rushes over, smiling brightly, out of breath. "Isn't this amazing?"

"People used to crowd these beaches," Ian says. "Before the war."

"Christopher said he spent time at the beaches in the east," I tell him.

"He lied. People don't leave the cities in the east any more than they leave them anywhere else. But he dreamed of playing in the ocean." From his pocket, he retrieves the leather necklace that he removed from Christopher's neck. "Enjoy the waves, kid," he says quietly before hurling the necklace into the surf.

We watch it bob on the ever-moving whitecaps until they swallow the pendant. Who knows in what strange land it'll finally come to rest? I hope it's somewhere far away.

After we take a silent moment, Tegan says, "Let's see what's in those bags."

We unzip the duffel bags and pull out several towels and a large multicolored ball.

"What is this thing?" Tegan asks.

"Come on, I'll show you," Ian says, grabbing it and running through the sand.

We all follow, and Ian turns around, tells us to spread out, and then bumps the ball toward Tegan. She hits it to me and it goes sailing. I have to chase it and, lifting my arms, I knock it over to Michael. He returns it the same way.

I can't believe we're laughing. We've all forgotten the world and the vampires and the dangers. Right here, it's just the waves, the sounds, the laughter, and the beach ball.

After a few minutes, I go sit down on one of the towels while Michael and Tegan walk down the beach, still passing the ball back and forth. Ian wades out into the water until it's circling around his calves. I wonder what distant memory he's recalling.

I can't help but think about Victor. We could never share a moment like this. The sun, so glorious, warms every part of me. It's like I never stopped to thank it for being there, always saw it as something that keeps the monsters away, instead of what it really is: perfection written in the sky.

I put my chin on my knees, my arms wrapped tightly around my legs, thinking that maybe I can freeze this moment. But the sun keeps moving, keeps setting. And it's time to go back.

When we return to the hotel, we discover Faith and Richard are in our suite. A white cloth-covered table cluttered with covered dishes is set out on the balcony.

"We thought since this is your last night here that something special was in order," Faith says.

"I brought something for you, Ian, from my private collection," Richard says. "The best scotch you'll ever find. I thought we might toast to better vampire-human relations."

Ian eyes him warily but the lure of good whiskey proves too much. "Sure, why not?"

"We'll leave the elders to their fiery brews," Faith says to me. "We'll have wine."

Maybe it's because we're near the sea, but we have an

assortment of seafood spread out before us. It looks to be real, which means it cost a fortune. Not that Faith can't afford it.

She lights candles on the table, and they flicker in the slight breeze. Tegan seems more relaxed, and I wonder if the time she spent at the beach distracted her from her bad memories of Sin. I catch her sneaking glances at Michael and when she realizes I spotted her, she looks guilty.

Hearing a clink of glasses, I watch as Ian takes a long swallow of the amber liquid. "Ah, excellent stuff."

"Only the best for you, Ian," Richard says. He shifts his attention to me, and I see something secretive in his eyes, something I can't read. A little warning bell goes off in my head, but this is Richard. Victor's best friend. He trusts him with his life. Has trusted him with mine.

"So what did you do today?" Richard asks.

I tell him about our trip to the beach.

"You should've seen it, Richard. It was . . ."

"Breathtaking? I have seen it. But never with the sun out. Tell me. Is the blue bright and beautiful with the sun reflecting off it?"

"Even more, it's . . . incredible. I wish all humans could see it. I wish we could tear down the walls and start over with the vampires."

"Who knows? Maybe this little trip will prove to be a start."

"Will you be returning to Denver with us?" Michael asks.

"No, I need to reconcile with my father and that's

going to take effort and time."

He doesn't sound too happy about it, but we will need all the Old Families to align with Victor in his battle against Sin.

"What about you, Faith?" I ask.

She pats Richard's hand where it rests on the table. I think she meant to make it a brief token of reassurance, but he turns his hand over quickly and captures her fingers between his. I expect her to pull away. Instead she gives him a soft smile. "I'm going to stay and help Richard make amends."

"What . . . the . . . 'ell?"

The slurred words have us all jerking our attention back to Ian. He's struggling to come up out of his chair, but he only gets halfway there before toppling over and crashing to the floor in a sprawl.

Tegan rushes over to him, touches the pulse at his throat. He snores deeply, and she gives Richard an accusing glare. "You put something in the scotch."

Richard finishes off his glass, making his point that he's immune to its effects. "I did."

Michael is on his feet, his stake drawn. "What's going on?"

Richard slides his gaze over to me. "You wanted to go with me to see my father, didn't you?"

My heart is hammering. "I did. I do. Absolutely."

"Ian wasn't going to let you go," Faith says reasonably. "And now, he'll have sweet dreams until you come back."

"I was going to distract him," Tegan says accusatorily.

"Oh," Richard says, looking sheepish. "Yeah, that probably would have worked, too."

"I didn't get a chance to tell them," I say, looking at Tegan. I wish I *had* shared our plans, since their methods are a bit extreme. But it's done now.

"And you forgot to tell me," Michael says. "I could have saved you all some trouble, because you're not going. It's too dangerous."

I walk over to him and lay my hand on his shoulder, feel him stiffen. We've shared so much, been through so much. "Come with me," I say. "I could really use your help out there."

"We don't need to do this," he says. "Ian is right. We have all the information we need. What's an Old Family vampire who lives outside the walls going to be able to tell us?"

"We won't know until we ask, until we talk to him. Like mine, your duty is to the city. We need to know *everything* about the Thirst, and *everything* about Day Walkers, and *everything* about Sin. No matter the cost."

"It doesn't always have to be you making the sacrifices."

"It does," I say. "Because I'm the only person who can. Who do I have now? Not my parents. Not my brother. I'm the person who can die for their cause, because I don't have anything to risk."

"But you do. We all do," he says, looking over at Tegan.

She steps over and takes his hand. "I'm not going. I'm going to stay and watch over Ian. I'll be fine. There are no vamps in the city, but there are plenty where Dawn is going. She needs you. You're a Night Watchman. She comes first."

I can see him struggling and realize that slowly during this trip his feelings have been changing, shifting from me to Tegan. And it looks like hers have been changing as well. I'm about to tell him to stay when he says, "Vamps or no vamps, keep all the doors locked, Tegan. We'll be back. I'll be back."

She smiles at him. "Just be careful."

He nods.

I breathe a sigh of relief, then look at Richard. "Can you at least move Ian to a bed?"

"Of course." He uses the amazing strength that vampires have to easily lift Ian over his shoulder and cart him to one of the bedrooms.

Faith touches my arm, bringing my attention to her. "I can sense that you're a little upset by our methods. He'll sleep for a couple of hours and be just fine. We should be back before he wakes up. This way was just easier."

"I guess it was . . ."

When Richard returns, he asks, "Are we ready?"

"Just to be clear," Michael says, "I want to go on record as saying I don't like this."

"Noted," Richard says. "Now, let's get out of here."

"How?" I ask. "There's only one entrance into the entire city, and that's the rails for the Night Train, which is closed with several feet of steeled gate and a dozen guards."

"I've been slipping in and out of this city for years," Richard says. "Don't worry."

* * *

Once we get outside, we go around a corner to where Richard parked his car. It's a beautiful, all-white, old sedan. It shouts glamour like nothing else I've seen on the streets. I expect a chauffeur in a top hat and leather gloves to come out and guide me into the luxurious backseat. But Richard opens up the back door and does it for me.

The inside is cream-colored leather, the softest I've ever felt. The stitching is perfect, the contours precise. Michael follows me in while Richard and Faith take the front.

Before long, we're gliding smoothly through the streets. The funny thing is, no one is looking. No one even seems to notice or care. They're so used to these kinds of sights that we're just another passing car. In Denver, people would have been turning their heads at every street corner.

An hour later, Richard has circled around to the only part of the city that isn't covered with lights and people.

"Good, it's still here," he says, driving toward a brick warehouse with a large metal sliding door. "Now, if only this still works." He holds up a remote and presses a button. The door rises. He drives through and the door clangs shut behind us.

The headlights illuminate the dusty floor, and then I see it: a ramp leading down. Slowing almost to a crawl, he follows it cautiously. Soon we're in a tunnel, and he puts his foot on the gas again.

"I built this deep beneath the city decades ago," he says. "It was the easiest way to get in and out after my father pissed me off."

"What would you do in the city?" I ask, somewhat claustrophobic.

"I'd just go to one of the nightclubs or a nice restaurant, surround myself with beautiful women. I swear, they're getting better-looking every year."

I look at Faith and as much as she tries, even she can't hide that tiny snarl at the mention of female "competition." Not that any mortal would be competition to her.

The tunnel is just large enough to fit the car, and several wooden beams are spread out every so often to help support the underground system. It doesn't seem the safest in the world, and I wonder when it was last used. But before long, Richard is pressing a button on the remote again and another door is sliding open. A dull blue hue appears. When we emerge, the moon is up high greeting us, casting its gaze across the deserted fields. I glance back to see the city's Outer Ring of walls behind us.

There are no defined roads, but with Richard at the wheel, they aren't needed. Soon we all relax, lean back, and enjoy the surroundings as we're speeding along. I'm distracted by the mountains in the distance when Michael taps my knee and points forward. I notice something looming up ahead, and even without Richard telling me, I know what it is.

The manor is very different from Valentine's. It's old and deteriorating. Larger, but it's like the entire thing is collapsing under its own weight and history. Chunks of stone are absent from the towers, which only seem to be standing by some freak architectural design. Their edges rotting away, window frames hold no glass. The front door is off-kilter, a hinge giving way some time ago.

"Man, it has been a while," Richard says.

"It didn't always look this way?" I ask.

"No. But my father's been growing lazier over the years, more complacent. The servants are obviously following his lead."

Richard brings the car to a halt so it's facing the manor, its lights revealing a crumbling foundation and vines crawling up the sides, as if a great tentacled beast lay in the ground trying to swallow the manor whole.

If Richard is nervous, he certainly doesn't show it as he opens the front door. Stepping in, we're greeted with black shadows fighting against the bit of moonlight pouring in through the windows and a handful of holes in the roof. Michael turns on his flashlight, and the extra illumination reveals Richard's concern.

"Now this is strange," he says. "The lamps aren't even on. Father was very adamant that they never go out."

As we begin to cautiously move forward, the wind picks up and I feel it crawl across my body from the hundreds of tiny openings throughout the decrepit great house.

"It seems abandoned," I say.

"I doubt that," Richard says. "Father has just become more of a recluse. That's all. He'd never leave this place."

Michael stays right behind me, sweeping his flashlight around us any time we hear a noise. I figure we're safe, though. Richard and Faith, leading the way, have highly attuned senses. If we were in trouble, they would know.

As we pass rooms, I steal glances into places that may have once been beautiful but are now haunted by decay and rot. Ragged, moth-eaten curtains hang at the windows. In the art gallery are torn paintings and smashed marble statues. The library shelves are nearly empty, the books strewn across the floor like some new and uneven carpeting. Bedchambers reveal flipped mattresses and armoires reduced to rubble.

Richard grows more tense, resting his hand firmly on the stake strapped to his belt. Taking the cue, Michael wastes no time withdrawing his own.

At the end of the hallway, a pair of great double doors greets us. Richard hesitates, maybe contemplating what he'll say to his father. Maybe more afraid of what his father has become. Driven mad, perhaps? Led to destroy his own manor? He wouldn't be the first Old Family to lose it. It isn't common, but their minds can be as fragile as a human's sometimes, cracking along hidden fissures they didn't even know existed.

Richard opens the door.

The massive room is empty except for one throne made entirely of stone. The only light shining upon it comes from a hole in the roof that must have been deliberately placed, because the moon falls perfectly onto the elaborate chair. The arms and back are covered in ornate designs, carved by some master artisan's ancient hand. But where the Great Carrollton Lord should sit, there is nothing except dust.

"He's not here," Richard says.

"We haven't checked all the rooms," Faith says in an attempt to comfort him.

"No. He isn't here. This place is empty."

"Not quite, young Carrollton."

The air is sucked out of my lungs as a new chilly voice responds to Richard.

From behind the throne, a pair of hands emerges, and then arms, and finally the head of a demented vampire. He crawls across the throne like a spider, his feet and hands never hitting the ground, but gliding across the seat of the Old Family vampire.

"Maurice?" Richard says. "Maurice, is that you? Where is Father?"

"Gone, young Carrollton," the vampire says. He wears only a faded loincloth, the rest of him pale and naked. Thin beyond all imagination except for a large jaw that would only fit on a man twice his size.

"But you're his most trusted servant," Richard says. "Surely you know where he went."

"Oh, I do, young Carrollton. He's all around us."

Maurice reaches down and rubs his hand along the dusty chair, pulling his fingers up and licking them.

It isn't dust. It's ash. Vampire ash.

"Why?" Richard asks, immeasurable calm in his voice.

"Because he saw the future," Maurice says, scaling the throne until he is perched on top with a balance that is mystifying and somehow adds to the small vampire's grandeur.

"The future? No one can see that."

"You can," Maurice says. "Just look around, and you'll find that you are . . . surrounded by it."

Michael slowly moves his flashlight up, tracing it across the ceiling, where the stonework slowly gains texture, moving from flat rocks with grooves to fully formed limbs and heads.

The ceiling is composed of living, breathing vampires. And they have their eyes focused on us.

Chapter 26

Maurice's mouth opens into a gaping black maw; rows of fangs send spittle flying as he lets out a massive roar that pours from his chest. The Infected are everywhere. The vampires descend from the ceiling, landing without grace, but with purpose. The need to feed has taken over their minds, and they only want to drink from Richard and Faith. Michael and I are mere inconveniences who will be dealt with quickly.

"We can't fight them all," Michael says.

"We aren't going to fight any of them," Richard says. "Run!"

Michael grabs my arm and we begin sprinting, but the hairs on the back of my neck are prickling and I know the vampires are chasing us. Michael eventually lets go of my arm and pulls out another stake, running farther ahead to clear the path of any vampire that gets in his way. His speed is incredible, his endurance something beyond human.

A vampire infected with the Thirst drops in front of us. Michael wastes no time dispatching him with a quick blow, so vicious and savage it's like he's possessed. I can hear Richard and Faith still close behind, but they, too, are fighting off this horde of the damned.

As we near the entrance to the manor, Richard leaps in front of us, kicking the door so hard that it nearly flies off its last hinge. He jumps into the car and starts it up. We get inside just as a vampire pounces on the hood.

The vampire's claws slam into the windshield, causing a fracture. Faith, maybe more annoyed than frightened, pulls out a stake and rams it through the glass, right into the vampire's chest, striking a deadly blow. The Infected quickly rolls off.

As Richard speeds away, the vampires have no intention of letting their prey go. They're scurrying after us, keeping a close distance.

"Speed up!" I yell, staring out the back window.

"I'm going as fast as I can," Richard says. "This baby was built for luxury, not speed. Besides, it's not as though I have a smooth road to work with."

He's right. Without a road, we're bumping over terrain littered with potholes and unseen branches and puddles of mud. Richard can only go fast enough to keep the terrifying monsters out of arm's reach, but not much more. They're close enough that I can see their eyes, and our reflection in their black pools.

We reach the secret entrance to Richard's tunnel and dive in so fast that all four tires leave the ground for a moment and the top of the car catches the roof of the entrance, causing sparks to fly. I look back. With their increased strength, the vampires stop the door from closing and they pour in.

The narrow passageway slows us down even further, and our pursuers take advantage. Before long, they flood the tunnel, running across the ground and crawling over the walls. Like insects, they can defy gravity. Some flatten themselves and take a path across the ceiling in an attempt to be the first to reach us.

A solid thud. A vampire on top of the car. He smashes Michael's window and reaches in, but before he can grab hold, Richard swerves the car into the wall. The vampire is dashed against the rocks, releasing a grotesque howl before crumpling away and falling below the rampaging horde.

That's when a terrible thought occurs to me. "They'll get into the city," I say. "They'll kill everyone!" Even though human blood is worthless to them, they will show no mercy to the inhabitants of Los Angeles.

Richard looks in the rearview mirror, perhaps counting, perhaps gauging. But he must come to the same conclusion.

As a vampire latches onto the side, Richard slams the car again into the wall, but clearly aims for one of the supporting wooden beams. After that, he hits every single one he can find. We lose speed, and the car's lights go out—destroyed by the very wooden beams he deliberately runs into. But we keep just enough ahead.

Richard's plan becomes clear. He's trying to cause a cave-in and destroy his tunnel forever.

A large, crucial wooden trestle is just ahead when Richard says, "We had some good times, friends."

He then rams into it so hard that we nearly stop dead in our tracks, but it's enough to begin the inevitable. The roof begins falling, rocks hitting the top of our speeding car. I look behind us as the entire tunnel begins to crumble under the weight of several feet of earth. Eventually, the vampires panic, and unsure whether to run back or continue their pursuit, they hesitate. And that's all it takes for the tunnel to bury them.

We emerge out of the other side and Richard slams on the brakes to prevent us from hitting the brick wall just outside the large metal door. I turn my head sharply to see that the once-clear tunnel is now nothing but a mountain of dirt and debris, impossible to dig through.

Chapter 27

The car barely makes it to the front of the hotel, two of the tires flat, lights missing, and the hood wrecked. Just as we stop, the side-view mirror falls off. I would laugh if I wasn't shaking so badly. We rush through the lobby and get into an elevator.

I can't imagine what Ian's going to say when we tell him what we've discovered. It should at least deflect some of his anger toward me for disobeying his order not to leave the city.

We burst into our suite and the first thing that I notice is that Ian is awake, sitting in a chair. Tegan is beside him. Thank God.

"Ian, Lord Carrollton is dead," I say. "The Thirst, it's everywhere."

When he doesn't say anything, I notice two men

in black suits standing near the door, stakes drawn. They must have been there when we rushed in, but I was too distracted to notice them. Faith, Richard, and Michael all have stakes drawn and have gone into defensive stances.

"Director Matheson is requesting an urgent meeting with you and your party," one of the black-suited men says. "Including the two vampires you brought with you into this city."

How did they find out about Faith and Richard?

Faith, of course, doesn't look concerned at all. Richard, on the other hand, does. He knows how serious a crime this could be: Knowingly bringing two vampires into the city could result in death to us all.

They pack us into two different black sedans and drive to the Agency. I'm with Michael and Tegan. Looking out the window, the night has never seemed so dark.

Once we arrive, we trudge like a funeral procession up the steps, through the lobby, and into the elevators.

The entire ride up, not a single word is spoken, by us or our handlers. When the doors open, we're led to Matheson's office. Our escorts let us inside, shutting the door behind us, not following us in. I know that I'm going to have to rely on my delegate skills to get us out of this.

Matheson looks up and smiles.

"Thank you so much for coming. Beautiful evening, isn't it?"

If he's angry, he certainly isn't showing it.

"Matheson, I can explain," Ian says, stepping forward.

"Oh, there's no need," the director says, standing up and laughing jovially. "I know you well enough, Ian: You'd never do anything to endanger my city. Bringing two vampires, especially two well-groomed and beautiful Old Family vampires, is nothing to worry yourself with."

Okay, now I'm confused. I look around and everyone else seems puzzled, too. Except for Faith, who seems happy with the compliments.

Matheson walks over to the window and looks out over the towering buildings, the same way Clive does. Maybe it's a director-required skill. Though I imagine he sees something very different. Success.

"Look at it," Matheson says. "So beautiful. When the first brick was laid, the mason could have never dreamed how high his wall would reach. Nor could he realize how easily it would all crumble."

Matheson steps back from the window and his mood is beyond somber, as if he's about to deliver the news that a loved one has died. He paces slowly toward his desk, his hands clasped behind him, eyes on the floor. He takes his seat and seems far older than he really is, slowly easing himself down like he might break at any moment.

"Why did you call us here?" I ask.

"For your . . . final present." He presses the intercom button on his desk. "Send him in, please."

"Yes, Mr. Matheson," a voice responds back.

The director pulls his finger back from the button as if it weighs a hundred pounds, dragging it along the desk.

Silence everywhere. Even from outside. The entire city has stopped just for us.

The door opens, and the devil himself strides in.

"Hello, Dawn," Sin says.

Chapter 28

"Sin," Tegan breathes, and for all her talk of wanting to stake him, she seems capable of doing little more than staring at him in shock.

"Ah, my favorite human," he says. "I was so hoping you'd be here."

"You . . . you—"

"Business first."

He isn't the teenage impostor who stepped into our classroom a little over a month ago. His hair and eyes remain unchanged, though a new darkness silhouettes his entire being. The raggedy jeans and T-shirts have been traded for an outfit more suited for an Old Family vampire. A complex series of buckles and straps wrap around his body, tying together a well-fitted bondage of toughened leather and metal plates, clearly meant to protect his vampire heart. On top of it is a long coat that brushes the floor, blacker than the eyes of the Infected who have taken over the countryside. The high collar nearly touches his ears in a throwback to some great count that he must be descended from. And, most fearful of all, on his right hand, a gauntlet made of interlocking metal plates that starts at his elbow and climbs down to terrible claws that line the tip of each finger. It's large and cumbersome, yet seems a natural extension of his evil presence.

Ian and Michael immediately draw their stakes.

"Don't," Sin says, giving fair warning.

But they don't listen. Ian takes the lead, wasting no time with two stakes flying in. But Sin catches his arm, and with a swift kick, sends Ian back.

Michael runs on pure emotion, wanting to kill the vampire who tricked him, who betrayed him, who made himself seem like a friend. The vampire who bit Tegan, and nearly killed me.

Sin punches him hard in the gut and all Michael's air rushes out of his lungs. Then, with a backhanded slap from his mighty claw, Sin sends Michael falling to the floor, blood arcing into the air. Across Michael's face, four deep streaks reveal torn flesh and bone.

The action seems to have snapped Tegan out of her shock. I can see the anger burning brightly in her eyes as she rushes to Michael's side.

"You're getting old, Ian," Sin says. "Your body's been through too much, your mind too fogged with scotch. And Tegan, well, I still haven't gotten your taste out of my mouth—neither your lips nor your blood. Finally, Michael, I can add more scars to your face. You'll only have to live with them for a short time, because I'll be more than happy to end your foolish life."

"You bastard!" I shout and reach for my stake, but Richard holds my hand tightly. "Let me go!"

"Don't . . ." Richard says.

"You'd be wise to obey the Carrollton," Sin says. "He's only looking out for you."

"I'll kill you!" I shout, letting my anger run free.

"Not like this," Richard whispers into my ear, his tone as harsh as it is quick. "You're a delegate first, even without the title. That's your strength."

I take a deep breath, and listen to his words. He's right. My emotions rarely control me, and I can't start letting them do so now. Sin just took down two hunters with ease; what chance would I have?

Ian and Michael get back up, and I can see them contemplating another assault. But Sin has crossed the room, his arms behind his back, his clawed hand dripping Michael's blood.

"Dawn, you were very naughty to leave Denver without telling me. Poor Eris has been beside herself with guilt, feeling as though she failed me. My disciples don't like to disappoint me."

"How many is that? Two, three?" I taunt.

"You have no idea. But you will. Very soon you will understand everything. As for the rest of you, you're free to go; just leave Dawn."

"You're outnumbered," Michael says, his face deadly serious, and made even more so by the thick crimson running down his cheek and collecting onto his shirt like wet paint.

"Me? Outnumbered?"

"Michael's right," Ian says. "Two hunters and two Old Family vampires, you won't stand a chance."

Sin walks over to the window and presses his hands against it, the metal claw making a sharp tapping sound.

"It's a beautiful city, isn't it?" he says. "At least, the people are beautiful."

"You talk too much, Sin," I say.

"Isn't it strange," he asks, ignoring me, "that all the people are so young and healthy and gorgeous? That they don't seem to ever sleep? That they're happy? How can that be?"

"That's only the Inner Ring," I say. "Most of the population live in constant starvation."

"Yes, the poor Outer Ring. The ugly ones. The . . . unchosen."

"It isn't their fault that they're out there."

"Oh, but it is. Because it isn't just a wall that divides them. The real difference runs through their veins. It's in the blood."

He taps on the glass some more, as if satisfied that he's made his bizarre point.

"Look outside," he says, "and I think you'll find that it isn't I who is outnumbered. It is you."

He walks over to the desk, that disturbing calm

following in his wake, as I rush to the window to trade places with him.

The entire Inner Ring, every person I can see, as far off as the farthest building, is looking up . . . at me. It's like they're a single organism, a single mind. A thousand, at least, gazing up, unblinking. My skin wants to crawl off as their hungry eyes devour me.

But it isn't their eyes that concern me. It's their fangs.

All of them have fangs.

"No," I say without wanting to, a pathetic little whimper, a plea for this to not be happening.

The others join me and stare at our nightmare come alive: The city is made of vampires.

"Day Walkers," Sin says. "Each one chosen by me, each one turned by me. A small army at my fingertips."

Impossible. But then it dawns on me.

"The Outer Ring is where they get their blood," I say. "Those walls aren't meant to keep vampires out; they're meant to keep humans in."

Sin smiles. "It's the future, and you're looking at it. At least, part of it. Human colonies, just waiting to be feasted on."

"How?" Richard asks. "This must've taken—"

"Twenty years," Sin says, anger in his voice. "Twenty long and patient years. This city surrendered early, and I started almost immediately when the walls went up. I saw within it an opportunity to share my gift. The young and beautiful, I promised they could be that way forever. And best of all, they could walk in the sun. Who would turn that down? Immortality, strength, beauty, health. Things that the New World Order would never allow humans. The VampHu might as well have said, 'Humans will forever be miserable cretins!' It might as well be the law! So I promised them a life worth living. A few resisted the offer, and they were quickly dealt with for fear of them spreading the news. But each of the Day Walkers out there is loyal to me. They aren't like the Lessers once controlled by your pathetic father, Richard, who he starved and allowed to run rampant. They aren't like Valentine's Lessers, who are controlled only through fear. They love me because to them, I am God!"

He turns toward Matheson, who pulls his lips back to reveal a pair of fangs.

"Good boy," Sin says, slapping him playfully on the cheek.

"You're insane!" I shout.

"Now you must see my proposal in a new light," Sin says, leaning on the corner of the desk. "Give me Dawn, and the rest of you will leave tonight. Resist, and not only will I still get Dawn, you will be killed."

"What are you going to do with her?" Faith asks, a strong sense of protection running through her voice.

"It doesn't matter!" Michael shouts, the blood still dripping from his deep lacerations. "She isn't going with him."

"Quiet down, child," Sin says. "The adults are talking."

"Fuck you!"

"Maybe I'll scar the other side of your face. Give you some symmetry."

"Try it!" Michael pulls out another stake.

"I'll go!" I shout. Everyone turns toward me and Sin's smile makes me want to vomit.

"You always were the smart one," he says.

"Just let them leave."

"Of course."

"We can't trust him, Dawn," Tegan says. I know she has a special hatred reserved for him.

"You're welcome to stay, too," Sin says, looking at her. "We can pick up where we left off. Then again, I already got what I wanted out of you."

I think Tegan might just rush in with her fingernails in place of a stake, but I touch her elbow to calm her down.

I feel the weight of Ian's hand on my shoulders as he leans in.

"We can get out of this," he whispers.

"Protect the rest of them," I say.

"No. I'm here to protect you."

He looks over at Richard and nods. The Old Family vampire nods back, and before I can do anything, everyone, except for Tegan and me, attacks Sin.

Chapter 29

They catch Sin by surprise, and he has to scramble to dodge the incoming blows. He's so fast, though, that a single strike could easily kill Michael, and I watch it all with terror beating an unsteady thread in my pulse.

Sin is pushed back nearly to the wall when he makes a charge, clearing a path through his attackers. His massive gauntlet cleaves the air, barely missing limbs and necks.

He turns around just in time to see Richard running at him.

The Old Family vampires collide—quickly and violently. Richard uses all of his force to take Sin through the window. The glass explodes into the room, and the pair hurtle together through the night air. Wind rushes through the opening, swirling the tiny glass shards like snowflakes.

Matheson's scream is cut short as Faith stakes him. He

falls into a heap at her feet. "You go with the rest of them!" she shouts at me, and then turns toward Ian. "Meet us in the alleyway."

Ian nods, and Faith jumps out the window, a pure creature of the night, to join her friend at the bottom. I don't even look over, knowing that time is precious, and that they've bought us our only chance to escape this place.

We take the elevator down, which gives us a few seconds to catch our breaths.

"I would've gone," I say. "This isn't worth the risk."

"Yes, it is," Michael says. "We didn't come all the way out here to lose you now."

"I'm not worth all your lives. I'm not that important."

"How can you say that?"

But before I can respond, the doors open. Only we're not on the lobby level. Guards there may have tried to stop us, so we've taken a different route. We rush down a dim hallway to the stairwell. Three flights later, Ian kicks open a red emergency exit door and we scramble into the alleyway behind the Agency.

We don't have to wait long. An Agency car comes barreling down the tight corridor, Faith at the wheel. I can only assume she overpowered the driver and confiscated it.

She stops the car right in front of us. "Let's go!"

We pile in and she drives off, the back tires spinning and squealing. At the end of the alleyway, she stops again. Richard stumbles and limps over to the passenger-side door and opens it. Blood is soaked into his shirt.

He climbs inside. "We have to get to the Night Train,"

he says through shortened breaths. "Sin is still after us; I couldn't finish him off. Not with the entire city coming in on me."

"You did great," Faith says, leaning across the seat and kissing him passionately on the lips, her foot slamming into the gas pedal, one hand on the wheel.

"Is the conductor even on the train?" I ask.

"No," Ian says. "I can drive it, but I'll need all of your help."

"What about the passengers?" I ask.

"If they're in the city," he says, "they're already gone."

He's right; I just hate to think it's true. They bought a one-way ticket to a dream future, and just ended up in the wrong city at the worst possible time. It's a cruel fate, one far beyond our control.

As Faith swerves through the city streets, the Day Walkers begin to come out of the alleyways and buildings; they drop from rooftops and land inches away from our speeding vehicle.

A few try to latch on, but Faith is too good at the wheel, and she's able to knock them off with rough swerves.

The large train station looms before us, and I remember Matheson's comment that the Night Train had already been turned around and was waiting for departure.

Faith brings the car as close as possible to the steps. It's still running as we all climb out and make a dash down the stairs. The city is alive right behind us, all its citizens moving and acting as a single hunter. I glance back briefly and see a tidal wave of vampires mimicking the ocean this morning. Their noise is rhythmic and daunting, powerful forces rolling within their ranks.

Inside the station, the massive steeled train awaits us.

Ian quickly gives us our orders: Richard has to decouple the front engine so that we can move faster; Tegan will shovel coal into the furnace to give us speed; Michael and Faith will guard the front and buy us as much time as possible.

"And I'll drive," Ian says.

"What about me?" I ask.

"You get inside."

I want so badly to help, but now isn't the time to protest, not when seconds can mean the difference between life and death.

We execute our responsibilities and move like clockwork—a clock that ticks loudly and keeps bad time, but clockwork nonetheless. Faith and Michael draw their stakes and stand guard, their knuckles turning white in preparation for the onslaught of Day Walkers that will be upon us any moment. Richard opens the coupling latch and grits his teeth as he withdraws the heavy steel pin holding the cars together, his vampire strength doing a job that would require three men.

I jump into the engine compartment, which is divided into two halves: the front with the levers that control speed, where Ian sits; and the back, which contains the furnace, the engine itself that moves the black behemoth. Near the furnace is a large stockpile of coal, which Tegan is loading into the flames by shovel. I want to help, but there isn't enough room for more than one person to stand in that clustered hovel.

It's going to be very cramped in the compartment. My shoulders graze the edges of the tight space.

I hear the screams of vampires. Faith and Michael are fighting desperately just to stay alive. They're losing ground, having to push the Day Walkers back rather than strike fatal blows. All we need is time.

"Dammit!" Ian yells.

I leap the few feet to the front of the train. "What is it?"

"The gate's down."

He points to the large metal shutter at the front of the train station.

"How do we open it?" I ask.

"Up the stairs, in the control room," he says, heading for the exit.

But I shove past him and jump from the engine. Looking up, I run for the set of thin industrial stairs leading to a small room with windows. Ian has to drive this train.

He shouts for me to stop, but I'm far away when he realizes what I'm doing, and the fighting coming into the station is deafening. The weight of the city is squeezing into this place!

Taking two steps at a time, I climb the stairs. At the top, I swing open the door. Inside the small room, a dozen controls greet me. Stealing a glance out the window, I can see the entire scene playing out from a new vantage point. I watch Michael and Faith getting pushed back ever farther. No sign of Ian, so he must be back inside the engine, making his final preparations. Black plumes are rising from the steel Goliath. Richard, done with the decoupling, has joined the fight, but even he can't make a difference. The sea of vampires coming in is unstoppable.

I run my fingers along the controls and easily find the lever labeled "Front Gate." I pull it back and watch the front shutter slowly ascend. I then see a giant red button: "Outer/Inner Walls." It must be for the gates separating the Inner from the Outer Ring, and the Outer Ring from the outside world. An emergency switch in case they have to be opened from here.

I slam my hand down on it. Hoping it's enough to get us out of here.

When I reach the bottom of the stairs, I look up to see the vampires pressing in. Now the gap between them and the train is but a few feet. And as I run, it begins to grow smaller. I can see Faith jumping into the engine, followed soon by Richard. The train is moving, and I have to pump my legs just to gain any ground at all. As I near the engine, Michael leaps on, and holding on to a handle, leans forward, his hand out, reaching for mine.

The gate is up. They can't slow down. It's like a dream where no matter how fast I run, I can never catch it.

My fingers stretch out and just graze Michael's.

"Come on!" he shouts.

All I have in me is one final push, one final leap, one chance to risk it all.

I jump forward, grasping desperately for Michael's hand.

All I grab is air, and I fall to the ground, a distance that seems infinite.

I hear Michael's scream. "No!"

I look up as the vampires surround me, and want to tell Michael to stay with the others. They're so close to getting out of here alive.

But I don't get a chance. Michael hurls himself off the train. The vampires crowding around me turn to see Michael rushing at them. He dispatches all of those in his way, making a last, useless dive for me. There are too many of them. Far too many. And soon, just as I begin to get to my feet, I'm kicked hard in the stomach. Falling down, I see Michael join me. The look on his face says, "I'm sorry."

And the Night Train clatters away.

Chapter 30

The vampires don't kill us. They don't even strike. A few particularly bold vamps disarm Michael and throw his stakes onto the other side of the track, well beyond reach. Then they wait. They stand like exhausted statues breathing the air, which is fouled in the wake of the Night Train's burning coal.

"What are they doing?" Michael asks, the blood from his scored cheek giving him a menacing look.

"They're waiting for Sin."

Soon the vampires begin to part.

"You should've taken my deal, Dawn," Sin says, emerging from the crowd. "Michael would have been saved."

"It was worth it," Michael says, "just for the chance to kill you."

"We'll see if it's still worth it, when I'm done with you."

Sin snaps his fingers. We're quickly bound with rope and shoved into the back of a waiting stretch limousine. Sin climbs in and sits across from us.

"Enjoy the luxury while it lasts," he says. "It will be a very long night."

We straighten ourselves up and try to get comfortable in the seats, but with our hands tied it's impossible.

Michael grits his teeth and fights the ropes, his entire body twisting, trying to find a way out of the binding.

"It must be difficult to do that with so much blood in your eye," Sin says.

He leans out of his seat and comes toward Michael, a strange hunger in his eyes.

"Let me help you," he says, his voice soft as his claws grab Michael's chin and force his head to the side. He leans in and in one lap, runs his tongue across Michael's cheek, licking off the blood. "You're better tasting than I thought."

He shoves Michael back against the seat before returning to his own place. Hatred burns in Michael's eyes.

We arrive at the Agency. The door opens and a vampire pulls us out of the car. Sin follows. We stand dumbly, awaiting instruction because there's no point in resisting right now. I have to think, but until I know his ultimate plan, I'm lost.

The entire city of vampires closes in around us. They look normal now, just like they have for the entire time I was here. Walking their streets, all they wanted was my blood, yet they held in their fangs.

Sin jumps on top of the limo and spreads his arms wide.

"You've done well tonight," he says, speaking to the crowd, who offer no applause, just obedient silence. "Enjoy the rest of the evening as you see fit. As the world turns, vampires fear the day, and humans fear the night. But we Day Walkers fear nothing. And soon, they will *all* fear us."

A roar of triumph goes up before they disperse. We're ushered into the building. Stopping at the elevator, Sin takes our arms and pushes us in. The vampires who brought us stay rooted to their spots, and the door closes on just the three of us.

Sin pulls out a key, places it in the elevator pad, and hits a red button labeled V.

"I hope you aren't tired," he says, speaking to our reflections. "You're about to see the Perfect World; I'd hate for you to miss it."

I expect Michael to say something, maybe break his bonds somehow and fight Sin here and now. But he just looks down at the floor. He's giving the appearance of surrendering, but I know him well enough: he's taking stock of our situation. We're only going to have one chance to gain our freedom. We both know it. We just have to figure out when to take it.

"So you knew we were here all along," I say.

"Of course I did. Did you like your little trip to the beach? That was my idea. I needed a little more time to arrange things."

When the door opens at the very bottom, Sin walks ahead and we follow him down the long, white corridor. A single door at the end requires a key card, which Sin produces. He warns us, "Try anything, and I'll make you watch as I kill the other."

He turns us around and slashes the rope binding our hands. I bring my arms forward, rubbing my wrists, relieved that the tension is no longer there.

Sin slides the key card, the door opens, and the Perfect World nearly drops me to my knees.

Chapter 31

The room is gigantic. As wide and long as the building itself, it must be several stories high, the ceiling just barely within view. Filling the room are hundreds of glass chambers, small prison cells. A door leads into each one, and inside, nothing but a single chair.

"Do you like it?" he asks, pacing himself slowly like a tour guide, his arms up as if presenting the greatest work of art ever bestowed upon man.

"What is it?" Michael asks.

But I know. Clive mentioned it, and now I know what I was seeing in Victor's nightmare.

"The V-Process," I say. "This was built during the war."

"That's right," Sin says. "This is where humans were reborn into Lessers. Of course, it was never used for that purpose. As part of the surrender terms that Los Angeles made, it had to construct one of these. It was unauthorized, Lord Carrollton's secret. Somehow, it made him believe he had some kind of control over the city. To him, having the constant threat of turning people was just as good as actually doing it. He was a fool. Soon the city built walls around itself, and this place sat idle."

"Until you arrived," I say. "That's how you've been turning people so quickly."

"Right again."

He leads us through the maze of cellblocks, each one consisting of twenty or so, forming little streets that divide the space and give it some sense of organization. At the center lies a gigantic silver disk the size of a car. Sin operates a control panel on it and the disk rises, revealing stores of blood within its chilled chamber.

"Gallons and gallons of me," he says. "Original. Old Family. Day Walker. The most valuable blood in the world. I take candidates, strap them each to a chair, hook them up with an IV of this. Then stop their heart with a simple, massive electric shock. The final step: releasing *me* into their bloodstream. And when they open their eyes, not only are they Lessers, they're Day Walkers."

Horror slams into me, and I realize that he's still growing his army. It's the reason Jake and the others from Dallas were brought here. Not to give blood as they thought, but to become monsters like Sin. I wonder if they've already been turned.

"You have your army now," I say. "So what? It won't be enough. You have a few hundred? Maybe a thousand?

When the Night Train reaches Denver and the story is told, this city will be doomed. The humans can't do anything but wait inside their own walls, but what about the other Old Families? Did you ever think about that, Sin? Fourteen Old Families who don't like the idea of Day Walkers running the show."

"You don't think I know that!" he snarls. "I was cast out by my own father because I was a *freak*! And every other Old Family sees me that way. But they'll all beg for forgiveness when I'm done. Not that I'll give it to them."

"You can't possibly take them all on," I say.

"You aren't thinking big-picture, Dawn. This is just the first step. Come see the second."

He leads us down another row of cells and as we head toward the end, the sound of screaming begins. Low at first, so low it could be mistaken for some kind of auditory phantom, but it grows and grows until I want to cover my ears.

Sin stops and turns to look into one of the cells. Inside, strapped to a chair, a vampire with an IV in his arm is being fed blood.

"Vampire blood," Sin says. "I don't want just Day Walkers."

"You want Thirst-infected Day Walkers," I say, losing my voice at the conclusion.

"Now you see the grand scheme. You met one in the laboratory. His reaction to ingesting Old Family blood was interesting, wasn't it, Simon?"

Simon steps out of the shadows. His arm isn't in a cast

and when he smiles at me, I realize why. He's a vampire. He's already healed. Like everyone else, he was playing a part.

"I believe you've met my lead scientist. He's been researching all the intricate possibilities of the Thirst."

"It's so unpredictable," Simon says.

"And I need it to be predictable," Sin says. "I need to always be able to control it, just as I controlled the one who was closest to your heart."

"Brady," I say, tears fighting to surface. The vampire in the cell—his eyes blackened, his jaw extended, his teeth razor sharp and lined like fence posts—he's twitching uncontrollably, just like Brady did. And he moves from laughter to screams of rage as easily as a coin moves from heads to tails.

"Brady gave me the idea, in fact. I gave him the power of the Day Walker, and he transformed himself into a monster by taking vampire blood and sparing humans. I was angry at first, but then I saw how he stalked the countryside, and how quickly and mercilessly he killed vampires. I owe all of this to him really. And this," Sin says, pointing at the monster, "is the future. The final step in vampire evolution. Stronger than Lessers, nearly as strong as Old Family. And they can walk in the sun. Can you think of anything on this earth more powerful?"

"Yeah. I can," I say, turning to him and smiling. "Victor."

His raw strength might not be quite what Sin's is, but he is rational and calculating. He's not as volatile as Sin. He'd never reveal his frustration or anger by yelling. He'd never lose control, but Sin appears to be on the verge of doing just that.

Sin slowly nods, licks his fangs, and stares across the vast space of this chamber. And then backhands me.

Michael grabs me. I don't fall. I just glare right back at Sin.

"I'll cut your face next time," he says, holding up the other hand, claws dancing. "It's true. Victor is a nuisance. That's why I was in Denver in the first place. I got the summons from my father to help create chaos within the city. I didn't really care about that; I didn't even really care about the throne. All I wanted was Victor dead."

"You're afraid of him, aren't you?" I ask.

"Of Victor? He's an irritant, nothing more. He has this annoying habit of fighting to the end, no matter the odds. As long as he thinks he's on the side of good, he'll give his life if need be. I wanted him out of the picture before I started my ultimate masterpiece. Unfortunately, he's a little stubborn in his refusal to die. So I'll have to begin even while his heart still beats. Of course, if your brother gave me the inspiration for this, Victor certainly played his own part."

"How could he ever help you with such an insane plan?"

Sin turns toward me and smiles. The room presses in around me, and I feel the earth turning beneath my feet.

"You recognized this place," Sin says. "You said the

V-Process. I assume you think that stands for, what? Vampire Process?"

"What else would it be?"

He grins with relish. "Victor Process."

Chapter 32

It takes every ounce of strength I have to remain standing as my world threatens to crumble.

"Look around, Dawn!" Sin yells. "This is Victor's legacy."

Sin explains it was Victor's idea, the unprecedented notion of using facilities to turn humans en masse into Lessers. Victor designed the entire process: how much blood was required to turn a human successfully, how much electricity was needed to stop the heart, how soon to feed them their first blood afterward.

"No," I say. "That's impossible." But I remember how guilty Victor looked when Clive mentioned the process, how Clive had to explain it. I remember Victor jumping in to say the shock was meant to prevent suffering. Again, the guilt. "Victor said he was in charge of destroying all the V-Processing centers."

"He was. And who better than the one who created them, the one who knew where they all were, the one who knew *how* to dismantle them perfectly because they were based on *his* designs!"

"You're lying."

"It's the truth. Victor said it was the humane thing to do. After all, the Old Families just wanted to burn entire cities with the humans inside. Victor convinced the council that the humans could be turned, and in great quantities efficiently."

"Then he saved their lives," I say. "If they were going to be killed anyway."

"Are you hearing what you're saying?" Sin asks, stepping toward me. "Are you hearing this, Michael? He saved them? He damned them! He gave them lives as monsters, feasting on the humans they once called friends. That's what he did!"

I fall to the floor, images of Victor running through my head. But he's no longer holding me closely. He's the one constructing this place. He's the one making the monsters who rule the night. I feel my heart turning to stone and dropping through my chest, breaking on the floor, crumbling into dust, and being scattered across the earth.

Michael kneels next to me and puts his hand on my back.

I remember being trapped in Victor's nightmare. Now I understand, because it's become mine.

"Yes, yes," Sin says. "You two are very sweet. But I'm afraid we must be going."

I fight back the tears and stand up. I'm not going to cry

or think about the things I can't change, the things I never knew about Victor. Whatever Sin wants, I have to figure out a way to stop him from getting it.

"Where are we going?" I ask.

"Haven't you ever wondered why I chose Brady?" Sin asks.

"Every night."

"Good. Because you're about to find out. We're taking a carriage ride, something you're used to."

The carriage is led by six mighty horses, which gallop through the center of the city on the train tracks. We had to go through the Outer Ring, but moved so quickly that it was just a blur, the thunderous hooves blocking out the night screams.

Michael is beside me, Sin sitting across from us.

"Do you see those mountains in the distance?" Sin asks, his manner too friendly, like it was a month ago, in Denver. Before we knew what a devil he truly is.

"Yeah," I say.

"That's where we're heading."

"Is that where you plan on killing us?" Michael asks.

Sin just shrugs. "If I have to. I'm not picky on where I kill you. But there are things within that mountain that Dawn must see. You're simply along for the ride, Michael. In fact, you should consider yourself privileged. You will learn things that few know. Things that have evaded the pen of history for a very, very long time."

Sin pulls out a small attaché case and unbuckles it.

From within the metal box, he withdraws a syringe filled to the brim with blood. He injects it into his vein and presses down the plunger. The blood swirls away, driving deeper into him. He grits his teeth as if it were unpleasant. Taking a deep breath, he relaxes for several moments before putting it all away.

"Get some sleep," he says. "You're safe in here."

But you're not. Not if I can control my dreams. If I can reach Victor, I can warn him. I close my eyes. The motion of the carriage is so soothing, very different from the one I'm used to riding in. It's like being rocked. I drift off to sleep.

I wake up to the sound of the ocean. It's night, but there's so much blue light, as if the moon is closer than it's ever been. I'm sitting on the grass, hands wrapped around my tucked legs. The ocean is so beautiful.

Someone approaches from behind and sits next to me.

"I'm in danger, Victor," I say.

"I know. I can sense it within you. You've come back to this place because it calms you, but it isn't enough."

I listen to the waves, wanting desperately to relax . . . but it's impossible.

"Sin has Michael and me. I don't know where we're heading—somewhere in the mountains."

"I might know. And I'm already on my way. I'll save you, Dawn."

"You have to save Denver. Warn Clive—"

"We'll have time for all that."

I want to ask him about the V-Process, about everything Sin accused him of. But I'm afraid the accusation will shatter this dream, tear it apart, and leave me with nothing.

"I'm so tired," I say. "I'm tired of fighting. I'm tired of everything. I just want this to be over."

"I know." He places his arm around my shoulder. "But I'm afraid it's only just begun."

It takes us two nights to reach the mountains. They always seemed so close before that at times I thought they were running away from us. Eventually, though, we catch up.

The night is fresh, the air cool. Sin opens up a small compartment in the back of the carriage and produces two jackets, giving one to each of us.

"Your world is about to change, Dawn. Some of your questions will be answered, but many more will appear. Know this, however: I am not your enemy."

"You are. And always will be."

Sin looks genuinely disappointed, but begins walking up the mountain. We follow close behind. If Michael is planning a surprise attack out here, now that we're so far from the city, I'm not in on it. I look over at him. He gives me a small shake of his head. *Not now.*

The path is gravelly and I find myself slipping, though Michael is often there to help me. On one occasion, even Sin offers his hand. I don't take it.

We seem to be climbing up for miles, but when I look back, the carriage and its driver are easily seen. Sin's prediction that my world is about to change was ominous. And this place is the perfect setting for that. All the vegetation is gone, and nothing but stone and rock lie strewn about.

Eventually we reach an area that cuts directly through the mountain, and we're surrounded on both sides by walls of stone that reach into the sky. The passage narrows until we have to move sideways and I have the unreasonable fear that the mountain will suddenly move a fraction of an inch, and that'll be enough to trap me within it forever.

I look around the ground for any signs of litter or human foot traffic, but there's nothing. The place is oddly abandoned, like even Mother Nature is frightened to walk here. The passage eventually splits and then splits again, looping in on itself before taking a new direction. It's a maze, one that a man could find himself lost in for his entire life.

And I have a terrible feeling that I've traveled it before—in my dreams.

At the final juncture, a large rock, taller than any of us, seems out of place. Sin, with his metal gauntlet, stabs the rock and the claws sink in, sending tiny shrapnel onto the ground. I can see another set of four holes that matches exactly the ones he just delivered. He's been here at least once before.

With strength that only an Old Family vampire possesses, he slides the rock back, the bottom of the stone grinding against the rocky floor. A dark cutout in the mountainside greets us. Without a word, Sin walks through and quickly disappears. We could run, but how far would we get before he caught us? Sin didn't come this far just to let us slip away. He has it all planned. He's always had it planned.

So Michael and I go forward. We can hear Sin's footsteps just ahead, and my hands glide along the walls next to me, feeling the slippery, moss-covered rock. It seems to take forever, but finally the labyrinth opens up into a gigantic cavern, the only light coming from a tiny hole in the top letting in shades of moonlight. By some strange alignment of nature, the light plays off of the shining, rocky surfaces, bathing everything in a bluish hue, just enough for our eyes to adjust so we can see the entire domed room.

Sin is off to one side, standing very still, waiting for us to enter. Michael is holding my hand, not in a romantic way, but in a be-ready-to-run-when-I-give-the-signal way.

In the middle of the cavern is a throne carved of stone. And sitting in it, a vampire so ancient that even time itself must fear him.

"This is what I brought you to see," Sin says, holding his arm out, presenting the vampire.

I question whether he's alive, or if he's even flesh and bone, until the thing breathes ever so slowly. His body is large, like that of Valentine's, but his features are carved deep within his skin, making him appear to be composed of clay. His hair is white and lays loosely across his shoulders; his clean face allows the sunken cheekbones and sagging skin to show themselves. His eyes were maybe blue once, but are covered with a thin, milky white. Still, he can see me; I have no doubt about that.

"It . . . is . . . you," he says, his voice as old as the stones surrounding him. "Dawn Montgomery. You have found me, at last."

His words send chills up my spine.

"He's been waiting a long time to see you," Sin says. "In fact, you could say he's been waiting for two thousand years."

"Why me? Who are you? What's going on?"

"Patience," Sin says. "All will be explained."

"Many secrets lie within you, Dawn," the vampire says. "Secrets that could destroy. But I think that on some level, you always knew that. You always knew you were different. The call of the vampire has always been difficult to ignore, hasn't it?"

"I've never wanted to be turned, if that's what you mean. And I won't change that tonight!"

"But you're already turning," the vampire says. "Or should I say, you are *awakening*."

I grab my neck, not for fear of it being bitten, but out of fear that this has something to do with Victor and his bite, with Victor and our dreams. "What are you talking about?"

"Don't deny it," Sin says. "A change is taking place in your blood. Ever since Victor bit you."

"No," I say. "You're insane—he never turned me."

"He didn't need to," the ancient one says. "Because you've always been a vampire."

Chapter 33

Michael stiffens beside me, his fingers automatically tightening on mine. "No way," he mutters. "They're just playing mind games with you, Dawn."

"Yeah. I know." That's got to be it. Although I think the more logical explanation is that they've gone mad. Centuries of isolation have driven this thing to the breaking point, and Sin is just as demented.

"I can hear it in your blood," the vampire says, holding up his hand and closing his eyes, treating the sound of my beating heart like waves he can connect with on some ethereal plane. "Your veins are singing the song of Montgomery. They are singing the song of vampire."

"Montgomery?"

"That's right, Dawn," Sin says. "There were not fourteen original Old Families. There were fifteen."

"The lost family? You're saying it's real?"

"I'm doing more than saying. I'm showing you its existence. And you, my dear, precious, sweet, innocent Dawn, are its legacy."

I'm not sure if I jerk free of Michael's hold or if he jerks free of mine, but suddenly I'm standing alone, disbelief, anger, and confusion simmering through me. "That can't be."

"My blood is yours," the Old Family vampire says. "I am Octavian Montgomery. The last full-blooded vampire of the Montgomery clan."

"I'm not a vampire!" I shout.

"You are. Just as your father was, and his father, and his father. Not fully. That was what made us unique, the Montgomerys. We could produce children with humans."

"That's not possible," I say. "It can't be done."

"That is why they feared us!" the vampire cries, anger in his voice coming up from the past. "They knew how powerful we would become. Half vampire, half human. A dhampir, as we called them. They had the strengths of each, but without the flaws. They could walk in the sun, and relished blood, but did not require it. They weren't as strong as the Old Family from which they came, but they were strong enough."

"You're insane. If that were true, where are they now?"

"Dead. Killed. The other Fourteen Families were afraid, and none more than Alistair Valentine. He said we were an abomination, diluting the pure blood of vampires to create half breeds and monstrosities."

I remember my father writing of a plague. I thought he was referring to the Thirst. But what if he was referring to the Montgomerys and the vampires' desires to keep blood-lines pure?

"Long ago, I told Alistair that this new breed was the next step, that vampires and humans no longer had to live separate lives, that we could become one. But he wouldn't listen and he turned the others against me. They wrote a death warrant for the Montgomery family, signed by all of them. It was a promise not to rest until we were all destroyed."

The document my dad found. Could it be? The symbol. I drop to my knees, find a section of sand and dirt, and begin frantically drawing.

"Dawn—" Michael says cautiously.

"Just give me a minute." When I'm finished I shove myself to my feet, point at it, and challenge the old vampire. "What does that say?"

"Why, child, it says Montgomery."

My heart batters against my ribs; my knees weaken. He could still be lying, but why would he?

"But they didn't kill all the Montgomerys—is that what you're telling me?"

"All of my family was killed. Every full-blooded vampire, every dhampir was hunted down and slaughtered. Until it was just me. So I ran. I ran so far away that they never found me. And eventually, I learned to control my blood urges, and began portraying myself as a human. Soon, I took a human wife and we had a child. A dhampir.

He never learned what he was, or about the legacy that he had inherited. But he went on to have a child of his own, the Montgomery blood, the vampire blood, further diluted. And then he had a child, and then so on and so on, until your father was born."

"Daddy was a . . ."

"A dhampir. Didn't he ever tell you what *his* father did for a living?"

"He said he was a historian. He studied mythology and folklore . . . vampire folklore."

"Yes, this was before we were made known to the world. His father, your grandfather, was also drawn to the night, to the world of vampires, even without knowing what he truly was. His father was the same, and his father before him. It's all in the blood, Dawn. It's always been in the blood. And now that you've been bitten and blood-kissed, it has been reawakened."

I slap my hand to my neck. "How do you know about the blood kiss?"

He smiles wickedly. "Because you bear no scars."

I shake my head frantically. "No, I'm human. I'm not some dhampir, half-vampire freak!"

"You can't escape it," Octavian says, his voice stronger than ever, as if this is his last statement on earth and he demands it be heard. "Your destiny is as unchangeable as the stars above you. The blood within you is diluted, but has infinite potential. Nearly two thousand years of vampirism lay dormant, waiting to be awakened."

"In me?" I ask. "Then it must've been in Brady, too."

"Yes," Sin says. "That was why I turned him. He could have claimed his place as the head of the Montgomery clan, but he was too stubborn, too shortsighted to fully comprehend what could be. Rather than embracing his destiny as a Montgomery vampire, he chose to succumb to the Thirst. Such a waste."

"Did my father know?" I ask. "About the Montgomery heritage."

"He always suspected," Sin says. "He once stumbled upon an ancient tablet in which the names of the original vampire families were carved in Latin. Imagine his shock when he read fifteen names instead of fourteen. And imagine what he felt when he read that Montgomery was among them."

"It's a coincidence," I say. "Nothing more. It's a common enough name."

"Not long ago," Octavian says, "maybe even you could have believed that. But not anymore. Not now that the blood within you has been stirred."

"Victor caused that," Sin says. "When he bit you, the vampire blood was reawakened. And now it's coming to the surface."

"My neck," I say automatically. "It throbs when he's near. He—" I can't say it, not to them, but I remember how Victor found my blood so tempting.

"It's calling," Sin says. "It *wants* to be turned. It *needs* to be transformed. You have to embrace your destiny as the new head of the Montgomery family."

I look down at my hands, trying to see the blood running

through the blue veins. Could it be possible? I never understood why people wanted to turn. I never wanted to be a
monster.

Sin steps closer to Octavian, who seems so tired now.
That secret—he must've been waiting millennia to say it.
Now that it's been said, has he expired? Is he prepared for
the end?

"You can start all over again, Dawn," Sin says, before
looking up at me with compassion. "*We* can start all over."

"We?"

"Three Montgomerys remain," Sin says. "You. Octavian.
And me."

"What? No. No, you're a Valentine. Your father was—"

"Yes," Sin cuts me off. "Murdoch Valentine. But my
mother . . . my *mother* was Esmerelda Montgomery."

The missing link. *Proof*, my father had written. Proof
that there was another branch of Old Family vampires.
Faith told me her name when we were on the train.

Esmerelda.

"She seduced him. He didn't realize she was one of the
last Montgomerys. She thought he would side with her
against the other Old Families if he fell in love with her,
but when I was born, he couldn't see beyond his tainted
bloodline. It was forbidden to mate with a Montgomery. He
knew if the council found out that he would be executed.
He murdered her, but he couldn't bring himself to kill me.
Even so, he never forgave me for what I was. He kept me
confined in the darkest rooms of a distant manor, never
to taste the sun again. Until I grew strong, and began to

frighten him. He banished me, and I wandered the earth, tracking down all the Montgomerys, only to learn that all had been killed. Except for Octavian here, who I would not discover for some time. And one other: Esmerelda's brother—Jonathan. He was just a boy; I followed him until he became a man, and then a father. I followed the Montgomery bloodline until it arrived in you. Don't you see, Dawn. We're family."

I think of my father, and the secrets he knew. But he never could have guessed how deep those secrets went, where the bloodlines would end up, reaching far back until they converged into Sin.

"I had a family," I say. "But they died."

"I know," Sin says. "And I'm sorry for that. But everything has a purpose, Dawn. Look at how strong you've become since their deaths. You never would have been prepared to face your destiny as the head of the Montgomery family; not while their hearts still beat."

"Did you kill them?" I ask, the words barely escaping my clenched jaw.

Sin looks me in the eyes, doesn't say a word, and moves to the other side of Octavian. His silence tells me everything. And I imagine him gazing into my parents' eyes, my father's eyes . . . my father, who was related to Sin by blood. And this monster still killed them. How? How could he do such a thing?

"You see now the full scope of my plans, Dawn," Sin says. "With my army of Day Walkers, combined with the Thirst, I will be unstoppable. Cities will bow down or crumble. The Old Families will step aside and recognize their new god, or be destroyed. That will happen and nothing can be done to stop it. Surely you can embrace my vision—it's what you've always wanted. A way to fight vampires without preying on humans or losing the ability to walk in the sun. We'll be better . . . humans."

I can only stare at his madness. I thought it was the sun that made us different from vampires. But as wonderful as the day at the beach was, it isn't the ability to feel the sun that makes me human. It's something that goes so much deeper. It resonates in my core. I'm human because everything about Sin repels me. His desire to destroy an entire race of creatures—vampires who can walk only in the night—is too horrible to contemplate. There has to be a way that we can all live together: vampires, Day Walkers, humans. Not one of us is better than the other.

"I will be king," he says, "and I will need you by my side. Queen to the masses. You must become the head of the Montgomery family. It is your fate."

"You're insane!" I say.

"Hear me out, Dawn. Within you swirls thousands of years of Montgomery blood waiting to ignite. You will be powerful, more powerful than you could ever imagine. You can take care of your friends and those you love. I can't do this alone. I can't restore our family without you. Even you, Michael, can join us. I will need a strong, powerful Day Walker to lead my armies and I will give that to you. All I ask is your loyalty, and you can have the world."

"I don't see much appealing in this world that you're

designing," Michael says. "I'm not interested."

"You're a fool," Sin says, renewed anger in his voice. "What of you, Dawn? Will you embrace the gift I offer?"

"Why are you even pretending that I have a choice?" I ask. "If you want to turn me, you'll do it."

"No," he says, shaking his head. "You have a choice."

"Why? You didn't give Brady a choice!"

Sin clenches his fists, fury in his eyes. But it isn't directed at me; it's pointing toward himself.

"I know," he mumbles through gritted teeth. "I didn't give your brother a chance to choose, and I've regretted it every day since. I turned him before he fully understood his destiny. It was the worst mistake I ever made. And I'll never do that to you, Dawn." He holds out his hand, ready for me to lay mine on top. "Will you come with me? Will you embrace your legacy as a Montgomery? Will you stand beside me as we rule the world?"

I feel history surging through this mountain. How long did it take to forge and weather these rocks? How long has Octavian waited? Within my blood runs the entire Montgomery family. Millions of years to create this rock. Thousands of years to create me.

And only one second to decide my answer.

"No," I say. "*You're* the fool, Sin. You'll be stopped. You aren't powerful enough to take on the Old Families. As for your creations, you won't be able to control them. You act like you're their god, but when they see how weak you truly are, they'll come after you."

"You're right, I can't control them. Not yet. Not in

this weak, pathetic body. But you've already witnessed the beginning of my transformation. The blood I injected into my veins in the carriage wasn't human blood. It was vampire blood. I will become infected. I've been ingesting for months, waiting for the transformation, and I can feel it within me now, so close. So very, very close. Can you imagine, Dawn? Can you see it? An Old Family vampire who can walk in the sun, with the strength of the Thirst beating in his heart! Nothing can stand in my way! Our family will rise again!"

Brady flashes before me. He was so powerful. What if Sin fulfills his promise? What will he become when his fangs grow and his eyes blacken, and he only craves the blood of other vampires?

"You have one chance, Dawn!" he shouts. "One chance to prove your loyalty to me. Soon I will be strong enough to kill Victor with ease, but you can do it for me. Drive a stake through his heart! The cold heart that created the V-Process, that forged this world you hate. Kill him and take vengeance against the Valentine family for destroying the Montgomerys. Do this, and you may join me and save your friends. If you do not, you will all fall before me."

Sin circles Octavian again. "The Montgomery family will need a new leader." With his hand, he gently strokes the cheek of the old vampire, his sagging skin unable to escape time's relentless aging. "We will need a leader who isn't afraid to fight. We will need a leader who isn't content to hide inside a mountain while his entire clan is slaughtered."

I see Octavian close his eyes, perhaps acknowledging the truth, perhaps acknowledging the inevitable.

"Where were you, my dear Octavian, as your brothers were hunted down and killed? Where were you when your father was staked through the heart? Why did only *you* escape?"

Octavian gives no answer, but merely sits as still as the stone.

"You are a stain upon the Montgomery family," Sin says. "You may have escaped the stake for two thousand years, but you only did so through cowardice. I am ashamed that I share your blood. But then again, your blood can have other purposes. It's the reason that I provided you with sustenance, that I ensured you were strong enough to reach out to Dawn. I needed you, but now I have only one more requirement of you."

Sin's jaw drops and he sinks his teeth deep within the ancient vampire's neck.

"No!" Rushing forward, I grab a rock and throw it.

Not even distracted from his gruesome task, Sin deflects it easily.

I leap—

He jerks around. Crimson rains down his chin. With one arm, he gives a mighty swipe, catching me before I reach him, sending me flying back. Sharp pain batters me as I crash against a mound of large rocks.

I open my eyes to see Michael smashing a stone against Sin's head. Sin twirls around so fast that he's just a blur.

Michael screams, staggers back, and I see rivers of blood

across his chest. Dizzy and disoriented, I crawl over to him.

"Pathetic," Sin chides before turning to the elder Montgomery and once again plunging his fangs into his vulnerable neck. My ancestor, *our* ancestor, screams in pain as Sin drains his blood, Sin's throat working, swallowing it all.

I can feel the vampire's suffering. This Montgomery, the oldest of all, his pain is mine. I can't explain it, but my blood is screaming with his. I double over. My head threatens to explode. I yell, but it doesn't relieve any of it. Every heartbeat pounds my skull, memories of the Montgomery clan running through it.

And then it stops. I look up, and Sin is standing over his victim, who is slumped and motionless.

"It's happening," Sin says. "I can feel the Thirst running through my veins. Not long now. My power will be unmatched. I will be a vampire who the world has never seen before, and I will take my rightful place as the ruler of day and night. Victor will kneel before me. All the Old Families will bow and worship me."

He releases a bloodcurdling scream and leaps onto a high rock. This madman standing before us, bathed in moonlight, seems unstoppable. The pages of history were all written for this one moment.

Laughing maniacally as though he's forgotten all about us, he begins clambering up the side of the cavern and disappears through the hole in the ceiling.

"Let's get the hell out of here," Michael says, struggling to his feet and grabbing my hand.

He's weak, we're both weak, but we start running for our lives, for humanity, for those we love. From a great distance, Sin's laughter continues to echo around us, drowning out our footsteps.

The maze swirls around us; we turn at corners, head down widening corridors. Finally we reach the entrance and burst into the night.

Following the path we traveled before, we use the stars and our memories to guide us. Our feet never quite get traction as we slide and stumble, scrambling over the rough terrain, until we hit level ground. Barely taking the time to catch our breaths, we head into the vast openness that spreads out before us.

Picking up my pace, I think that if I run fast enough, I'll outrun what I am. I'll outrun the monster that I might become. I'll outrun my destiny.

But even as my legs churn and my heart pounds, I remember all the times that I told Victor that he couldn't avoid being the monster he was—that it was in his blood.

Now it seems that it's in mine as well.

And sooner or later, I'm going to have to face it.

Dying to know what happens next?
Read on for a sneak peek of

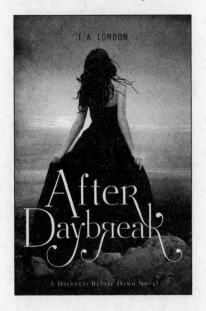

Chapter 1

With my arms wrapped tightly around Michael's waist, we ride out fast, eager to escape the mountains, desperate to escape Sin.

Warm liquid pools against my hands. Michael's blood. His chest is still bleeding, a four-strike wound from Sin's claws as Michael tried to protect me. I press my palms against him, trying to stop the flow. Before Sin clawed Michael's chest, he sliced open his cheek. The blood there has caked over, but the gashes must ache. We debated taking two horses from the coach, but Michael's injuries are weakening him. I wasn't certain how long he'd be able to ride if I wasn't holding him. If he falls, I doubt I'll have the strength to get him back on the horse. No way am I leaving him to the mercy of any vampires who are roaming the countryside.

Exhaustion threatens to claim me. I can't give in to its allure. I can only imagine how difficult it is for Michael to remain upright. We don't speak as the mountains behind us become mere ripples in the sky.

The clouds begin to change, lightening in shade, and then the moon fades. The sun rises, but it brings little comfort. It'll send most of the vampires into hiding, but it won't affect the Day Walkers.

Michael brings the horse to a slow canter, giving it a chance to catch its breath. "We should stop, check your wounds," I say.

Michael shakes his head. "Let's find some sort of shelter first. If I get off the horse, I don't know if I'll be able to get back on. Although . . . maybe you should go on alone, search for help. You'll be faster without me."

"I'm not leaving you."

"Dawn, you might not have a choice."

"I'm not leaving you, Michael." I make my voice as forceful as possible. I don't want to admit that he's right. We're the only ones who know the full scope and horror of Sin's plans. One of us has to return to Denver, to let the others know so they can prepare to meet the new threat.

Time passes. I don't know if it's minutes or hours. The sun beats down on us. It's so incredibly desolate out here. My mouth is dry; my lips feel as though they might crack if I talk again.

We have to find food and water, but where?

The horse slows to a plodding walk. Michael is drooping in the saddle. How much blood has he lost? How much longer can he ride?

Michael directs the horse to a steep hill and, kicking his heels against its sides, urges it up. We arrive at the top of the rise and look out over the vast expanse spreading before us. Thirty years of war decimated it. Ten years later, nature is still struggling to reclaim what it once owned—much as we humans are.

Michael raises a hand to his brow to shield his eyes from the glare of the sun. "In the distance there." He points. "Is that what I think it is?"

It doesn't seem possible, but through the wall of shimmering heat—

"It looks like a town," I say.

The Vampire Human Treaty, or VampHu, outlaws the establishment of any town other than the twenty walled cities agreed to in the settlement that ended the war.

"Maybe it's a mirage," he says, and I can hear in his voice his reluctance to hope.

"I don't think so. I mean, would we both be seeing it if it were?"

"Guess not. I've heard rumors that illegal towns exist beyond the walls, but I never thought to see one."

I hate to be the bearer of bad tidings, but we need to be realistic. Without the walls that surround the major cities to protect them, the humans in that town would be easy prey. "It might be prewar, and the odds are that it's abandoned, but that doesn't mean we won't find water or food there."

"I could use a drink."

He could use a lot more than that. He needs medical attention. Maybe we'll find something that I can use to tend to his wounds.

The horse isn't as sure-footed going down the hill, and I hold my breath, hoping it doesn't stumble. But we make it safely to level ground and the horse trudges forward.

The town, so small it seems threatened by the enormity of the surrounding desert, grows steadily larger. I spot a windmill, hear the clacking of the blades echoing over the plain as the slight breeze turns them. The tiny buildings begin to take shape, their odd placement showing no evidence of planning, their even stranger form indicating a lack of craftsmanship. Walls curve and bend at unusual angles, stone is missing from key foundations, and the road through the town's center is little more than well-packed dirt. The only impressive things are the thick, clay roofs, which seem to be attached to the unstable walls by some miracle of architecture.

As we near, we get a genuine surprise: men, women, and children. They walk along boarded paths, talk to others in front of their homes. People are working: patching walls, gathering water from a well beneath the windmill, sorting a myriad of boxes. I see smiles. I hear the din of laughter and conversation.

We must look pretty sorry when we arrive at the edge of the town. Michael's bleeding has worsened, our clothes are torn and dirty, and our poor horse is panting like it spent a year in the desert alone in desperate search of a cool lake.

A burly man with salt and pepper hair that matches his beard approaches. He must be a guard. A rifle is slung over his shoulder, and a sturdy stake-filled bandolier wraps around his barrel-shaped chest. With steel in his light blue eyes and his mouth set in a firm line, he gives us a measuring look before shouting, "Get Doc Jameson!"

A young barefoot girl with braids races off.

The man helps me slide off the horse, softening my landing. I nearly collapse when my feet hit the ground, my legs unsteady after the long ride. Michael tries to dismount, but his weakness is apparent as he begins to fall, and the man quickly catches him.

"Easy now," he says. "No shame in asking for help."

Michael leans on the man and we all walk into the center of town. People stop what they're doing to watch us. They're probably wondering what sort of trouble we've brought. I'm just as wary. How have they managed to exist in this isolated place?

A woman with red hair pulled back into a ponytail runs up to us.

"He's in rough shape, Doc," the man says.

"I'd say so." Her face sports a constellation of freckles. She's wearing a beaten and frayed lab coat. Maybe it was once white, but it's now the color of the dust. She doesn't look very old, and her movements are quick and efficient, her green eyes sharp as she surveys the damage.

"Get him inside," she says before turning her attention to me.

"I'm fine," I say, barely able to get the words past my

moisture-stripped throat.

"Don't be brave just for your friend," she says, examining my neck, and I know she's searching for bite marks. "I can take care of you both. Follow George. I'll meet you in the clinic."

I would've followed George no matter what. Michael's hold on the guard loosens with each step, his strength sapped. I slip under his free arm, determined to get him where he needs to be, even if it kills me.

The outside of the building is crude and simple, like all the others, but the inside is clean and tidy. On one side of a living area is an open office with a large desk. On the other, strings of beads serve as a doorway to a shadowed room. George walks straight through an opening that leads into what must serve as their infirmary. No tile or white sheets greet us, but care has been taken to ensure the dust and sand from outside don't creep in. George lifts Michael onto an examination table that looks to be salvaged from some ancient scrap yard and hastily repaired.

When George leaves, I step forward, take Michael's hand, and squeeze it reassuringly. The gashes on his cheek look angry, swollen, and painful. I can only imagine how much worse the ones across his chest are.

Dr. Jameson marches through the door, followed by a girl who looks to be about my age. Her blond hair is pulled back into a long braid. There is purpose in her movements as she sets a bowl of water on the counter. The doctor begins washing her hands while the girl arranges towels and instruments on a small table near where Michael is resting.

A dark-haired girl enters carrying two glasses with clear liquid in them. She gives me one. "I'm Amy."

"Dawn," I croak, before drinking the water. It's cool as it travels down my parched throat.

"Drink slowly," the doctor orders.

But it's difficult. I never expected anything that didn't have a flavor could taste so good.

With a shy smile, Amy puts an arm beneath Michael's shoulders and lifts him gently, taking the glass to his lips. He finishes it off quickly. She settles him back down, takes my empty glass, and leaves the room. I realize the other girl is gone as well. But I'm not leaving. Maybe Dr. Jameson recognizes my determination to stay because she simply ignores me and steps over to the table. "Let's see what we've got here."

Scissors in hand, she proceeds to cut away Michael's shirt to reveal the crimson furrows. I cling to his hand, more for my sake than his. I can't believe he was able to help us get away. He must have been—still must be—in agony.

"Nasty gouges," Dr. Jameson says. "On your face and chest. What happened?"

"Got into it with a cat."

She shoots him a warning glare. "Now isn't the time for jokes."

Michael looks at me, hoping maybe I'd crack a smile, but I'm too worried.

"Someone swiped at him with steel-tipped claws." The

weapon, so frightening, seemed like a natural extension of Sin's demented persona.

"You're lucky," Dr. Jameson says. "If not for your ribs, these wounds could have gone a lot deeper, sliced into your organs. You wouldn't be here now."

Dr. Jameson dabs alcohol over the torn flesh. I feel helpless while Michael takes in a sharp breath and cringes. He tightens his hold on my hand. He's nearly died for me so many times that I'm losing count. I wish I could do more for him.

"I'd love to offer you some anesthetic," she says. "But all I have is this."

She hands him a piece of wood, about the size of my forefinger, wrapped in rope. Michael places it in his mouth and bites down.

As she works a needle and thread through the wounds, she tugs tautly to close the openings. With every puncture, Michael grunts and tightens his jaw as he transfers the pain onto the piece of bark between his teeth. With my free hand, I brush my fingers through his short hair.

I lean over so he can hear me easily. "Remember when we were kids and we played on the swings? Go there, in your mind. Go to a place where there's no pain, no Sin."

He grows silent, and the doctor continues her work. I still feel the tension from his hand holding mine, but I can tell that my talking is distracting him. So I carry on, reminding him of all the good moments we've shared. He's been my best friend for so long. For a while he was more than that.

When Dr. Jameson is finished with his chest, she closes up the gashes on his cheek. "All right, all done," she says when she's completed her work.

I help Michael sit up.

"How do I look, Dawn?" he mumbles, trying to talk without reopening the wounds. "Am I still as handsome as ever?"

Fighting back tears for all he's suffered, I smile. He's made another little joke, but right now it's just a relief to know he's going to be okay.

"Chicks dig scars," I say.

Which he'll have. Forever. Four deep strikes across his cheek, nearly cutting to the teeth, sealed up by a railroad of stitches. In a few weeks they'll become small mountain chains of scar tissue. Then there are those along his chest, which the doctor is now covering with strips of gauze.

When she's secured the ends so the bandage won't unravel, she studies me intently. "Are you sure you're okay?"

"Just bruised a little."

She sits in a chair and sighs heavily, maybe slipping out of doctor-emergency mode finally. "So, who are you two?"

"Dawn Montgomery," I say. "Former delegate for the city of Denver."

"Impressive. And you?"

"Michael Colt. Bodyguard." Even away from Denver he's careful not to reveal that he's a Night Watchman. They're a clandestine group, their identities always held secret so their families don't become the target of the vampires they hunt.

"Well, you two are certainly far from home. What brings you here? And is there trouble following you?"

A lot, but while I want to reassure her, I'm too tired and can't think of how to be diplomatic. "I'm afraid we're a magnet for vampires."

"Who isn't these days? But don't worry," she says, holding up her hand. "They never bother us here. I'll have Amy get you some fresh clothes and show you where you can wash up while I get Michael settled in a bed."

"I'm not leaving Michael."

"He'll be in the room through that beaded doorway," Dr. Jameson says. "You can join him there."

"I'm not leaving him."

"I'll be fine, Dawn," Michael says.

"No. We stay together."

With a wry grin, he looks at Dr. Jameson. "She's stubborn."

"I'm getting that. Come on, then. I'll have Amy bring the water to you."

With Michael moving gingerly, we follow her back into the front room and through the beaded doorway into a room with three cots and no windows.

"What is the name of this town?" I ask.

"Crimson Sands," Dr. Jameson says.

I imagine this place is in a delicate balance, teetering on the edge of oblivion. The harsh landscape can dry out societies, dry out souls. How many towns have tried to be Crimson Sands and failed? How long has this illegal town survived, and how much longer can it?

"We'll get your horse watered and fed. I'll have supper ready for you when you wake up."

"Thank you. How long have you been living like this?" I ask.

"Five years."

"That's incredible."

"We survive by working together. Into bed now."

"We'll do what we can to repay you," Michael says.

"No need. Crimson Sands has flourished, relatively, on the kindness we offer each other. It's only right that we extend that kindness to those who wander our way. You could say it's our little way of reclaiming the world after such a devastating war."

"By showing that you never lost your humanity," I say.

"Precisely. Now please, no more talk. You need your rest. Just make yourselves comfortable and sleep as long as you like." She leaves, the wooden beads clacking in her wake.

With a deep sigh, Michael sits on one of the cots. "I think I'm safe here. You could get to Denver faster without me."

"You are turning me into an echo. I'm not leaving you. Now get some sleep and I'll keep watch."

"But—"

Before he can finish, the beads are clicking again. Amy sets a large bowl on a small table. "Brung you some water and clothes."

"Thank you."

"I'll help him put on the shirt I found for him." She

gives Michael another shy smile as she walks toward him. "Don't want to undo Dr. Jameson's handiwork."

While she's tending to Michael, blocking his view of me, I quickly remove my shirt. I wash my hands, face, neck, and chest. The gray T-shirt she brought for me is soft and faded with age, somehow comforting.

The beads smack again. Dr. Jameson is holding two mugs. "Decided you should have a little soup before you sleep."

She hands me one, then takes the other to Michael before leaving, ushering Amy out of the room as well.

I ease onto the bed across from Michael. I take a sip of the thick, creamy, tomatoey soup. "It's good."

"Yeah." He barely opens his mouth to take a long swallow.

"Are you in much pain?" Stupid question. I know he is.

"I'll be all right."

If he were dying, he'd say the same thing. Not only because stoicism is part of his training as a Night Watchman, but because it's in his nature to downplay his own suffering. Even when we broke up after going together for several months, he contained his anger and pain as much as possible.

I'm just grateful that we were able to become friends again after we separated.

Once we finish off the soup, I set both mugs on the table and return to the cot. "You try to get some sleep."

Reaching across, he touches my leg. "Are you okay? Sin and that old vampire in the cave laid some heavy stuff on you. Just so you know, I don't believe any of it."

I don't either. It's just not possible. "Thanks. I'm fine."

"I mean, your dad would have told you if you were . . . you know, a vampire."

If I was a vampire. I squeeze my eyes shut tightly against the obscene thought. I shoved back everything I was told. I wasn't ready to deal with it—not while Michael was bleeding, not until we were safe. Octavian, the ancient vampire in the mountain, claimed to be the last full-blooded vampire of the Montgomery clan. He claimed I was one of his descendants.

"Sin said I was a dhampir. Not exactly a vampire. More like some half-breed freak. But Sin has done nothing but lie to us. Why believe him now?" Especially when the truth could be so painful.

Michael pulls back his hand, rubs it on his jeans. He probably doesn't even realize what he's doing—wiping me off his skin. He still hates vampires as much as I used to. He lies down. "I don't think I've ever been so tired."

"Me either." I hear him snoring before I'm fully stretched out on the mattress, my eyes on the beaded doorway. I can't sleep, not for a while yet. I want to trust these people, but Sin has destroyed my ability to trust. He let us go so easily. What if he knew about this place? What if he has already made its citizens his disciples?

But if they answer to him, then why not just admit it? Take us captive?

Beyond the walls that surround us, I can hear the movement of people as they work: hammering, scraping, shuffling feet over the ground. It all sounds normal, safe. I fight to keep my eyes open, to remain on guard, but the past few days and the horror of last night have taken their toll.

If I give in and sleep, I could also reach out to Victor. Victor, the Old Family vampire who changed my life and worked his way into my heart. After being terribly wounded during a fight, Victor was forced to drink my blood in order to survive. Now we have a connection where we can visit each other's dreams. I shy away from the thought that this bond may be proof of my vampire heritage. What's important now is finding Victor.

I relax and succumb to sleep.

I feel like I've been floating forever. Then I find myself at a place that starts my heart racing.

The mountain.

I'm inside the cavern where Sin brought us, where I met the Old Family vampire who claimed to be my ancestor. The area is awash in blues as the moonlight spills in from a hole in the top. I see the throne where the ancient vampire sat. Now there is nothing except a pile of ash. The sun poured through earlier and destroyed his body.

A forlorn figure is kneeling before the throne, his fists clenched, his head bent.

"Victor!"

He turns toward me, and without a second's hesitation we embrace each other. Although I'm in his dream, I can feel him. He's solid, comforting.

"Dawn, you're alive. I was so afraid."

"I'm fine," I assure him. "But how are you here?"

Releasing me, Victor paces before the throne, combing his fingers through the ash of the vampire who once sat there.

"Jeff and I were here," he says. Jeff served as my bodyguard at the Agency. "After you came to me in the dream and told me Sin had taken you, I left Denver with him as soon as I could. But we were too late."

He throws a handful of ash onto the ground in frustration.

"We were so close . . ." he whispers.

"It's okay," I say. "Our blood kiss has brought us together again. In this place."

Victor nods, still investigating the throne and its ashen king. "What happened here, Dawn?"

I rush toward him and grab his shoulders, forcing him to stare into my eyes with his deep blue ones.

"I'll tell you everything when you find us." There's no time to discuss it now. Our dreams are so fragile that either of us might wake at any moment. We'll lose our connection and the ability to communicate. "Michael and I are in a town, not too far from here. To the southeast. You'll see a windmill. Come for us."

"What about Sin? Does he know where you are?"

"I don't know," I say.

I touch his face. The bristle along his jaw scratches my fingers. I've never understood how I can experience all these sensations when we're together like this. "I need you, Victor. Please, get to us as soon as you can."

"I will," he says, and I feel him move sharply.

It's like his body is being pulled from me by some invisible string, jerking him across vast distances. My hand passes through the empty air where he stood just a moment ago.

He's woken up, breaking our connection. He'll find me. I know it.

I walk over to the throne and stare at what remains of the ancient vampire.

What if I am a descendant of the lost vampire family—the Montgomerys—as Octavian claimed? It changes everything if I'm no longer human. What world do I fit in? The humans won't want me, and since the Old Families signed a death warrant to eradicate the Montgomerys, I'm pretty sure the vampires won't want me either.

Like him, I may be cast out, forced into hiding, and left to live my life alone.

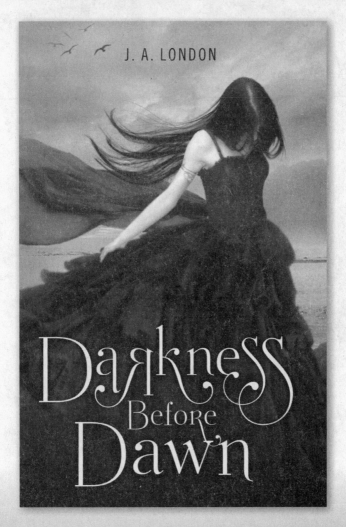

Loved *Blood-Kissed Sky*?

Then don't miss the Dark Guardian series from Rachel Hawthorne, part of the team behind J. A. London.